Praise for the Greenhouse

BITTER HARVEST (#2)

"Tyson's first-rate second Greenhouse mystery stars big-city lawyer turned small-town organic farmer Megan Sawyer, a kind, intelligent, and spirited woman with great integrity. In short, she's the sort of person cozy readers warm to and root for...Tyson populates the cast with a smug-but-attractive PR consultant, a temperamental-but-gifted chef, a shrewd and sexy Scottish vet, and assorted townspeople, whose motives are complex and believable. It's a pleasure to spend time in their company."

– *Publishers Weekly* (starred review)

"*Bitter Harvest* is a delightful read. It has everything you could want in a mystery—a spunky heroine with a charming love interest, quirky characters, a setting you desperately want to visit, and a plot that keeps you guessing!"

– Amanda Lee,
Author of *Better Off Thread*

"An exceptional cozy, *Bitter Harvest* offers up a veritable feast for mystery fans: a beautifully drawn setting, engaging characters, and plenty of twists and turns that will keep readers guessing. The suspense deepens with every scene...Tyson has crafted a fresh, intelligent, compelling story that's sure to satisfy."

– Cynthia Kuhn,
Author of *The Art of Vanishing*

"A perfectly-crafted smorgasbord of suspense, family drama and small-town intrigue."

– Liz Mugavero,
Agatha-Nominated Author of *Custom Baked Murder*

A MUDDIED MURDER (#1)

"Tyson gives us an evocative sense of place, a bit of romance, and dimensional characters with interesting backstories. Readers are left looking forward to the next book in the series and hankering for organic mushroom tartlets."

– Publishers Weekly

"Charming and entertaining cozy series debut...Megan is a spunky heroine who loves her family and wants to succeed. Readers of animal-centric cozies will flock to this."

– Library Journal

"A warmhearted mystery with an irresistible cast of characters, two- and four-legged alike. Tyson's small town setting is a lush bounty for the senses, and the well-structured plot will keep you guessing right up until the satisfying conclusion."

– Sophie Littlefield,
Edgar-Nominated Author of *The Guilty One*

"Tyson grows a delicious debut mystery as smart farmer-sleuth Megan Sawyer tills the dirt on local secrets after a body turns up in her barn. You won't want to put down this tasty harvest of a story."

– Edith Maxwell,
Agatha-Nominated Author of *Murder Most Fowl*

"A good story with well-developed, fun characters. And anyone who grew up in a small town will remember 'roots' like these quite well. This is the book to enjoy on a nice spring day—sitting back, relaxing, and discovering Washington Acres."

– Suspense Magazine

Bitter Harvest

The Greenhouse Mystery Series
by Wendy Tyson

A MUDDIED MURDER (#1)
BITTER HARVEST (#2)
SEEDS OF REVENGE (#3)
(Fall 2017)

Bitter Harvest

GREENHOUSE mysteries

WENDY TYSON

HENERY PRESS

BITTER HARVEST
A Greenhouse Mystery
Part of the Henery Press Mystery Collection

First Edition
Trade paperback edition | March 2017

Henery Press, LLC
www.henerypress.com

Trade Paperback ISBN-13: 978-1-63511-173-6
Digital epub ISBN-13: 978-1-63511-174-3
Kindle ISBN-13: 978-1-63511-175-0
Hardcover Paperback ISBN-13: 978-1-63511-176-7

Printed in the United States of America

For you, Ian.
I love watching you fly.

ACKNOWLEDGMENTS

So many people made this book possible. I owe much gratitude to Frances Black of Literary Counsel, my agent extraordinaire. Special thanks to everyone at my publisher, Henery Press, especially Kendel Lynn, Art Molinares, and Rachel Jackson. Thanks to Carol Lizell, my godmother, beta reader, and remarkable line editor, and to Rowe Carenen at The Book Concierge, whose hard work, insightfulness, and support help me through every release. Gratitude to Ian Pickarski, whose insights and advice on knife making and modifying lent an air of authenticity to *Bitter Harvest*. As always, thanks to my family, who walk beside me on this writing journey, offering encouragement, late-night caffeine, and the occasional plot twist. And, of course, I'm grateful for the crime writing community—my amazing readers, fellow authors, book bloggers, reviewers, and my friends at ITW's *The Thrill Begins* and *The Big Thrill*. I feel like I've come home.

One

The harvest moon glowed bright overhead, a burnt offering to the demons plaguing Megan's peace of mind. The woods beyond Washington Acres felt inviting—until nightfall. It was early October, the start of fall foliage season, and by day the leaves on the oaks, birch, and mountain ash shone bright in a rainbow of reds, golds, and deep oranges. But once darkness hit, the ghosts emerged. Or so it seemed.

Halloween was just a few weeks away, and the pace on the farm had finally lulled to a more comfortable frenzy. Most of the summer crops had been picked and sold, and what was left had been canned, frozen, stored, or donated. The fields were being turned over and planted with cover crops like clover and daikon radish. The fall bounty was just coming in, and Megan had enough pumpkins to supply a dozen fall festivals. Autumn had been kinder than the previous spring, and the October air was cool but not cold, dry but not arid. The farm's coffers, too, were full—well, at least not empty.

Megan should have felt content. Pleased, even.

Then why this feeling of unrest? Megan opened the door to the porch and stepped outside into the chilly night. Overhead, the stars were eclipsed by the reddish, eerie moon. Gunther and Sadie, her two dogs, ran out behind her. Gunther, a Polish Tatra Sheepdog, took off for his nightly rounds, checking on the chickens and goats and monitoring the perimeter of the farm just as Megan and Dr.

Finn had trained him to do. Sadie stayed pressed to her side. Megan reached down to pat Sadie, taking comfort from the dog's warm presence.

But she couldn't shake the image of the chair.

Oh, she knew very well that it was just a chair. A battered red Adirondack seat, the kind you see at homes all across the United States. Nothing scary about that. Except that this one wasn't parked on a patio or beside a pool in some suburban lot. It sat alone at the top of Potter Hill, in the woods—the same thick woods that bordered her property.

Megan had hiked up there yesterday, seduced by blue skies and the allure of those fiery leaves. Out of breath, with Sadie beside her and Gunther running up ahead, she reached the top of Potter Hill and spied the chair. Her first thought was one of gratitude— how nice it was to have somewhere to sit after a grueling climb. But after she lowered herself into the chair, she realized it was oddly positioned. It didn't take advantage of the sweeping view of the valley below or the red-hewn tree line in the distance.

It did, however, have a clear view of her house.

Megan had hopped out of the seat, still thinking it was purely a coincidence. Whoever had placed the chair there had done so on a whim, and they had probably paid no attention to how it was situated. But when she stood and examined the spot, she realized she was wrong. The ground under the chair's legs had divots where the base had worn into the dirt, and the grass and foliage near the foot area, thick elsewhere, had been trampled from frequent traffic. Where Megan's feet had rested, the earth was worn bare.

Spooked, she'd called the dogs and raced back to the house. In the comfort of her kitchen, she'd decided she was overreacting. So what if someone had been sitting alone on Potter Hill. So what if their chair faced this property. What could they possibly see from that far away?

But now, as she stared into the dark woods under the glow of the autumn moon, Megan realized her earlier angst had been warranted. With a good set of binoculars, someone could see quite a bit from that spot. Like her comings and goings. And the times she and Bibi were alone.

The Washington Acres Café and Larder was abuzz. Megan was happy to see a small line waiting to pay by the front register. She scanned the space, letting her gaze travel over the well-stocked shelves and back toward the kitchen. She spotted Alvaro Hernandez, the café's beloved, if not slightly grumpy, cook. Only today, "slightly grumpy" didn't quite capture it. The scowl that covered the bottom half of his face was rivaled only by a pair of tightly knit gray bushy eyebrows.

"Morning, Alvaro," she said.

Her chef grunted in reply.

The café had only been up and running for six months, but already it was starting to feel like a Winsome hub, a place where townspeople came to pick up necessities like homegrown vegetables, canned goods, and local pastured meats, and—increasingly—a place where they met to dine and socialize. In fact, the café had regulars, a number of men and a few women, who'd started to call themselves the Breakfast Club. They began meeting twice a week over the summer to plan for Winsome's Oktoberfest celebration, but even after most of the details had been ironed out, they continued to show up. And now they were there almost daily. That's what seemed to have piqued Alvaro's impatience today.

"More coffee, Alvaro," one of the men called.

"I'll have some too," another yelled. "And maybe a muffin. Cranberry orange."

Alvaro shot Megan a look of exasperation.

"I'll get the coffees," Megan said.

In the kitchen, she shuffled around the cook, making a fresh pot of brew. The air was rich with the aromas of sautéed onions and peppers and the pungent, sweet scent of cinnamon. Alvaro was pouring brown batter into muffin cups, his hands moving swiftly with graceful agility. He popped the muffins in the commercial oven and walked over to the sink. He was short and slender with a long, drawn face and a shocking mop of white hair. But his eyes—hazelnut brown and surprisingly kind—shone with keen awareness. Alvaro owned no poker face.

"I have to watch every ingredient when Ted Kuhl is here. All those allergies. And Albert Nunez is causing trouble again," Alvaro muttered under his breath. "Six cups of coffee." He waved a dishtowel, his face turning red. "No more. I should charge him for the third, fourth, fifth, and sixth."

"Alvaro—"

"That man's a freeloader." But Alvaro's voice had softened, as it normally did when he was speaking to his boss. "You want to make a profit here? You can't let these men sit and loiter."

Megan glanced out at the café section of the store. When she'd agreed to leave her Chicago law practice and return to her hometown of Winsome in Eastern Pennsylvania, she knew it would be hard reinventing the farm and the old store, but things were slowly coming together. She *wanted* the café to be a meeting place for the locals. Hadn't that been her vision all along? Sure, they tended to sit and talk for hours, sometimes racking up nearly nonexistent bills. And yes, they were loud. But they congregated at odd times, so there was usually room for other customers, and they were always polite. Alvaro was just sore that he had to keep an eye on these gents rather than cooking. The answer, perhaps, was to eventually hire another server—not to kick out her most loyal customers.

Suddenly a loudly yelled "Damn it, Lou," caught Megan's attention.

Albert Nunez seemed to be picking an argument with Lou Brazzi, Winsome's sometimes real estate attorney. Brazzi was giving Nunez a bemused smile, all the while stirring packet after packet of sugar into his coffee. Nunez caught Megan looking at him and lowered his head. He glanced sideways, at the opposite end of the long table, and tried to catch the attention of Ted Kuhl. Only Kuhl, one of the town's two beer brewers, seemed lost in thought.

Kuhl shared space at his end of the table with Winsome's other brewer, the owner of Otto's Brew Pub, who sat with his arms crossed on the table. A furious gash of a mouth marred his otherwise handsome features. Wearing gray wool pants, a white button-down, and a gray vest, Otto had the distinguished good looks of a man addicted to clean living and fresh air. He was usually a gentle man, quick with a kind word or compliment. Anger didn't suit him.

"It's not fair, Lou, and you know it," Nunez was saying. "Whoever gets that sponsorship has a helluva good quarter."

Brazzi shook his head.

"A lottery is a lottery."

"Not when it's rigged," Ted said. His eyes were bloodshot, his face ashen under the ruddy veneer.

It took Megan a moment to realize what they were talking about: Oktoberfest. Otto Vance had proposed the idea more than a year ago during one of the Historical Society sessions, and the town representatives jumped on it like ants on a donut. His vision had been modest—a few tents, some authentic German food provided by his brew pub, a band—but as with a lot of things, many hands made more work. After a year's worth of planning, the upcoming Oktoberfest was to be a week-long affair that would showcase the town's small businesses. The Society had hired a public-relations expert to run the festival, and businesses—including Megan's—were scrambling to sponsor specific events. Sponsorship meant advertising and exposure, and with several thousand visitors expected, a lottery had been put into place to ensure fairness. Apparently not everyone thought the lottery was working as intended.

"That's a serious allegation, Teddy." Lou's eyes narrowed. "You shouldn't be walking around saying that. It could get you into trouble."

"I'm already in trouble."

"You need some sleep." Nunez's voice was unusually gentle. The former union negotiator and rabid Phillies fan could be abrasive, but he stared at Ted with genuine worry. "Get some perspective."

"Blame me, go ahead. I'm not the issue here." Ted turned sharply toward Otto, who looked ready to pounce.

"Can I get anyone anything else?" Megan asked, interrupting before an argument could break out. She eyed the group.

Nunez turned his attention to Megan. He rubbed his ample belly. "Bonnie make any more of that apple strudel she's known for? With ice cream, maybe?"

"No apple strudel," Alvaro called from behind the counter. "You ate the last of it." The cook scowled, then disappeared into the pantry.

"You might want to find some friendlier help," Nunez grumbled.

"Don't even suggest that," Brazzi said. "We finally have someone around here who can cook."

"How about a slice of pound cake?" Megan said. "I think we have some left over from yesterday."

Nunez said, "Nah, not now. I'm okay, Megan."

The thick tension in the café caused Megan to pause outside of the kitchen. A look passed between Ted Kuhl and Brazzi. The lawyer mouthed something to Ted. Whatever Brazzi said, it caused Ted to stand up suddenly and storm toward the window. He stared outside, shook his head violently back and forth, and turned toward the table of men. His mouth struggled to form words that never materialized. After a painful pregnant moment, Ted let out a low moan. He pulled his wallet roughly out of his pocket and threw a twenty on the table.

Otto flew from his seat. He grabbed Kuhl by the arm and pulled him to the side, near the kitchen entrance. Noticing the alarm on Ted's face, Otto took a step back, but his hands remained clenched, his jaw tight. Megan busied herself folding dishtowels, but she could hear much of their conversation. She felt her own body tense.

"Knock it off," Otto said. "Let it go, for everyone's sake."

"We both know how that will end." Ted thrust his chest out. "Don't be a fool, Otto. This isn't what you wanted. It's not what anyone wants. Not really." Kuhl's eyes burrowed into Otto's, hot coals of accusation.

"Bugger off," Otto said.

"You'd like that, wouldn't you? 'Ignorance is bliss' and all that happy horse manure."

Otto closed the distance between him and Kuhl. He whispered something in Kuhl's ear, something Megan couldn't hear.

Ted stood there listening, hands clawed by his side, face red. While Otto was still speaking, Ted tore away and sprinted out of the café.

Megan glanced at the men around the table, noticing their reactions. She watched Brazzi watch Ted go, his face expressionless. She saw Nunez return to his newspaper. But Otto Vance sat back down, his brooding form throwing a shadow across the shiny copper table top.

Megan was about to speak when her cell phone rang. A glance at her screen told her it was Clay Hand, her farm manager. She looked back at the men, still wondering what had turned these Dr. Jekylls into Mr. Hydes, and continued into the kitchen to take her call. Oktoberfest had everyone on edge. Like the harvest moon, surely this too would pass—and tempers would be back to normal.

In the relative privacy of the café's kitchen, Megan answered the call.

"Hey," she said. "What's going on back at the farm?"

"I hiked up to Potter Hill, but there was no chair."

"You're joking." Only she knew he wasn't. Clay's voice was dead serious.

"I wish I were. There is no chair. In fact, I couldn't even locate the spot you referred to."

"Maybe you were in the wrong area?"

"Top of Potter Hill, facing the farm. We zig-zagged our way

back and forth across the area—and nothing. Two of Bobby's men were with me." Clay got quiet for a second. "Are you sure that's where you saw it?"

Megan's spine stiffened. She knew what she'd seen and where she'd seen it, and the fact that it was gone now made her that much more concerned.

Appearing to read her mind, Clay said, "Look, I have to ask because I know Bobby will." Bobby was Chief Bobby King, Winsome's youngest-ever police chief. "Plus," Clay continued, "I'd almost prefer if you'd misplaced the chair's location, because if it's gone the day after you spotted it, that means—"

"That someone saw me up there." Megan finished his thought. What she didn't add was, *because they were probably spying on me.* She was pretty sure Clay was thinking it.

"Yeah."

The silence that ensued was thick with unspoken memories. A bloodied, battered body in Megan's barn. An intruder with murder on their mind. And something Megan would remember but Clay would not—a secret separating her from the rest of Winsome. From the rest of her family. Was it possible whoever placed that chair on Potter Hill knew about the treasure buried somewhere on Washington Acres' property? Megan figured anything was possible. History had taught her that.

The steady contented activity from Alvaro's corner of the kitchen had stopped, and the café was suddenly quiet. Megan looked over to see Alvaro watching her, his lined face scrunched with worry. Megan immediately regretted having the conversation in the kitchen. She also regretted not taking a photo of the chair when she'd had a chance. She'd been too spooked to stay there— and now her haste was backfiring on her.

"Look, Clay," she said, forcing her voice to sound cheerful, "it's no biggie. It was a folding Adirondack chair. Someone probably enjoyed a picnic at the top of Potter Hill and packed it up when they were done."

"Uh-huh," Clay said, sounding thoroughly unconvinced.

"Besides, we have a ton to do. Washington Acres Café and Larder won one of the restaurant lottery spots, so Bibi is baking later this morning and Alvaro will have his hands full. If we win the farm sponsorship, none of us will sleep for the next few weeks."

"When will you hear?"

"Should be later today." Megan glanced at Alvaro, now back to chopping. "I need to go, Clay. I'll leave here shortly. And then we can tackle the remaining pumpkins and take inventory."

"In case we win?"

"Whether we win the lottery or not, with so many expected visitors in Winsome over a week-long period, our produce will sell—through the farm or through the café."

"Still, it'd be a real boost if we won that lottery. Help to get our name out there. Whoever sponsors is in all the advertisements and brochures."

"True." Megan considered the scene she'd walked into in the café. "It seems everyone feels that way. Funny how a little healthy competition can turn friends into frenemies."

Two

By the time Megan left the café, she'd forgotten about the lottery and the Oktoberfest celebration. The next two hours after Clay's phone call had been taken up by a mad rush of customer orders, a broken bathroom faucet, and a trip to the hardware store. With the bathroom finally back in working order, Megan finally turned into the driveway at Washington Acres. Sadie ran to greet her, a worshipping Gunther trotting behind.

Megan bent down to pet the dogs, then headed toward the door that led to the enclosed porch and into the kitchen. Clay was up at the barn—she could see him sorting pumpkins into the bin for Saturday's farmers market. She glanced at her watch. It was nearly noon. The day had already gotten away from her.

Megan was just pulling the door open when her cell phone rang. She pushed her way into the big country kitchen, dropped her belongings onto the table, and glanced at her phone. A number she didn't recognize.

She answered. "Hello?"

"Megan Sawyer of Washington Acres Farm?"

"Speaking."

"This is Ophelia Dilworth. From the Oktoberfest committee."

"Ah yes, the PR person. Good afternoon." Megan opened the kitchen window, letting in some fresh air and allowing her gaze to wander toward Potter Hill. From this distance, she couldn't see the spot where the folding Adirondack had been, but she could make out the fiery cluster of trees near the top where it had sat. Until someone moved it.

"Megan, you have an incredible farm. I love, just love, what you're doing there."

Megan closed the shades and tried a window on the other end of the kitchen. Perhaps the chair had simply been moved, not taken. She scanned the hills for a small dot of red—not easy to ferret out in a sea of changing foliage. "Thank you."

"And I think—the Oktoberfest committee thinks—that you will be in a *perfect* spot to represent Winsome at a huge event like this. In a few years, that is."

Megan closed the curtain abruptly and spun around on her heels. She leaned against the counter. "In a few years?"

"Yes." Deep, dramatic sigh. "I'm sorry to tell you that Washington Acres was not chosen as the farm sponsor. It's not that you're not doing a good thing—you are, obviously, and we're all rooting for you—but the committee feels that the farm is too young to take on such a large responsibility." Ophelia Dilworth had a voice that simply *dripped* with disappointment for Washington Acres. "And with so many people expected, it *would* be a large responsibility."

"What farm was chosen?"

"Plus, you're a female farmer going at it alone."

"My grandmother is here. And I have help."

"Yes, but you're still the boss, which makes for an even better human interest story. We'll find a way to highlight what you're doing over there—"

"What farm was chosen, Ophelia?"

There was a long pause, during which the sound of a chainsaw buzzed through the open window.

"The Sauer farm."

Incredulous, Megan sat down at the table. She rested one arm on the worn Formica and rubbed her temple with the other. Her head was starting to throb. "Glen and Irene Sauer?"

"That's them. A lovely couple."

Lovely was not quite how Megan would describe the Sauers. That decision made no sense. Megan could understand if one of the other, more established small local farms had been chosen, but Sauer? Glen Sauer had been Gunther's abusive owner before the local vet rescued the pup. Megan felt no love for the Sauers, but beyond their treatment of animals lurked another problem—their sheer size.

"Megan, I knew you'd understand. Just like me, you want what's best for Winsome. This was no easy decision—the committee really struggled—but we all want to put Winsome's best foot forward. Or clog in this instance." She laughed at her own Oktoberfest reference.

Only Megan wasn't listening, her mind still swimming over the committee's unexpected decision. "Ophelia, the Sauers grow mostly corn and soy—not the variety of vegetables you'd need for something like Oktoberfest. And their operation is much larger than the guidelines the committee itself set forth."

"Yes, well, we revisited those guidelines, and we decided they were too limiting."

"The Sauers run a huge spray and grow operation, on top of a national beef and poultry lot. I understand if you don't want to take a chance on Washington Acres, but there are other farms the committee could choose. Smaller family-run operations like Mark Gregario's place, Diamond Farm. I thought that was what this was all about. Buy local, eat local. Show the wholesome variety of what Winsome has to offer."

"We never required the sponsoring farm to be organic, if that's what you're getting at. Even your farm doesn't have its certification."

"But it will. It just takes time. And besides, that's not the point."

"Then what is the point?" A condescending impatience had crept into the perfect sing-song of Ophelia's voice.

"Oktoberfest is supposed to showcase Winsome's small businesses. Winsome is a historic town with a proud agricultural history. That means small family farms and local produce. You've managed to choose the one farm that defies that tradition."

"We've picked the one farm that can supply all of the products we need for the event. Vegetables like corn as well as meat. Reliably, and without question."

Megan could name two other farms—humanely run farms with a strong local reputation—that could do the same. So why Sauer? But arguing with Ophelia was clearly pointless. Sadie, sensing Megan's distress, pressed against Megan's leg and nosed her way into Megan's lap. Megan rubbed the dog's ears absentmindedly.

"The Sauer farm's national distribution could be viewed as a plus. They have standing broader than Winsome. We're trying to get your town on the map." Ophelia stopped chattering long enough to take a breath. "Look, I actually called with other news." Ophelia's voice had lost its edge and was back to its practiced sincerity. "We'd like to highlight Washington Acres in the Oktoberfest program. We'll do a spotlight piece on you and the farm. Female farmer and all that."

Megan didn't immediately respond. She knew the committee was buying her agreement. Sauer Farm was the wrong farm to sponsor the event—for many reasons, including the fact that they didn't meet the committee's own original parameters. Well aware that Megan had been a lawyer, the committee must have figured a spotlight would keep her quiet.

And it *was* a tempting offer. She could use all the publicity she could get. But not that way.

"I don't think I'm interested."

"Don't be like that, Megan. Think of your farm. Of Winsome."

The kitchen door jingled and Clay entered with a hearty "hello." Dirt streaked his face, and his normally worn but pressed clothing was also caked with mud. Seeing Megan was on the phone, he frowned, and mouthed, "Sorry."

"I have to go, Ophelia."

"What's your answer? Would you like to be featured in the brochure? Come on."

"I really am not interested."

"Just think about it."

"Fine."

Ophelia huffed her annoyance. "You don't have much time though. We're already late going to press. I need to hear from you tomorrow at the latest. Okay?"

"Yes, sure," Megan said. Clay was shifting from foot to foot. He glanced at his watch. "I'll call you then." Megan hung up. "What's going on?" she asked Clay.

"It's Porter. He went to pick up more baling twine and now his car won't start. I need to go jump it for him."

Brian Porter was the newest addition to Washington Acres. A young veteran with anger-management issues, he started working on the farm a few months ago at the request of Dr. Denver Finn, the town veterinarian and Megan's sort-of boyfriend.

Megan said, "You look like you're in the middle of something."

"Turning over beds so we can plant more cover crops." Clay glanced down at his clothes. "That bad?"

"Pretty bad. How about if I jump Porter's car and you finish what you were doing?"

"You don't mind?"

"I don't mind." Megan's mind wandered back to her call with Ophelia. "I could use a distraction."

Clay gave her directions to where Porter was stranded. "What was that call about?"

"You don't want to know, and I don't want to keep Porter waiting. I'll fill you in later."

Megan pulled behind Porter's truck and jammed her own pickup into park. It was a warm October day, and the mid-day sun beat down on the pavement, heating her face and reflecting off Porter's silver truck like sharp shards of glass. He'd stalled on Horse Buggy Lane, a long stretch of nowhere that adjoined Curly Hill Road and passed only the Jenner solar farm, the back side of Lyle Lake State

Park, and an abandoned kennel. Seemed like an odd way to get to the hardware store, but then, Porter was an odd bird.

Megan grabbed the jumper cables from the truck bed cabinet and walked over to Porter's vehicle, which had been pushed to the side of the road. Porter was sitting on the curb, smoking a cigarette and looking put out—a sullen, tattooed James Dean in his dark blue jeans and white t-shirt.

He said, "I get paid for this time."

It was a statement, not a question. Megan, still feeling argumentative after her talk with Ophelia, swallowed a biting response. Porter was a recovering alcoholic and a troubled former soldier. Like her late husband, Mick, Porter had seen the Middle East from the vantage point of the trenches. Unlike Mick, Porter came home—in one piece physically, if not mentally or spiritually. But despite Megan's misgivings about Porter's ability to stay clean, she'd found that he'd proven himself useful at the farm. She'd pay him for his time now, if only because he needed the cash more than she did.

She tossed the jumper cables his way. Porter shook his head. He tossed the cigarette on the ground, saw the look of annoyance on Megan's face, and picked it up again, holding it away from him like it was poison.

"Flat tire. That's why I stalled. I stopped to check the tire and couldn't start the car again."

"Do you have a spare?"

"Nope."

"Clay didn't mention the flat. I don't have a spare with me."

Porter shrugged.

"Doesn't matter."

The reason it didn't matter came rolling along the otherwise deserted stretch of road and pulled up behind Megan. A shirtless Dr. Daniel "Denver" Finn climbed out of his 4Runner. "Afternoon," he said to both of them before disappearing behind the vehicle. He came back carrying a tire.

"Think you forgot something," Porter mumbled. He stood,

stuck the cigarette butt in his pants pocket, and took the tire from Denver. "Ain't it a little cold to be showing off?"

Only Megan could see a gash running down the side of Denver's torso. And a bruise blossoming along his lower ribcage, an angry red bullseye in the middle. "You got gored," she said.

"Aye," Denver replied in his Scottish brogue. He rubbed a hand along his flank and winced. "Porter here caught me on the way back from a neighboring farm. The bull got the best of me."

"Ouch," Porter said, suddenly fascinated.

Megan took a long look at the veterinarian, trying not to stare. His dark auburn hair, tousled on a good day, formed a mop of waves atop a ruggedly handsome face. The beginnings of a beard shadowed his jawline. Her gaze traveled down his well-muscled torso, and she redirected it—with difficulty. They'd been seeing each other on and off since the spring and she'd told him she wanted to take things slow. Only standing here, on this beautiful fall day, with Denver looking wounded and devilishly strong at the same time...she thought maybe they were taking it *too* slow.

Porter cleared his throat. "You two gonna stop staring at one another and help me get this tire on? Doc? I could use a hand."

"I don't think that's a good idea." Megan glanced at Denver. "He needs a doctor."

Denver shook his head. "Just a few bruises."

"And a lot of dried blood." She touched the spot above the gash gently and Denver winced again. "He got you good."

"Aye, you should see my shirt. It fared worse than me."

"That doesn't make me feel better."

Sirens began to blare in the distance.

Porter grinned.

"Ambulance is coming for you."

The sirens wailed louder, getting closer. They were joined by another sort of wail—fire trucks.

"Something must have happened." Megan turned back toward Denver. "Please. Go see the doctor and get that wound cleaned up. I'll help Porter. We'll be fine."

Denver opened his mouth to argue, so Megan stepped closer. She balanced on her toes and kissed his lips lightly.

"Unfair means of persuasion," Denver murmured.

"Holy hell, you two. Get a room," Porter said. But he was staring at the vet worriedly. "She's right, Doc. You'd better get that looked at. You don't need an infection."

The sirens wailed louder.

"Damn," Porter said. "I wonder what happened."

Denver looked out toward the trees bordering Lyle State Park, and Megan followed his stare. Nothing beyond the sentry line of pines was visible. The sound was coming from the direction of the adjacent solar farm.

He said, "Probably a car accident."

Megan agreed. She rooted in her car for the first-aid kit she kept in the glove compartment. The small box in hand, she tossed him a fresh roll of paper towels from her truck. He unfurled a few and pressed them against his side. She applied antibiotic and a square patch of adhesive bandage and declared him fixed up—for now.

"Let's get Porter back on the road, and then I'll run by the clinic, Megs." Denver smiled. "So ye will stop nagging me."

They worked quickly, getting Porter's truck running well enough to make it into town and to a garage. It took Megan a second to notice the sirens had stopped.

"See you back at the farm," Porter said to Megan. He thanked Denver and drove off.

Denver paused by his Toyota.

"Will I see ye tonight?"

"I'd like that."

He nodded, eyebrows knit into a frown. He was still shirtless, and the skin on his chest was coated with a light sheen of sweat, despite the cool air.

"Ye look pretty, standing there with engine grease on your nose."

Megan smiled. "I do my best to look attractive for the boys."

Denver's eyes narrowed. His mouth twisted into that maddening half smile. He moved closer. "*All* the boys?"

Megan placed a hand on that chest, felt the muscles—hard and real and alive. "Just you."

He nodded. For a moment, it was just the two of them. Megan could hear the blood rushing through her veins. Her mind flitted to Mick. She felt the pang of guilt, pushed it away.

The sirens started again, breaking the spell.

Denver's gaze strayed back to the road. "That would be Bobby King," he said. "I recognize the wail."

Not good, Megan thought. She watched Denver drive away and started her own engine. The sound of sirens still shook her up. The sound of the Chief's sirens sent a shiver straight down her back. She forced the truck into drive, reminding herself that what happened months ago was over. The chair meant nothing. The sirens meant nothing. Winsome had moved on—and so would she.

Three

Megan drove back toward the farm. Instead of fading, the sirens screamed more loudly. She hoped it wasn't a forest fire in the state park. It had been dry as of late, and with the fallen leaves and a summer's worth of wooded debris, it would only take one careless hiker. But as she neared the giant solar fields that lined one side of Curly Hill Road, she saw it was the solar field—not the park—that was at issue. She rolled down the window. No outward signs of a fire.

She was slowing to get around a half dozen official vehicles when she spotted her grandmother's Subaru tucked between an ambulance and a police car. Pulse racing, stomach suddenly knotted so tightly she thought she would be sick, Megan pulled the truck onto the grass, jammed it into park and hopped out. She rushed to a cluster of firefighters standing by the side of the road, hands on hips, mouths moving. They quieted when she approached, looking at her expectantly.

Winsome's fire department depended on volunteers, so she recognized most of the men standing in this circle. She took solace in their facial expressions; none of them looked panicked when Megan approached. If Bibi had been hurt, they would show it in their faces.

"Megan," one of them said. "Come to collect Bonnie?"

"I just happened by and saw her car. Where is she? What's going on?" Megan pointed toward the far end of the solar field where a cluster of police and firefighters were gathered. She recognized Chief Bobby King in front of one of the solar panels. Most of him—and whatever he was looking at—sat beyond her field of vision.

"There's been an accident," one of the firefighters said. He kept his voice low. "Bonnie was first on the scene."

"What kind of accident?"

The man glanced around the tight-knit circle, clearly struggling with how much to say. One of the other men nodded, and the firefighter finally replied, "A person died."

Oh no, Megan thought. Her grandmother had been through enough—but now to come across an accident? And at a solar field? What in the name of glory was Bibi doing at Jenner's solar farm? And who had been killed? And *how*?

"I can't say anything else, Megan. You know that. It's up to Chief King to fill you in if he sees fit." He started in the direction of the ambulances. "Let me take you to Bonnie."

Megan followed him around a fire truck and to the first ambulance. She found Bibi sitting on a stretcher, arms crossed defiantly over her chest. Her white hair was pushed back from her face, and the hem of her pink cotton blouse hung partway out of the waist of her pants. She wore a "Winsome Rules" t-shirt over the blouse, and Megan could see a smudge of what looked like blood along the seam. Normally not one to show emotion, Bibi's eyes were red and puffy. One hand clutched a balled-up tissue; the other rested on her silver phone. She was scowling at a blood-pressure cuff that hung flaccid from the outstretched hand of a very young EMT.

Bibi caught Megan's eye. Her frown deepened. "I told them not to bother you. I'm fine." The EMT leaned in with the blood-pressure cuff and Bibi pulled her arm away. "I said I'm *fine*."

"Would you give us a few minutes alone?" Megan asked the paramedic.

"Certainly." She looked relieved.

Megan waited until the EMT was out of earshot before asking her grandmother what happened.

"They didn't need to call you. I'm fine."

"They didn't call me. I just happened to come by."

Her grandmother raised her eyebrows. "Really?"

"Really." She laid a hand on her grandmother's shoulder. "Bibi, you're sitting on a stretcher in the middle of a solar field, surrounded by a score of Winsome's finest." She looked over at Bobby King, who was now headed slowly in their direction. "Please tell me what happened."

"I drove by, saw something, and called 911." She lowered her head, and her thin shoulders looked frail under the light material of her shirts. "Well, I tried to call 911, but I kept hitting the wrong dang buttons on that new phone you made me buy."

Megan felt a wave of affection—and concern. "What did you see?"

"Enough to know I wanted my phone to work."

Megan wanted to hug her *and* strangle her. Bonnie Elizabeth Birch could be one stubborn lady when the mood hit, and the mood always seemed to hit when she was trying to protect Megan. But Megan wanted to know what was going on before Bobby arrived. She knew from experience that once the Chief was involved, Bibi would be as selective about her words as a savvy politician in a news conference. Bibi liked Bobby King, but she didn't trust the police—or anyone in authority.

"Did you see what happened?"

"No." Bibi sighed. "Only the aftermath."

"So you drove past, saw something, and called emergency services. That's it?" Megan peered into her grandmother's eyes, searching for an indication that Bibi was holding back, trying to protect her granddaughter. She saw a spark of something and leaned in. "Bibi."

"I may have gotten close enough to touch the body."

"Touch the body?"

Bibi sighed. She closed her eyes, then opened them, focusing her very sharp attention on Megan. "I had to see if he was alive."

Megan glanced over Bibi's head, looking for Bobby King. He'd stopped to talk to the ring of firefighters, but his gaze was on Megan and Bibi. On the other side of the road, a Hummer was pulling up to the curb. She recognized Marty Jenner's jowly face through the windshield. Once the owner of the solar fields began grilling everyone, there'd be no answers. A Philadelphia investor and recovering attorney, Marty had a way of making the Winsome townsfolk feel small and extremely protective of their own.

"Who was it, Bibi? Who was killed?"

"I'm not sure. The body...was turned over." Another blink, this one longer. "I just saw blood." Bibi kept her voice steady, but the shake in her fingers gave her away. "Lots of blood." She frowned. "I felt for a pulse, but I knew it was pointless. He was...he wasn't...he couldn't have..."

"It's okay. Never mind." Megan reached out and grabbed Bibi's hand. She had more questions, but King had renewed his journey in their direction, and she could tell now wasn't the time to pepper her grandmother with queries. She waited until King reached them, which only took a few seconds.

"Megan." Bobby nodded a curt greeting. He looked hard at Bibi. "Thank you for calling us, Bonnie. I'm curious though—how did you know he was here?"

"I already told your people this."

"They said you saw color in the field, called 911, stopped to investigate, and that's when you found the body. Is that right?"

Bibi nodded.

"Nothing else?"

"No."

"You spy anyone leaving here, Bonnie? Someone running away? Maybe pass a car on the road?"

Megan shot him a questioning look. He returned the stare with a subtle shake of the head that said *just asking routine questions.*

"No," Bonnie said. "No one. No cars. Nothing."

The corners of King's mouth turned down. Tall, blocky, and blond, Bobby King was Winsome's youngest-ever police chief, but he was quickly becoming a seasoned professional—mostly out of necessity. Winsome had seen more action in the last year than in the entire decade before it. It was baptism by fire for King and his crew, and while Megan didn't always agree with their approach, she gave King props for hard work and ethics. He wanted to do the right thing.

"Bonnie, what brought you by here to begin with?"

This was the question Megan wanted answered. Curly Hill Road was four miles from the farm and seven miles from the café. Unless Bibi was headed on a roundabout route to the hardware store, was visiting Porter's house, or had decided to go for a hike, there was no need for her to be out here.

"Porter," Bibi said. "Brian Porter had a flat. His car died."

"Brian called you?" Megan asked. It made a certain sense. He'd called Clay. And Denver. Maybe he was getting impatient and decided to beg a ride from Bonnie too.

"Brian didn't call me," Bibi said. "Otto did."

Both Megan and King looked at her in surprise. "Otto Vance?" they said together.

Bibi nodded. "He drove past Porter coming the other direction. Said he didn't have time to stop, but wanted to let Megan know the boy needed assistance. Otto called the café. Only you'd already left, so I came out." Bibi glanced at Megan. "I was going to pick Brian up, but I came in from Curly Hill Road and never got to him.

King chewed his lip again. "You're sure it was Vance who called the café?"

"Of course I'm sure."

"Did he tell you where he was headed? Vance, I mean."

"No, just told me about Brian."

King frowned. "Did he sound upset?"

"Rushed, maybe, but not upset." Bibi let out a sigh. "Oh, I don't know, Bobby. When I heard Porter was out there with a flat, I left the café and got here as quickly as I could. I wasn't thinking about Otto. Now that I'm thinking about it, maybe he did sound upset or annoyed. He was kind of breathing hard."

Megan turned to King. "You think Otto had something to do with this?"

Bobby stood up straighter, forcing his full six-and-a-half-foot frame into military posture. "Not purposefully." King squinted in the direction of the pack of police officers, who were now talking with Marty Jenner. A body lay inside a bag nearby, the vague outline of a human form the only hint to its contents. "That body over there belonged to Otto Vance."

Megan glanced at him in surprise. Bibi let out a low moan. King placed a paw-like hand on her arm.

Softly, he said, "Bonnie, this means you may have been the last person to speak with Otto. You can understand our interest in interviewing you."

Bibi waved toward the scene behind them. "Do you think it was an accident?"

"I'm not sure why Otto was here. There's really no reason for him to be at the solar fields—unless *he* stopped to check something too." King placed a hand on his hip, squinted up toward the sun. "But yes, looks that way."

"He hit his head," Bibi said. "At least that's what I saw."

King nodded. "Coroner will have to corroborate, of course, but it does look like an accident. Seems he fell hard—very hard and at a very bad angle—and slammed his head into the sharp corner of a panel. Happened very recently, by the look of it."

"Where's his car?" Megan asked.

"One of my men found it in the state park lot."

Odd. Megan thought back to the scene at the café earlier that day, the spoken and unspoken tensions in the room. Otto's vitriolic words. Ted's Kuhl's reaction. An accident?

Megan sure hoped so.

Four

"You didn't notice anything odd at the café?" Megan asked her grandmother for what felt like the umpteenth time. "More arguing? A fight? Something we may have missed?"

"Oktoberfest has everyone agitated. But I heard the same noise that I hear every day. Grown men with nothing better to do than pick at each other."

"They love to argue. It keeps them going," Megan said. "And I suppose those grown men pay our bills."

Bibi sat in the kitchen chair and picked up her needlepoint. She stared at it, then put it back down. "I know," she said noncommittally. She glanced up at her granddaughter. "I really didn't hear anything else, Megan. I wish I had. I *want* to help."

"I know you do. I'm sorry for all the questions. I'll end the inquisition."

Bibi nodded. "You heard Bobby King. It was an accident." She brightened, bringing out the wrinkles around her eyes and drawing her sharp intelligence into focus. "Otto probably saw something while out on a walk—maybe an injured bird, solar panels can be bad for birds. And Otto had a soft spot for small creatures. I remember that about him. From the time he was young he could be counted on to help a bird or baby squirrel. One time your grandfather even found him with a bear cub. Its mother had died." Bibi shook her head at the memory. "Poor Lana. And those kids. He was a young man, Megan. Too young. At least to my standards."

Megan nodded. Otto *did* like animals, and he *was* too young.

Only what if his death had less to do with curiosity about a solar farm or a hurt bird and more to do with the all-too-common human foibles of greed, lust, or jealousy?

Megan thought about Otto racing past Brian Porter, calling Bibi rather than stopping himself. In a small town like Winsome, people went out of their way for neighbors. Even if they were late to something. And someone like Otto...who would save a bird? The fact that Otto didn't stop caused Megan to wonder where he was headed in such a hurry.

Bibi went on: "In any case, we'll send flowers. And maybe some cakes. I'm sure the Vance family will have people coming and going for days. They'll appreciate some cakes."

Megan nodded.

"Cakes would be good."

"I just wish I hadn't been the one to find him," Bibi said. "Maybe someone younger or faster could have gotten to him sooner. Maybe he would still be alive."

"I don't think so, Bibi. It sounds like he died instantly, based on what Bobby King said."

Bibi traced a swollen-knuckled finger down the length of her needlepoint. She stabbed the center of a flower with a sharp needle, pulling the bright red thread through the other side. "Such a waste," Bibi said heavily. "Much too young."

"Do you think maybe you're reading too much into things?" Clay said. His voice was kind but firm. "After what you went through, it would be easy to read motive into everything." Clay was referring to the body she and Denver had found in the barn last spring—a body that had been bludgeoned to death. A body that threw the town of Winsome into a tailspin.

It was later that evening. Clay and Megan were tending to the Pygmy goats, Heidi and Dimples. Each tiny goat wanted attention, and they took turns ramming their small heads into the back of Megan's legs while she was cleaning their heated pen. She stopped periodically to pet them, marveling at how much personality could fit into such a small package.

"After all," Clay continued, "it's been a rough year." His eyes pierced her own. Not a trace of pity or doubt—only concern. "One could forgive you for seeing nefarious intent where there is none."

"I know what I heard and saw. Don't forget, once upon a time I was paid to decipher people's motives and behaviors. That training doesn't just disappear."

She was referring to the years spent as an environmental attorney in Chicago, working for a big firm that defended corporations against claims of environmental malfeasance. Not quite the work she'd envisioned when she decided to go into environmental law, and after Mick's death overseas and her father's departure to Italy to be with his new girlfriend, she'd decided to change course.

When her father asked her to take over the farm and café and stay with Bibi, she'd agreed. She hadn't enjoyed practicing law, but something good had come out of it: a better understanding of human nature, boils and all.

Clay spread fresh hay on the floor, then flopped down next to Dimples. The goat immediately climbed on his lap and started chewing the cuff of his long-sleeved t-shirt. Clay didn't seem to mind.

"I'll take a ride by Jenner's place tomorrow," he said eventually. "See if there is anything curious about the panels. Something that may have caused Otto to stop on his way elsewhere."

"I'm sure the police are investigating that."

"If they have it in their heads that his death was an accident, they may not." He shrugged. "Can't hurt to take a look."

Clay was an engineering student and a die-hard tinkerer. When he wasn't studying or at the farm, he was inventing stuff in his apartment, which sat over the café in town. Megan had no idea what Clay created up there, but every day that the café building remained intact was, in Megan's mind, a good day.

"I would appreciate that," Megan said. "You're right, it can't hurt."

Clay nodded. He lifted Dimples up so that she was eye level and said, "Can we talk about the chair you found on Potter Hill?" He placed Dimples back on the floor and scratched behind her ears. "You've been under a lot of stress lately—"

"Stop. This isn't about stress, or Duvall's murder last spring, or anything other than facts. I know what I saw. Someone had a chair at the top of the hill and it was situated toward the farm." She wrapped her arms around her chest. "The angle gave a perfect view of the driveway. I know because I sat in it."

"That's what I wanted to talk about. I believe you. I just don't want to add to the stress." He picked up Heidi, looking into her eyes for signs of wateriness or discharge. Once she'd nestled into his chest, he glanced back at Megan. "You may have a stalker."

"I know." Megan sat heavily on the ground across from Clay. "The fact that whoever it was removed the chair after I discovered it worries me the most."

"Because they might have been watching you?"

"Or they were heading there at the same time and happened to see me." She thought again of treasure hunters and human greed. "Neither alternative is comforting."

Clay stood up and wiped his hands on a terrycloth towel. "I talked to Porter."

Megan looked up. "Porter?"

"I know he seems gruff and difficult, but I think he cares about you. He and I are going to take turns heading up there periodically. To make sure whoever it is doesn't set up camp somewhere else." Clay smiled. "It was Porter's idea."

"Absolutely not."

Clay glanced at her with surprise. "Why not?"

"You both have enough to do around here. If someone wants to spy on the farm, let them. All they'll see are dogs, goats, chickens, and a lot of boring farm work."

"And you." He softened his voice. "Doesn't that bother you?"

"Of course it does." Megan glanced at her watch and pulled herself upright. It was getting late. She saw the worry in Clay's eyes and tempered her position. "Fine, if you think it will help, go up occasionally. But if you see something, bring in King. I don't want any vigilantism, especially not from Porter."

Clay nodded his assent. "It does make me wonder why someone would want to watch Washington Acres."

Megan thought about the letter she'd found last spring, now tucked away in a small safe in her room. She thought about Otto Vance and whether her stalker could be related to what happened on that solar farm. The frown on Clay's face told her he had been contemplating Otto's death too. Before either of them could say anything to heighten the anxiety further, Megan stood and opened the gate to the goats' enclosure. She walked out into the cool night air. Gunther had been waiting outside the gate. He wagged his white tail furiously at the sight of Megan. She knelt down to pet him, using his calming presence to quiet the jitters in her mind.

Clay followed Megan, securing the gate behind him. "I'm going to close up the barn and head home. Will you and Bonnie be okay?"

Megan smiled at her farm manager. How someone so young— someone who'd had such an unorthodox upbringing—could be so chivalrous was always a mystery to Megan. Clay had Captain America Syndrome. But she was grateful he was in her life.

"We'll be fine."

"See you tomorrow, then."

Megan nodded and headed back toward the house. She paused in the driveway, outside the porch that led to the kitchen. The harvest moon lit her path, and she looked up, toward the hills beyond the farm. Toward Potter Hill. Was someone up there now, using their vantage point to watch her walk along the yard, enter her house? Maybe they had binoculars. She could almost picture a man sitting in the shadows, a lit cigarette by his side. Faceless, brooding. Megan jutted her chin forward and lifted her head. On impulse, she stuck out her arm. She wanted to follow with her middle finger but something held her back. Instead, she held up her hand, palm side toward Potter Hill. She refused to feel cowed on her own property. If someone was there, she was sending a message: I know you're watching. And I am not scared.

Inside, she double locked the door. She wasn't scared. Not really.

But she wasn't stupid either.

Five

"It's clean, Megan." Clay wiped a lock of dark hair from his eyes. He looked like a slightly more rugged Jake Gyllenhaal—in overalls. "I don't know what Otto was doing at Jenner's solar field, but I didn't see anything out of place."

"Had King placed crime tape in the area?" Last year when Duvall was killed in the barn, King had left crime tape up for days. Knowing how he was treating the scene of Otto's death would give them some inkling about what he'd found. Or what he suspected.

They were loading pumpkins into the truck to sell outside the café. Megan was standing in the truck bed and Clay was swinging the pumpkins from a pile on the ground into the back, where Megan was trying to sort them into some semblance of order.

He handed her two small ones and shook his head. "Not that I could see. Whatever happened there yesterday, there was no evidence of it today."

"Hmm. Did Clover mention anything?" Clover Hand was not only Megan's café/store manager, but the mostly on-again girlfriend of Police Chief Bobby King—and Clay's sister.

Clay stroked his chin with one slender hand. "She didn't mention Otto when I spoke with her last night." Clay pulled an especially large pumpkin from the dwindling pile and tossed it effortlessly onto the truck. "I've got this one." He jumped onto the truck and pulled the large fruit toward the side of the bed. That done, he said, "I did witness something odd though."

"Oh? What was that?" Megan leaned against the truck in need of a break. The sun had just come flaming over the horizon, and a hush had fallen across the farm. It was only seven thirty in the morning, and the air was brisk and cool, an icy undercurrent a harbinger of the freezing months to come. She took a swig of water from the bottle resting on the edge of the truck and waited.

"That Ophelia woman? The woman running Oktoberfest? I saw her with Glen Sauer."

"That's not really news." Megan told Clay about her phone call with Ophelia and about Sauer's appointment as the farm sponsor for the late October celebration.

"I guess that explains it." Clay paused. "I wonder why they're bending the rules for him."

"Because he convinced them to? Because he has by far the largest farm in the area?"

"Maybe." He didn't sound convinced.

Clay placed the last of the pumpkins in the truck bed. Megan jumped out and they pulled the gate up, securing it into place.

Megan said, "Something's still bothering you?"

"Just the way they were talking."

"What do you mean?"

Clay's brow creased, as it always did when he was thinking. Behind him, the old barn loomed, its stately form a reminder that all was not always as it seemed in Winsome. "Glen wore an angry scowl and Ophelia seemed to be doing her best to appease him. She's a looker, and he can be...well, he tends to leer. Made me uncomfortable, I guess."

"I haven't met her in person. Do you think they were fighting?"

"Maybe. I don't know. I'm not sure why the town hired her. I mean, I get that the Oktoberfest celebration is a big deal. The town is spending a lot to have the week-long event come off without a hitch. But did we really need a PR specialist to run the show?"

"The committee must have thought so." Megan was not enchanted with committees, especially ones that were self-appointed and self-important, as many of Winsome's seemed to be.

"The funny thing is, this was Otto's baby—yet he didn't seem that involved in the whole affair."

"I sensed some tension about that," Clay said. "Resentment that his brewery was chosen as the beer sponsor. A little too cozy." Clay was retying his work boots. He stopped to look up at Megan. "Do you think what happened to Otto could be related? People get funny when it comes to this stuff. Maybe a fight that went awry?"

Megan thought again about the argument at the café amongst the Breakfast Club members. Ted Kuhl's anger over not being chosen as the beer sponsor, the obvious disagreement between the men about how the business lotteries were being handled. "I have thought of that, but I don't want to believe Otto's death has anything to do with Oktoberfest. I know people can be petty, but to allow something so silly to end like that..." Megan shook her head. "A terrible thought."

"Well, we may never know." Boots retied, Clay picked up the handles of a wheelbarrow and started back toward the barn. "Want to take some of the garlic to the café with us? Alvaro could use some, and I think we're almost out of it on the shelves."

"Sure." They'd had a strong garlic harvest the past summer, and scores of braids of Music, Chesnok Red, and other varieties hung from the depths of the barn, enough to last for months. "Have you talked to Ophelia yourself?"

Clay swung around, toward Megan. "No. Why?"

"Just something you said earlier. About why she's here in Winsome."

"The committee hired her PR firm to help with Oktoberfest." He tilted his head. "What's there to know?"

"Why Ophelia? How did they find her? How much is she charging? Just seems sort of extravagant for such a small town."

Clay smiled. "You forget, Megan, we're still on the East Coast, in the northeast corridor. Lots of money around here—and I'm sure the committee has set its sights on bringing some of that money to the good people of Winsome."

Including Sauer farm, Megan thought.

"Perhaps it is that simple."

"But as for why Ophelia specifically, got me." Clay had reached the barn entrance and was maneuvering the wheelbarrow through the wide doors and into the building. "Ask Merry Chance. If anyone would know Ophelia's qualifications, it's the town busybody."

Megan found herself too busy over the next day to seek out Merry, but on late Friday afternoon of that same week, the town's nursery owner and expert on all things Winsome stopped by the farm looking for eggs.

"The store is out of them," Merry said, eyeing Megan over the top of her fuchsia readers. Her tone let Megan know that running out of eggs was a grave sin. "Perhaps you have more here?"

"I'll have Brian bring you some. How many do you need?"

"Two dozen. I'm making my famous quiche for a church fundraiser this weekend."

Megan texted Porter, asking him to fetch two dozen eggs from the cooler. Merry was standing on the front porch. She peered around Megan, straining for a glimpse into the kitchen. "Is Bonnie home?"

"She is. Would you like to come in?"

"Oh, I don't want to bother you, Megan. But it *would* be nice to get off my feet for a spell."

"It's no bother. My grandmother is making herself dinner. I'm sure she'd enjoy the company." Megan choked the words out. Bibi didn't care for Merry Chance any more than she liked hemorrhoids or arthritic knuckles.

"Oh, good. Then I'll just wait inside for those eggs." Merry clutched her light blue purse tight to her light blue sweater-clad bosom. "You look nice. What's the occasion?"

Megan glanced down at her brown skirt, brown boots, and the vintage ruby-and-brown print blouse she'd picked up in SoHo. Not particularly dressy. Considering she spent seventy-five percent of her time in blue jeans, she supposed this outfit looked like an upgrade to the rest of Winsome. "As a matter of fact, I'm having dinner out this evening."

Merry smirked. "With a certain Scottish veterinarian?"

"Perhaps."

"I'm glad to hear that." Merry touched Megan's arm lightly on her way inside. "It's not good to be alone all of the time." A shadow fell across her face. "Trust me."

Inside, Bibi was at the stove, heating a pot of water. When she caught sight of Merry, she shot a furtive questioning glance at Megan, her lips pressed into a frown.

"Merry's here for eggs," Megan said quickly.

"And maybe a cup of tea," Merry chimed in. "If you don't mind a little company, Bonnie."

Bibi didn't answer immediately. Megan knew Bibi wouldn't outright lie and say she didn't mind, nor would she hurt Merry's feelings. Instead, Bibi filled a kettle with water and placed it on the gas stove, letting time take away the need for a response. Then she reached into an overhead cabinet and pulled the tea box down.

Bibi said, "Earl Grey, green, English Breakfast, or some ridiculous ginger vanilla chai concoction Megan picked up in Chicago?" Bibi's inflection on the last words said that while she thought ginger vanilla chai tea was ridiculous, she was proud to have a granddaughter well-traveled and sophisticated enough to pick some up.

"Ooh, I'll try the chai tea."

Bibi's frown deepened, but she placed a bag in a navy-blue "Winsome Rules" mug—a leftover from the days when Megan's father owned a Winsome souvenir shop—and swung her head in Megan's direction. "Would you like some tea too?"

"None for me, Bibi. I can't stay long."

"Ah, yes." Bibi smiled. She liked Denver Finn, and she let Megan know it at every turn.

Bibi pulled another mug from the cabinet—this one had tiny Christmas ornaments and ornamental lights painted on it and "Jingle some bells in Winsome!" written in red script along the rim—and dropped a chamomile tea bag inside. When the teakettle went off, she poured water into the two cups and placed them on the table.

Megan heard a sound coming from another room. "Is that your phone, Bibi?"

Bibi paused, listening. "Yes. It's probably your father, Megan. Let me grab that. I'll be right back."

"I'll get it for you—"

With a hard glance at Merry, Bibi said, "No, no. You two talk. I'll only be a minute." She disappeared into the hall.

Megan added honey, cream, napkins, and two spoons to the table setting. "Have a seat, Merry."

Merry sat heavily in one of the four chairs around the kitchen table. She poured honey into her mug and while she slowly stirred her tea, said, "It's a shame about Otto."

This was the entrée Megan had been waiting for. She was glad Bibi was out of the room. Bibi didn't need a reminder of what she'd witnessed.

Casually, Megan said, "It is a shame. Have you heard any more about what happened?"

Merry took a long sip of tea, eyes wide over the rim of the cup. She dabbed at her mouth with a napkin. "I heard it was an accident. He fell and hit his head on one of those solar panels, and, well, you know." She leaned in, feral interest gleaming in her eyes. "But what was he *doing* at the solar farm? I wonder if something illicit was happening. I've heard he and Lana had been having marital issues."

Lana was Otto's widow. A six-foot-tall former beauty queen, Lana Vance was also the brewery manager and head bartender.

Megan said, "Otto didn't seem like the cheating type." And he didn't. He'd been part of the café Breakfast Club since its inception, and Megan had never seen him so much as glance at another woman. Not to mention that a solar farm would be an odd place for an extramarital dalliance. But who knew? Stranger things had been known to happen.

"They never seem like the cheating type." That shadow again.

Megan wondered whether Merry was talking from experience. She'd been a fixture in Winsome for so long that Megan never bothered to question Merry's history.

She felt a wave of shame at her own self-centeredness. A wave that crashed abruptly when Merry said, "How about Bonnie? She was the first on the scene. She probably knows something."

"My grandmother didn't see anything...only Otto."

Another sip of tea, another feigned innocent glance over the rim. "Why was she there?"

"She was heading to pick up Brian Porter. He had a flat tire. She happened to see Otto."

Merry looked disappointed, as Megan knew she would. Mundane altruism wasn't exciting. "Well, it is strange, Otto at the solar farm. There's a story there. I'm certain of it."

Megan sat down across from Merry. She wanted to shift the conversation away from Otto's body before Bibi came back, so she said carefully, "There does seems to be a lot of tension in the air in Winsome recently."

"Oh, absolutely. It's Oktoberfest. I'm as excited about it as anyone, but it certainly brings out the worst in people. You should see the committee members. No one can agree on anything. And to think, this was all Otto's idea." Merry brightened. "Although he would have liked that it's bringing attention and money to the area."

"Not for everyone," Bibi said. She came quietly into the kitchen and sank into a chair at the table. "Lottery my ancient derriere. That Ophelia woman seems to be picking and choosing her favorites for the sponsorship positions."

Merry, whose nursery had been chosen to sponsor the event—not a particularly big deal as hers was the only flower gig in town—looked suddenly uncomfortable.

Megan said, "I'm sure Ophelia is just doing her job. It can't be easy."

"Seems pretty easy to me," Bibi quipped. "Put some names in a hat and draw them out. Presto. Random drawing."

Merry's color deepened. Megan stifled a smile. As usual, Bibi had gone right to the heart of the problem. "Do you know who brought Ophelia in?" Megan asked.

Looking relieved to be on safer footing, Merry said, "Her firm came recommended to the committee. She's a PR generalist and event coordinator, but very good at her job. From what I hear."

"Who recommended the firm?"

Merry frowned. "You know, I'm not sure. I think Roger Becker may have suggested her, although I'm not sure how he knows her. She certainly comes with a business pedigree."

"Is the Oktoberfest committee happy with her work?"

"Oh, very. She's bright and tenacious and understands today's market. She's really taken the lead, allowing the rest of the committee members to focus on their own tasks."

The back door rattled, and Clay came inside carrying a small shopping bag.

"Sorry," he said to Megan. "Goats escaped. Again. I have Porter chasing Heidi in the woods, so I come bearing eggs." He held the bag out to Merry.

Megan glanced at Merry. "They're little escape artists."

Bibi stood. "You'll want to get your eggs home before they go bad."

Megan fought the urge to roll her eyes. The eggs would be fine. Bibi was just ready for Merry to leave. Merry took her cue and accepted the bag.

"Can you put this on my tab at the café?" Merry asked.

"Sure." Megan paused, still thinking about Ophelia. "Merry, do you know why they changed the rules regarding the sponsorships? The lotteries were supposed to go to smaller businesses with local markets, but the Sauers were awarded the farm spot. That's fine— I'd just like to understand why."

Merry blinked her eyes once, twice, three times—before the blush returned to her cheeks. She raised the bag of eggs. "I should go."

Megan pressed. "It seems odd that they moved the goal post at the last minute, making it easier for large operations to be considered. I'm sure there is a strategic reason for the change, but Ophelia hasn't been able to articulate it. I'm just curious."

But Merry was already out the door. "Talk to Ophelia again about the lottery, Megan," she said over her shoulder. "I'm sure if you ask nicely, she'll share her insights. The decision was hers, after all."

After everyone left, Megan dumped the tea bags into the sink and washed the cups and silverware while she waited for Denver. Bibi was standing by the window, looking out into the yard, a melancholy expression on her face.

"Penny for your thoughts," Megan said, echoing the trite saying she'd heard so many times as a kid.

It took Bibi a long moment to respond. "That was King on the phone."

"And?"

"He wants to talk to me again. They think it was an accident, but they need to button up some loose ends."

"Did he say what those loose ends were?"

"Just details about the time I found him, timing of the call to the café, that sort of thing." Bibi turned around to face Megan. The lines around her mouth looked deeper, her shoulders sagged under the weight of her sweater. "It sounds as though he went for a walk, ended up in the solar field, and tripped."

"You don't believe that now?"

Bibi wrapped her arms around her chest. "I don't know what to believe."

"What bothers you?"

"Something. Nothing. I guess that's the problem." She met Megan's gaze, but the spark Megan knew so well seemed diminished. "I overheard part of your conversation with Merry. Why was Otto at that farm? Why did he pass right by Porter? His fall may have been an accident, Megan, but that man was in a rush to get there. And unless he had a newfound love for energy science, I'm afraid someone else was involved."

Megan nodded. "I had the same thought. You're wondering who is that someone?"

"And why aren't they coming forward?" Bibi rubbed her upper arms with hands that had seen more than eight decades. "King wants this put to bed. But I'm old enough to understand that a person scared to come forward is a person up to no good."

A knock at the door interrupted Megan's next statement. They'd been so engrossed that they hadn't heard Denver pull up.

Bibi opened the door for Denver. She smiled when she saw him, and said in a lighter tone, "You two have fun. Just be careful. Please."

"We will, Bibi."

Bibi nodded. She walked to the sink, her shoulders hunched. Megan closed the door and locked it, willing her grandmother to also stay safe.

Later that night, under the glow of the moon, Megan asked Denver Finn what he thought about Ophelia Dilworth.

"Only met her twice," he said. They were sitting outside on his deck, close to one another under a wool blanket. The night air was sharp with moisture, and Megan could almost smell winter setting in. Denver's five dogs were curled in various spots on and around the blanket. Megan had her head on Denver's shoulder, and he stroked her hair with gentle rhythmic motions, his thoughts clearly elsewhere.

"Did she strike you as competent and trustworthy?"

"Aye, I guess." He tilted his face down to look at Megan. Megan was again struck by his rugged handsomeness, his fiercely intelligent eyes. "Why are ye asking me this, Megs? Did she do something to bother ye?"

"Not exactly."

"Well, ye don't quite seem yourself. Why might that be?"

Denver's accent got stronger when he was upset or tired. Tonight he looked exhausted. He'd spent the afternoon overseeing the breach birth of a foal. The foal and mare lived after hours of worry and struggle, but when Denver showed up at the farm, she'd sensed his weariness. She offered to make him dinner at his house instead of going out, an invitation he eagerly accepted. So after a light meal of salad niçoise and white Burgundy, they headed out to relax on the deck.

"I mean it," Denver said. "Something's bothering you. Even a country vet can see that."

Megan smiled. Leaning against his solid frame, she told him about the Sauers' farm and the Oktoberfest celebration. "Seems strange, doesn't it? Sauer isn't even that well-liked by most of the people on the committee."

"He's a cash cow though. Pun intended." Denver's face contorted in distaste. He'd stopped providing services to the Sauer farm last year after rescuing Gunther. "No matter their rationale, that's not right," he said. "Challenge it."

"I tried to. I sound like a sore loser."

"Don't ye do that, Megs. This farm is your baby. They broke their own rules when it was convenient for them to do so."

True, but Megan knew from talking with Ophelia that they would simply find a way to justify their actions. Her eyes were feeling heavy. Denver's body felt so warm, a stark contrast to the biting fall air. She considered telling Denver about the conversation she'd witnessed between Otto Vance and Ted Kuhl, but she was suddenly too sleepy to form the words. She hadn't mentioned the chair on Potter Hill either. She told herself she didn't want Denver to worry, but she knew deep down it was more than that. If she told him, she risked resenting his reaction, and he'd be in a no-win situation. He knew about the treasure on her property too, so he knew as well as anyone what a stalker could mean. Whether he told her she was being paranoid or he tried to talk her into being more cautious, she would be annoyed. She didn't want to go down either path with Denver. Better to say nothing. For now.

Megan sensed Denver looking at her, felt the caress of his breath against her cheek and the strength of his arm underneath her. He was waiting for her to make a move. A kiss, a gesture, anything to indicate that tonight she'd stay. It wasn't just concern about leaving Bibi home alone that stopped her. She wanted to stay. She'd wanted to for a while now, but once their relationship went in that direction, there was no going back. She wasn't ready. Sex for her wasn't simply a physical act, and the emotionality of it wasn't something she could deal with. Not just yet. But would he wait? She hoped so. She'd rather have him move on than betray her own needs though: two unwanted consequences, but one was worse.

Forcing her eyelids to open, she stretched, then disentangled herself from the man and the blanket. She stood.

"I should go."

"Aye, it's getting late." Voice flat.

Megan asked, "Will I see you later this week?"

Denver unfurled to his full six-foot-plus height. "I'd like that."

Megan stretched on tippy toes and kissed his lips. "We can have dinner in or out, doesn't matter to me."

One dog barked, another wound its way between Megan's ankles.

"There may be more privacy out," Denver said. "Git, ye wee pains."

Suddenly feeling somber, Megan said, "I forgot. Otto's memorial service is coming up next week. Want to come with me and Bibi?"

"Ta. That would be nice." Denver rested his head atop Megan's. "Shame, that. He was a good man."

It seemed a rhetorical statement, and Megan didn't respond. She stayed like that, entwined with Denver, feeling the beat of his pulse in time with her own. He was the first to pull away. Megan held on as long as she could before heading back to her car. Time to go home. Alone.

Six

As much as she tried, Megan couldn't get the Breakfast Club—and the tension between Otto and Ted Kuhl—out of her mind. She replayed that morning over and over, looking for some clue as to why Otto might have driven right past Porter and ended up at the solar farm. Bibi was right, something was missing—but she came up empty every time. It didn't help that Bibi seemed not to be herself since the accident. Her grandmother was pale, withdrawn, and more snappish than usual. Megan knew finding a body could do that to you. Accident or not, Otto's time was cut short, and it was Bibi who'd first had to witness the grisly aftermath. Only Bibi's current state of mind seemed related to more than finding Otto. It was as though the incident made her feel unsafe, insecure in the town she'd called home for her entire life.

Megan wished there was something she could do.

At the café the next morning, Megan asked Clover if she'd heard anything more about the investigation into Otto's death. The café was unusually quiet, and Clover was waiting on a man Megan didn't recognize. He was sitting at the lunch counter, drinking coffee and reading *American Angler* magazine. Clover topped off the cup and he thanked her, pulling the mug to his lips with fingers crisscrossed with burn scars.

"Far as I know, it's been ruled an accident," Clover said. "Otto fell and smashed his head. Killed him instantly."

"No signs of struggle?"

Clover arched well-shaped eyebrows. "No, why?"

"Just wondering."

"You think someone did something to make Otto fall?"

"I just think it's odd that he drove past Porter, who was clearly stranded on the road."

"That bothers you?"

"It's out of character."

"You always did see patterns." Clover made a "hmm" sound. "Maybe he was having an affair. He left his car at the park and met whoever it was at the solar fields."

"That's what Merry Chance said."

"Oh, man, now I sound like Merry." Clover leaned against the cashier's counter, her scantily clad backside dangerously close to knocking over a display of Sunny's organic mango lip balm. "Seriously though, you have a good sense for people. If you think there's more to it, we should tell Bobby." Clover chewed on her bottom lip, looking thoughtful. "Although his force is stretched thin right now. With Oktoberfest and all. I'm sure he's hoping this was just an accident."

Megan shook her head. "I don't have anything concrete anyway." Megan forced a smile—no use telling tales when she didn't have a complete picture. "Looks like you and Alvaro have things under control. I'm going to head back to the farm and work in the greenhouses. Need anything?"

Clover shook her head, sending long silky brown hair in all directions. "Nope." Her eyes widened suddenly. She snapped her finger. "Actually, yes! Ted left something here yesterday. I was going to give it to him this morning, but I must have missed him. Mind dropping it off at his house on your way?"

Clover walked around to the back side of the checkout counter. She reached underneath and handed Megan a thick manila file folder. "Here you go. Just let him know he left it under the newspapers." She waved her hands, flashing nails like neon daggers. "I didn't even open the file. Whatever he has in there remained safe in my keeping."

"No problem." Megan eyed the folder warily, wondering what

was inside. She would drop it off—a good excuse to talk to Kuhl. She'd known Ted for years, since she was a little girl. If nothing else, maybe he could help her get over this feeling that all was not right in Winsome.

Ted Kuhl lived with his daughter, Emily, in a row home on the outskirts of the Winsome town proper. Like most of the residences on the street, the house was a plain-faced unit, more utilitarian than elegant, with a white stucco exterior and a concrete porch bordered by a black wrought-iron railing. A welcome mat greeted Megan at the front door, its blood-red and sun-yellow daisies faded nearly to gray. Megan knocked, and the door swung open almost immediately. Emily Kuhl stood before her, her face registering first relief, then disappointment, before finally settling on fear.

"I'm sorry to disturb you," Megan said. "I was hoping to see your dad."

Emily flashed a half smile. "Yeah, well, join the club."

Emily pushed open the screen door and Megan followed her into a cramped living room. The house smelled of disinfectant and furniture polish. Green shag carpet graced the floor and two brown plaid love seats faced one another across a battered pine coffee table. Stacks of books covered every square inch of a small desk at the back of the room. Emily traced Megan's gaze.

"Business books, brewing guides, recipes. Dad's a nut when it comes to research."

"I can see that."

Research, Megan knew, for his fledgling brewery, Road Master Ale. The brewery he wanted to showcase at the Oktoberfest celebration. She turned to look at Ted's daughter. Like her father, Emily Kuhl was tall and gangly. A severe ponytail twisted thick blond hair into submission. Somewhere in her late twenties, Emily had moved back home with her six-month-old daughter, Lily, after the breakup of her short-lived abusive marriage—facts Megan had overheard at the café. Today the frayed hems on the sleeves of

Emily's khaki sweater gave testament to raw nerves. Even now she was picking at the loose ends like some people worry a scab.

"Would you like to sit down?"

"I don't want to keep you." Megan pulled the file out of her tote bag. "I just stopped by to return this to your father."

Emily glanced at the file without comprehension. She took it, opened it, and then stared back at Megan in disbelief. "Where did you find this?"

"Clover found it at the café. He'd left it under his newspapers."

"Today?"

"Yesterday. Clover meant to give it to him today, but she missed him."

"So he was there? For breakfast?" Emily looked to be on the verge of tears. "Tell me he was there."

"I can't say for sure. I didn't arrive until later. None of the Breakfast Club—his group of friends—was there, but maybe they'd already left, including your father."

Emily's skin paled to the color of raw milk. She fingered a large gold cross that hung around her neck, twirling the chain around her fingers.

"Emily, are you okay?"

Megan didn't know Emily well—just well enough for idle chitchat and to say hello when they bumped into each other at the farmers market—but clearly the manila file had jostled a nerve.

"Would you sit? I'd like it if you'd sit." Emily swallowed. "I think I need to sit."

So Megan sat. She waited while Emily fetched two plastic cups of ice water.

"What's going on?"

"I don't know. I haven't seen my father since he left for the tap room yesterday. He never came home last night."

"No call, email, or text?"

"Nothing."

"Did you check his business lines? Maybe he tried to contact you through Road Master."

Emily shook her head. "Did that—nothing."

Megan refused to jump to conclusions. "Let's call the café. If he was there this morning, Alvaro, our cook, will know."

But a quick call to the café was inconclusive.

"Alvaro doesn't think your father was there, but he was so busy he couldn't say for sure." In actuality, the cranky cook had said, "I'm too busy to babysit our freeloading customers, so how would I know?" but Megan chose to paraphrase.

"He wasn't there. If he had been, he would have asked for the file. He would never have purposefully left this there." She raised the file, opened it, and fanned through the contents. "This has been his life for the last three years."

"The brewery?"

Emily tore at the hems on her sleeves frantically. She nodded. "After Mom died, he sold the house and moved into this dump. He used the garage out back to home brew at first. People told him he was on to something, and he believed them. He put every cent he had into Road Master, rented the tap room, thought he could grow Road Master into a national brand." She slumped against the back of the couch. "At first I thought it was a good distraction, a way to deal with grief. But he became more and more obsessed."

"And then the town turned down his bid to serve at Oktoberfest."

"He saw Oktoberfest as his ticket to building his brand. Even though he could still sell, he wouldn't get the advertising and attention the sponsors get." Emily's eyes darkened. "Otto is established, has a bigger operation. Plus, Oktoberfest was Otto's idea to begin with. But Dad's beers are *better*. Otto brewed beer so he could have a microbrewery that complemented his tavern. My dad is all about the beer. He deserved that shot."

"There are other things he can do to promote his brews."

Emily shook her head. "Not like that. Thousands of people in one spot over the course of a week? The name of the brewery slapped on every billboard, every advertisement? Talk about exposure. When the committee chose Otto Vance, my father was heartbroken. Irate. He asked for a spotlight piece, a mention at the chili cook-off. Anything." She met Megan's gaze. "I think he took it personally. As though the whole town didn't believe in him."

Megan could see that. She understood how valuable a sponsorship could be if the Oktoberfest celebration drew in the kind of crowds the committee was expecting. Washington Acres Café was selling food at various events across the week-long celebration, but it would be the Sauers' name on the brochure cover, the billboard, the newspaper articles. That kind of exposure could trigger sales beyond Oktoberfest, so Ted's disappointment made sense. But Megan could also see that a man so obsessed, so hurt, might act out in desperation.

"Does your father blame anyone in particular?"

Emily looked surprised at the question. "I don't know. Not particularly. Maybe the committee overseeing the Oktoberfest. And his competition, of course."

"Otto?"

Emily nodded. "He felt sure that Otto had made the committee block him so the competition would be limited. Honestly, he was so upset that he was directing his anger everywhere. It was hard to determine what was real and what was paranoia." She frowned. "He just hasn't been himself—and it seems to be getting worse."

Clearly the thought that Otto's death and her father's plight were related had never crossed her mind. That or Emily was an excellent actress. "Why would your dad have brought his business file to the café?"

"I have no idea. Maybe he was meeting with someone about a loan. He's run out of money. Maybe he's still trying to convince someone on the committee to allow him to take over the brewery sponsorship."

Now that Otto was out of the way, Megan thought. But was Ted Kuhl—quiet, diligent, wounded Ted Kuhl—capable of doing something so heinous? No. The thought was ridiculous.

Then why this constant hammering tension in her belly? Megan finished her water and rose to leave.

"Don't go." Emily's eyes widened, panicked. "I thought...maybe you could help me figure out where to look. You being a lawyer and everything."

"Former lawyer." Megan smiled gently. "I don't know where your dad could be, Emily. He's probably out nursing his hurts and needs time alone. If he shows up at the café, we'll call you. I'll ask Alvaro and Clover to be on alert."

Emily sat there. Teeth gnashed at a bruised bottom lip.

"Is there something more?" Megan asked. "Something you're not telling me?"

Emily nodded. Megan could hear light whimpering coming from somewhere deeper in the house. Emily glanced backwards, seemed to be weighing her choices. Finally she said, "Wait here. Please."

When she returned, she had Lily on her hip. The baby was chubby and rosy and happy—all the things a baby her age should be.

Emily shoved something toward Megan. "Look at this."

It was a single piece of lined paper, ripped out of a three-ring binder. At the top was a small silver key taped onto the paper with clear Scotch tape.

The paper had several sets of numbers on it. Megan eyed Emily questioningly.

"They're his bank accounts, and that's the key to his safe deposit box."

"He left these for you?"

Emily nodded. "When I came home from work yesterday, these were on the dining room table."

"With anything else?"

"No." Eyes darted toward the doorway. She hugged the baby closer to her breast.

Megan sighed. She could tell Emily wasn't telling her everything—but why should she? She didn't know Megan well. She was simply scared and looking for someone safe to confide in. "Emily, have you called the police?"

"No." That alarm again. "Why would I call the police?"

Megan waited for Emily to draw the conclusion herself. Eventually Emily said, "In case he hurt himself."

"That's what you're worried about, isn't it?" Megan asked gently.

Emily rested her head against the baby's. She didn't answer, but watery brown eyes spoke for her.

"Do you want me to do it for you?"

Emily shook her head. "I'll call. I promise."

Megan hated to do it, but she asked the question that had been plaguing her since she saw Otto's covered inert form carted away from that solar farm. "Do you think there could be another reason he's left?"

"What other reason could there be?"

"Do you think your father is capable of hurting someone else, Emily?"

"No. Never." Emily pulled her shoulders up, standing at her full height. She turned Lily away from Megan and shook her head violently. "Himself? Maybe. He hasn't been the same since my mother died. But someone else?" Comprehension dawned in her eyes. "Like Otto Vance? No way. Not even by accident, if that's what you're insinuating."

"I'm not insinuating anything. I'm simply asking you a question. Your father left you those accounts for a reason." Megan paused. "Please call the police. Have them look for him. I'm sure he's fine and just nursing his hurts, but just in case."

"I will."

The trusting warmth was gone from Emily's voice now. Megan left, feeling as though she'd stolen a treasured doll from a child. She too wanted to believe Ted Kuhl was fine—and incapable of anything worse than anger and rage at a world that had let him down. But there were a lot of coincidences here. And a man didn't simply leave home for no reason.

* * *

Megan returned home to find the house empty. She'd intended to work in the greenhouses planting a new round of lettuce seeds for winter harvest, produce Alvaro would use at the café. Despite Sadie's excitement at seeing her and Gunther's insistent kisses, Megan didn't feel like being at the farm. Not now. Emily's reaction and the reality that Ted Kuhl was missing weighed heavily on her.

Although the police were looking at Otto's death as an accident, when she added up three bits of information—Ted's anger about Oktoberfest, Otto's strange behavior the afternoon he died, and Ted's sudden disappearance—logic told her there was more going on here. Bibi was right. Connecting the dots seemed to indicate that Ted had something to do with Otto's death. A fight or a push, perhaps. He could have been the person who fled the scene. It didn't have to add up to murder.

Megan bid the dogs goodbye and climbed into her truck. She wasn't sure where she was going, she just knew she needed to go *somewhere*. She caught a glimpse of the dogs' faces peeking through the window. She exited the truck, wrote Bibi a quick note, and loaded the dogs into the pickup. She'd drive and think for a while. Maybe with some time to mull, her brain would sort things out.

Seven

It was after four when Megan pulled into her aunt's driveway. She was partly relieved, partly apprehensive to see Sarah Birch's car in the lot. Her paternal grandfather's sister lived in a storybook cottage outside of Winsome. Thick woods of mature trees horse-shoed around abundant flower and vegetable gardens. Elaborate fairy gardens peeked out from under foliage, their miniature leaf beds and walnut-shell cradles suggesting more whimsy than Sarah might admit to. With the fiery leaves and the last of the fall-blooming perennials painting starbursts of deep purple and bright orange, it was easy to see why the famous mystery author secluded herself here. Although only minutes from Winsome and less than an hour from Philadelphia, her home felt eons away from the chaos and uncertainty of the world.

Megan and the dogs climbed out of the car. Sadie and Gunther ran ahead, circling the gardens and nipping at each other's legs. Megan made her way to the door. She was about to knock when the front door opened and her Aunt Sarah rushed out of the entryway onto the small porch landing.

"Megan, you gave me a scare! I was just about to leave and wasn't expecting to see someone on this porch. But I am so very happy to see you."

"Good to see you too," Megan managed. She hadn't known Aunt Sarah at all until about six months ago, so it was hard to muster enthusiasm for a woman who'd been nothing but a vague ghost of a memory for most of her life.

Sarah scanned the yard, spotted the dogs frolicking by the woods, and said, "Would you like to come in? The dogs are welcome too."

"If you need to leave, I don't want to hold you up."

"No, that's fine. I was just heading out to get a bottle of wine. It can wait."

"If you're sure." Megan called to Sadie and Gunther. Gunther, better trained every day, came immediately and sat before her, the obedient livestock guardian dog. Sadie looked at her, sniffed a flower, peed next to a bush, and then trotted her way toward the house, stopping twice to investigate something interesting. For Sadie, obedient livestock guardian dog was clearly not a career aspiration.

"He's a beautiful dog," Sarah said, pointing toward Gunther. "A Great Pyrenees?"

"A Polish Tatra Sheepdog. Like a Pyrenees, but slightly smaller and pure white." Megan bent down to pet Gunther and his tail wagged furiously. "When he's not muddy, that is." He licked her and she smiled. Hard to believe this was the same downtrodden pup who'd been so mistreated by Sauer only months ago.

"Well, we're letting the chill inside. Come in for something to eat. And I have water and cookies for the dogs." She looked at Megan over the bridge of her prominent nose. "Can they have ginger snap people cookies?"

"You've met my grandmother. She says no table food for the dogs and then feeds them when no one is looking. So yes, one cookie is fine."

Megan followed Sarah through the dining room and into the kitchen. Her aunt had renovations completed last spring and the house was back to order—mostly. Books, half-finished sketches, and piles of manuscript paper still cluttered the flat surfaces.

"Ignore the mess," Sarah said. She pointed to a white table in the bright cozy cottage kitchen. Blue milk paint-coated wainscoted cabinets paired nicely with bright white trim and pale yellow walls. Colorful Mexican majolica tiles formed one countertop, worn three-inch maple butcher block the other. Something simmering in a crock pot smelled of garlic and smoky cumin.

"Vegetarian chili," Sarah said. "You're welcome to stay for dinner. I'm making cornbread too."

"No, thank you." But that would be a great combination for the café, Megan thought—something to please Winsome's growing vegan population. Maybe Alvaro could add that to the menu for the Oktoberfest cook-off.

"Are you sure? I have plenty."

"Bibi will be expecting me."

"Coffee or tea, then? I have some coffee on, but tea will just take a moment."

"Coffee would be great."

Sarah tossed a ginger snap to each of the dogs and then placed a plate of cookies on the table. She poured coffee. "Cream?" When Megan nodded, she placed a ceramic pot of cream, a matching small ceramic pot of sugar, and a tiny pewter spoon on the table before sitting down.

Megan studied her aunt from across the table. Sarah, her grandfather's sister, had Megan's father's green eyes and square jaw, but her stare was intelligent, serious, and rather shrewd— unlike the *joie de vivre* of her father's easy countenance. Sarah's long graying hair hung in one ropey braid down her back. Today she wore black wool pants cut wide and loose and a red-print kaftan that skimmed the blocky lines of her torso. Her hands were big and thick-knuckled with clean short nails. No-nonsense working hands—like Megan's.

Megan wanted to fight this feeling of kinship with an aunt who had betrayed her, but try as she might, she couldn't muster anger— only bewilderment.

"Megan, you seem unsettled," Sarah said. "Everything okay with Bonnie?"

"My grandmother is fine. So is the farm."

Sarah took a sip of coffee and cocked her head sideways, waiting.

"I'm struggling with a bit of a moral dilemma, and I was hoping for some insight from you."

"A moral dilemma? Of the intellectual or emotional variety?"

"Is there a difference?"

Sarah smiled. "Depends on your attachment to the underlying problem."

So different from talking with Bibi, Megan thought, for whom many things were black and white, cut and dry, right and wrong. Lawyers were used to working within the gray—and so, Megan figured, were crime authors. That's what had brought her here.

Megan started with a question. "You and Ted Kuhl knew each other in school?"

"We did indeed—although we were four years apart."

"How well do you know him now?"

"How well do I know the man little Teddy has become? Not very well, I guess. Why?"

Megan shared her concerns with Sarah—from overhearing the conversation between him and Otto, to Otto's behavior toward a stranded Porter, to Ted's recent disappearance. "Something is off."

"You think Ted had something to do with Otto's death." It was a statement, not a question.

Megan looked toward the window. Nodded. "He might not have been the cause, but I think he knows something at least."

"And only you overheard their heated conversation. You're afraid you misinterpreted what you heard, and you don't want to get an innocent man in trouble if that's the case."

Again Megan nodded. She kept her gaze on the window, then on Sadie as Sadie quietly groomed Gunther's neck in the corner.

"And to complicate factors, you're just getting established here in Winsome. People like your café, the farm is coming along well, and the hoopla from the happenings of last spring has finally died down," Sarah continued. "You don't want to make waves for yourself in such a small town by being the one to suggest Otto's death could be more than an accident."

Megan looked at her aunt, surprised. She was right, of

course—although Megan hadn't even realized she was feeling that way. She felt her face flush.

"So for you it's not simply an intellectual exercise, but an emotional one too. You have something to lose."

"I guess I do." This certainly wasn't helping her feel any better.

"Megan, I think you know the answer to your dilemma." Sarah stood to refill the coffee cups. Megan's sat untouched. Sarah dumped it and poured her a fresh cup. "You can't control what these townspeople think of you. And as for Ted, if he's done something wrong—no matter how understandable his disappointment with life—justice should prevail."

"And if he hasn't done something, and I make his life even worse—"

"You didn't cause the argument you overheard. You didn't leave town in a manner suggesting wrongdoing or guilt. Stop taking responsibility for others' actions."

Megan chewed at her bottom lip, thought of Emily, and stopped. "You're right."

"Of course I'm right. You asked whether there was a difference between an emotional or intellectual moral dilemma. The key is to remove the emotionality and treat any dilemma as an intellectual exercise."

"Like you did when you helped my mother leave, all those years ago?"

Sarah paused mid-sip. She quickly regained her composure, set her mug down, and nodded. "Yes, Megan. Exactly like that." She leaned forward, her face a study in tranquility. "Would you like to talk about your mother?"

Yes. No. Maybe, Megan thought.

Her mother had abandoned her when she was only eight years old, leaving her in the hands of her very capable and loving grandmother, a stern grandfather, and her loving but not-so-capable father, Eddie Birch. It was only last spring that Megan discovered her aunt was living again in Winsome, that her aunt was a famous mystery author, and that Sarah had been the catalyst to her mother's departure. It had been a lot to take in then. It was still a lot to take in.

Megan mustered her courage. "Why did you help her?"

"Because she was trapped and miserable and it was the right thing to do."

"Intellectually."

"Yes."

"But what about me? What about your young niece and the fact that her whole life would be turned upside down? Didn't that come into play in your decision at all?" Megan could feel her voice rising in pitch and she struggled for control, but these were questions that had been plaguing her for months. "How could your decision be made so coldly?"

Sarah leaned forward. She very deliberately made eye contact with Megan. The look on her face was one of understanding and empathy—not anger or pity. Somehow that made it worse. "Your mother loved you, Megan. I loved you—love you still. You are looking at this through the eyes of a hurt little girl, not a grown woman. To understand, you must force a different perspective."

"I don't think I will ever understand how a mother could leave her child."

"Do you understand that people make mistakes? That sometimes those mistakes have unintended consequences?"

"Like an unplanned child?"

"Like a forced marriage."

"You're saying my mother was forced to marry my father? Certainly not by him—or my grandparents." She seemed suddenly unable to control her anger. Bibi would no more force a marriage than kill a child. Sarah was rationalizing her own hand in all of this.

"I'm saying this situation is much more complicated than you think. No decision was made coldly or rashly." Sarah placed a napkin over her cup. "Now isn't the time to talk about it. Clearly."

Her words were gentle but firm and Megan knew she was being reprimanded. A million conflicting emotions soared through her body. She landed on frustration—with herself and her aunt.

She rose to leave.

"You're angry," Sarah said.

"No, I'm not angry."

"You have a right to be angry. What I'm asking you to do takes an incredible amount of strength and courage. To remove yourself from the equation, to look at what happened from the vantage point of objectivity." Sarah sighed. "It takes will and insight most people can't muster."

Megan mulled Sarah's words. She called Sadie and Gunther, both of whom rushed to her side.

"Thank you for the coffee."

"I hope you'll come again, Megan. I really do."

Sarah followed Megan to the front door. She placed a hand on Megan's shoulder—strong and warm and unwanted.

Before leaving, Megan turned to face her. "There are multiple sides to every story, Aunt Sarah. My mother has one, and perhaps from her vantage point her actions were justified. You have one. And I'm sure you felt you did the right thing based on the facts and circumstances at the time. But I have one too." She met Sarah's gaze, refusing to be silenced, even by her aunt's calm intellectual gaze. "I was the only one with no control. I didn't ask to be born. I couldn't really speak for myself. So while I am busy mustering this perspective you demand, who is speaking for me?"

Once at the truck, Megan glanced back to see Sarah watching her from the doorway. It was too far to see the expression on her aunt's face, but her silence had been all the answer Megan needed.

"I just don't know, Megan. The coroner believes it was an accident. No signs of foul play." Chief Bobby King rubbed his temple. He looked tired and cross. "You're sure about what you heard between Vance and Kuhl?"

"I know what I overheard, but I'm not certain of the context." Megan sat forward in the uncomfortable steel chair. They were in King's office in Winsome's humble police station, and she was beginning to think coming here was a mistake. "Did Emily call you to report her dad missing?"

"She called, but said she was afraid he'd done something to hurt himself."

Megan nodded. "He's run off, Bobby, and that's what I'm worried about. He argues with Vance, next thing you know Vance is dead. Coincidence? Maybe. But now Kuhl's missing. And he left Emily his bank information."

Bobby King perked up at her last statement. "She didn't mention that when she called."

"I don't know what it means and neither did she." At least nothing she would admit to. "Will you follow up?"

"Sure, we'll follow up."

"But you don't think it's anything."

"No, I don't." He sighed. "Look, it's Oktoberfest, Megan. The festival may have sounded like a great idea at the time, but with so many people expected to flood this little town, someone has to keep everyone safe. Do I have time to chase after vague theories? No, not really. So I just hope this isn't another wild goose chase."

"*Another* wild goose chase?"

"First the chair up on Potter Hill, now suggestions of aggression between Otto and Ted? Murder is a strong accusation."

"I never said murder, Bobby. You're putting words in my mouth. I said there could be a connection, one that warrants investigation by the police. And that chair was there, facing my house."

Bobby didn't respond, but the look on his face was enough. He was humoring her at best—that was all. Megan grabbed her purse.

"Look," Megan said quietly, "if you don't want to consider the connection between Otto and Ted, at least help Emily find her father. She seemed pretty distraught."

"Megan, are you telling me how to do my job?" King folded his hands in front of him on his desk. "Because if you are, I don't appreciate it."

"You know that's not the case."

"Do I?" He took an audible breath and let it out loudly. "Here's what we're gonna do. You're going to go back to farming and running that wonderful café of yours—love Alvaro's breakfast burritos, by the way—and you're going to let us deal with Otto and Ted and whatever else may be going on in Winsome. Okay?"

Megan felt the hot sting of angry tears. She refused to get emotional—not here, not in front of King. She'd made what he thought of as irrational suggestions and managed to bruise his ego. The only recourse left for her was to do as he asked—or not. She preferred the not, but with her cards held closer this time.

"Sorry to have bothered you," she said curtly.

"Ah, Megan, now don't do that. You know how highly I think of you and Bonnie. And after last spring, I know you're more than capable. I'm sorry if I hurt your feelings, but with Oktoberfest coming up, we're swamped and—"

"Oktoberfest. Is that the only thing anyone can talk about? There are bigger things to think about, Bobby. A man has lost his life, and my grandmother was the one to find him. And now a Winsome man has gone missing. Ignore my concerns, but help Emily. Tell me you'll do that."

She waded through King's silence for only a moment before leaving. It was the second time that day someone from Winsome let her down. She hoped it would be the last.

Eight

Lana Vance surprised Megan with a phone call three days before Otto's memorial service. The coroner had not yet released his body for burial, but Lana wanted to hold a ceremony now for closure. And she wanted Alvaro and the farm/café to cater a memorial lunch at their spacious Winsome estate.

"He loved your place, Megan," Lana said. Her voice, laced with the accent she'd inherited from a childhood spent in Sweden, sounded heavy with grief. "He enjoyed spending time at the café with his friends. It was a safe place for him. I know it is short notice, but maybe some German-inspired salads and sandwiches. He was a simple man. He would like that."

How could Megan say no?

And so she skipped the memorial service at the local Lutheran church and went instead to the Vance home to set up with Clay and Clover. The Vance family lived on nine lush rolling acres of property. Their house, originally a simple Colonial in line with the historic roots of the area, had been added on to multiple times until it was a four thousand square foot sprawling abode with a large sunporch and an in-ground pool. Otto's German heritage was everywhere, from the ornate hex sign over the pool house entry to the black and white prints of Berlin, Munich, and Cologne in the kitchen.

The day was crisp and clear and warm. Lana had designated

the sunroom and the grounds around the pool for the luncheon—and it looked like the weather would continue to cooperate.

"Why aren't they having it at the brewery?" Clover whispered while they folded white cloth napkins and laid them beside a stack of glass dinner plates. "The brewery has the space. And they serve food."

"I thought that was curious too," Clay said.

Megan had been wondering the same thing. "Maybe the memories are too painful." She glanced at her watch. "Alvaro should be here any moment with the food."

"He's been preparing for two days, taking time away from the things he's making for Oktoberfest," Clover said. "But he wouldn't tell me what he was making. What's on the menu?"

"Lana wanted to play on Otto's Germanic roots, so Alvaro and I designed the menu around that. Warm German potato salad, thinly sliced chicken schnitzel, spaetzle with Gruyere and caramelized onions, bratwurst and sauerkraut, a field green salad with walnuts and goat cheese, and an assortment of pastries and cookies."

Clover looked surprised. "Alvaro agreed to make all that?"

"He grumbled, but yes, he agreed." Megan glanced at Clover. "In fact, he designed the menu."

Clay smiled. "He liked Otto. Even if he'd never admit it."

Megan heard a vehicle pulling up outside. "Speaking of our angel, I think he's here."

Alvaro's 1997 van belched its way into the driveway next to the sunroom. They rushed out to meet him, and together they placed the food on the white-clothed tables. Two vases of yellow roses—Lana's request—acted as the centerpiece alongside pictures of Lana and Otto, their five grown children, and their six granddaughters.

"That should be enough food for two towns," Alvaro mumbled. Still, he left and came back in with fresh-baked pumpernickel bread and homemade Bavarian pretzels—not even on the menu. He straightened out several of the dishes and nodded to himself.

"Thanks, Alvaro," Megan said.

"Don't thank me for doing what I'm paid to do," Alvaro said, but Megan heard the hitch in his voice. "I'll be at the café if you run out of something."

"Otto was such an integral part of this town," Clover said after Alvaro left, her eyes moist. "A lot of people will really miss him."

Megan agreed. He wasn't a showy man, or a leader, but he was always there with a kind word or a creative suggestion—like Oktoberfest. The brewery drew patrons from Winsome and other local towns, as well as passersby. The beer wasn't great—Emily was right about that—but it was decent, as was the food. Thinking of Emily caused thoughts of Ted Kuhl to come unbidden to her. Would Emily attend the memorial service? Ted? They had been friends after all. Megan had hoped to join Bibi and Denver at the service to pay her respects and to see for herself, but it wasn't meant to be.

Guests started arriving fifteen minutes later. Clover had volunteered to run the buffet, so Megan wasn't needed. She changed into a plain black vintage dress and patent leather heels and went to look for Bibi and Denver. She found them together by the pool, watching the floating orchids and candles Lana had placed on the water.

"Ta," Denver was saying to Bonnie, "I'd like that."

"Like what?" Megan asked. She slid between them, gave her grandmother a kiss, and smiled at Denver. "What did I miss?"

"A lot of tears," Denver said. "It was a sad service."

Bibi nodded.

"And I was just inviting Dr. Finn here back to the house for some coffee and cake after the luncheon."

"Were you now?" Megan asked.

"Can't have our only veterinarian going hungry." Bibi shot a sly smile at Denver. "Right?"

"Aye," Denver said, patting his flat stomach. "Wouldn't do at all."

"There's plenty of food inside," Megan said. "In case you're starving. From being a bachelor and all."

Denver laughed, Bibi didn't. Leave it to her grandmother to matchmake during a memorial luncheon.

The back door opened, and a group of people spilled out onto the stone patio, all carrying dishes piled high with food. All except one woman, that is, who carried only a glass of white wine. Many sets of eyes were on her—including those of a number of the gentlemen standing nearby. She was young, petite, and slender. Chin-length straight brown hair accented a heart-shaped face. Megan saw almond-shaped brown eyes with unnaturally thick lashes. A pertly sculpted nose. A long, graceful neck. She would have been a beauty had it not been for her mouth—thinly lipped, tight, with what appeared to be a permanent scowl. In fact, she had the look of a woman who'd just sucked her way through an entire basket of lemons.

"Who's that?" Megan whispered.

"*That* would be Ophelia Dilworth," Denver said.

"So that's Winsome's PR expert," Megan mused aloud. "Not what I'd envisioned."

"Aye," Denver whispered. "A bit of a priss behind the scenes, I bet. The kind of person who's sweet to your face right before she chops you up and buries you in her flower garden."

Megan laughed. "I take it you're not a fan."

"Anyone who chooses Sauer over you is my sworn enemy." He smiled, softening his words. "There is something about her. I can't put my finger on it."

After excusing herself, Megan left to check on Clover and the buffet. From the sunroom window, she watched Ophelia make the rounds outside the courtyard. The young woman stopped to talk with Clay before moving on to the town's newest zoning commissioner, Roger Becker. It wasn't long before the PR specialist was holed up in a corner talking to Denver too.

Megan swallowed a stab of jealousy. She had no right. Still, she wished Denver looked a little less animated and Ophelia a little more homely. Megan tore her gaze from the pair outside and back on the chicken cutlets, warming in a tray over a Bunsen burner. It was then she saw Ophelia and Denver had another observer. Lana Vance was standing by the stove, a chef's knife in one hand, a knife sharpener in the other. The knuckles wrapped around the knife handle were bone white—matching the pallor of her face.

Megan stayed to help Lana clean up.

"I want to thank you for doing this," the older woman said. She was washing glasses in the remodeled kitchen's oversized apron sink despite the empty dishwasher a foot away. "Otto would have approved."

"Alvaro did the heavy lifting. As much as he complains in general, I think he had a soft spot for your husband."

"He wasn't the only one." A shadow fell across Lana's fair features. "He could be charming."

Megan wrapped the last of the leftover salad and placed it in the refrigerator. The house, so lively just an hour ago, echoed with the tap of her shoes against the old pine floors. Megan knew from experience that the echoes would seem louder, the emptiness more pronounced, in the coming days. Lana would need to keep busy. If cleaning helped with that, so be it.

Megan reached for the mustard to tuck it into the refrigerator when a wailing sound from Lana stopped her. Sobs racked her client's shoulders, and big angry tears trekked down her cheeks.

Lana's fist balled. She punched her arm, then her palm. "I. Hate. Him." She closed her eyes, scratched at the raw skin on her forearm.

Megan sprinted to her side. "Hey," she whispered. Louder, "Lana, I'm right here. It's okay." She placed an arm around Lana and led her toward the living room. It was like leading a rag doll.

Megan knew this feeling. She remembered the bewilderment, the hurt, the rage of losing Mick. It did get better—eventually. The anguish eased, the loneliness abated. It all devolved into a constant dull ache rather than searing torture.

Lana said, "He was screwing her."

Megan's eyes widened. "Her?"

"That slut. Oph-ee-lia." Lana repeated the name twice more, leaning in to the rhythm on her tongue. "Oh-pheee-li-a." She spat, "God, how I hate her."

Megan felt the urge to defend Otto, but what did she know? She stayed quiet, not wanting to feed Lana's angst. The other woman's body stiffened beside her.

"I hate him for doing this to me," Lana said. "Oh, lord, I'm sorry, Megan. I just don't know who to talk to. Otto was everything to me. We'd built a life together. We were going to sell this house and travel." Another sob. "And to leave me like *this*."

"Are you sure, Lana? You may be jumping to conclusions."

"They'd been texting and meeting."

"That could mean anything. Oktoberfest had been Otto's idea. He was a sponsor. They were probably just meeting over business."

"When her name came up, he'd blush, stumble over his words. You knew my husband. Kind? Yes. Strong? Absolutely. A good liar? No."

"Still, there could be another explanation."

Lana turned, looking Megan in the eyes. "A woman knows when something's not right. I'd been meaning to confront Otto for weeks, but I never found the time. Or the courage." She shuddered. "Maybe if I had—"

"You can't allow yourself to think that way."

This time Lana laughed—a crazy, eerie laugh. "What else am I supposed to think? Middle-aged man, younger woman. It's so common, it's cliché. What's not cliché is him dying at the end." She flexed her hand. "Unless the betrayed wife is the one to kill him."

Nine

Megan kept this newest information to herself. Not only was she not sure what to do with it, she didn't want to betray Lana's confidence. She couldn't keep her mind from wandering to Lana clutching that chef's knife. She didn't think Lana was capable of committing murder—even in a fit of rage. It had been angry talk, born of a desire to have answers to questions she could never now ask. Still, with Otto's death so fresh, everyone seemed suspect— including an aggrieved and angry wife.

Perhaps Lana's suspicions explained why she chose to have the funeral lunch at her home. The house was Lana's territory, filled with the evidence of her husband's love and devotion to family. She couldn't very well bar Ophelia from coming, but she could let Otto's mistress—if that's what Ophelia was—know who'd really won in the end.

Only it felt like no one had won.

"You're awfully distracted today." Porter's voice broke through her reverie. They were planting arugula in one of the hoop houses, and Porter was on hands and knees in the dirt. "Something wrong?"

It was unusual for Brian Porter to pay much attention to anything beyond his own needs, so Megan was startled by the question.

"I'm fine," she said. "Why don't we finish this row and call it a day in here."

"Suit yourself." Despite the cool weather, he wore a sweatshirt with the sleeves cut off. The tail of a tattooed dragon snaked down his arm. Megan studied him, looking for signs he was drinking again. He seemed self-possessed. And calm.

As they walked back toward the barn, shovels and seeds in hand, Porter surprised her again. "I headed up to the hill yesterday," he said, "when you were all at the funeral. Thought I'd make sure no one was watching you again."

Megan's heart swelled. "And?"

"Nah, nothing. Some flattened areas in the brush, but that could have been deer or bears. I think maybe he's on to us now."

Megan nodded. She turned away so he wouldn't see the emotion in her eyes. "That's what I figure," she said.

"Don't worry. I'll keep an eye on the hill. Bastard returns, you'll know it."

"Thanks, Brian."

He waved a hand in her direction. "What's next? Turn over the pumpkin patch?"

"That'll work."

Porter headed one direction, Megan another. She watched him walk toward the back fields, purpose in his gait.

It took Megan twenty minutes to locate Ophelia's Oktoberfest headquarters. The PR specialist had hunkered down in the front two rooms of an office building otherwise occupied by a trusts and estates lawyer and the town's only newspaper. Her offices had a temporary feel to them: apartment-white walls, dingy grey Linoleum flooring, and the total absence of personal artifacts. However, they didn't lack Winsome flair. Three giant whiteboards were covered with photos, reports, and timelines. The center whiteboard read "Winsome First" above an illustration of a beer mug labeled with "Vance Brewery" in black letters and a black steer with "Sauer Farms—Winsome Born and Bred" in small white letters along its back. The themes of the event were clear: beef and brew. The stars of the event were equally evident: Sauer and Vance.

Only Vance was dead.

Megan waited until Ophelia Dilworth was finished with a phone conversation. In the meantime, she thumbed through several area brochures, happy to find Washington Acres listed in the back of one under "produce" and again under "eateries." At least the farm had been included, even if the café's address was wrong.

"Can I help you?"

Megan turned to see Ophelia standing, looking at her expectantly. Today the younger woman wore a pale green sweater that highlighted the deep cocoa hue of her eyes and a pair of skinny dark denim jeans. Brown riding boots, crafted with expensive Italian leather, hugged slim calves. Again, Megan was struck by the incongruity of Ophelia's mouth. It was a stingy slice of a mouth, and right now it was set in an impatient frown.

Megan held out her hand. "I don't believe we formally met. I'm Megan Sawyer."

Ophelia's grip was flaccid, her hand soft and malleable. "Washington Acres, yes. Glad you came. I assume you've reconsidered the spotlight feature?"

Megan shook her head.

"Then you came to talk about Sauer Farm." Ophelia smiled, although it was annoyance, not joy, that shone in her eyes. "I thought we put that subject to bed."

"You put it to bed. I merely let it nap."

Ophelia didn't laugh. Didn't even crack a smile. She walked around her metal desk, stopping at the center whiteboard. "As you can see, operations are well under way. We're ready for a slew of tourists in a week, and you know they'll buy your stuff as well as Glen and Irene Sauer's. It's a great opportunity for the entire town, Megan, and I know you'll get onboard."

"I'm not here to talk about Glen and Irene Sauer. I want to discuss Otto Vance."

Ophelia looked at her blankly. "I'm afraid I don't understand."

"What will happen now that Otto's passed away? Will Vance Brewery still sponsor Oktoberfest?"

"Of course."

"I'm not sure it's an 'of course,' Ophelia. Vance was the heart and soul of the brewery. The master brewer, the business manager, and the president. I thought a big part of the celebration was to showcase the sponsors in the town and have those sponsors provide products, demonstrations, and seminars."

"Vance has several kids. One of his sons is a master brewer, and his daughter, Hedy, has an interest in the pub." Ophelia smoothed the corner of a brochure template despite its steam-iron edge. "Or Lana can do it."

Megan studied the younger woman. She definitely sensed a tone of defensiveness. Was Lana right about Ophelia and Otto? Did it matter?

"Have you considered giving the spot to Ted Kuhl?"

Ophelia's lips twisted in surprise. "No, why?"

"He had petitioned for the sponsorship too."

"We never took him seriously."

"No?"

"He's only a level two brewer. He can't serve food. And frankly, his beer isn't as good."

"It's quite good. He's won three awards. That's three more than Otto."

Ophelia pranced toward her desk. She pulled her chair back and slid gracefully into the seat. Wearily, she said, "Megan, if you're here to question every one of the committee's decisions, I suggest coming to a meeting and doing it with the full group directly." She examined her nails, one by one. "Or maybe, since you have so many complaints and ideas for improving the process, you can ask to be part of the committee."

Megan blanched internally at her snarky attitude, but she refused to react.

"I *was* part of the initial Oktoberfest discussions, and there was a lot of excitement about showcasing our small artisans and businesses. Sure, some of them are less glossy and professional— but so what? You come on board and we have made a hundred and eighty degree turn, preferring big operations to small, and changing the rules on the run."

"Vance Brewery is still a relatively small operation."

"Sauer isn't."

"Always comes back to that."

"No, it doesn't. I don't care about sponsoring the event—I really don't." And she meant it. "But Sauer is an animal abuser and an unethical man. No one in the town can think he's the right choice to represent Winsome."

"Obviously you're wrong." She smiled. "I couldn't have chosen him alone."

Megan paused. She was right, of course. If nothing else, the other committee members would have had to back her.

Ophelia tore her gaze from her nails long enough to say, "Megan, go home. Get some rest. The café is cooking for several of the events. Enjoy the community feel, bask in the recognition. Next year maybe Washington Acres will be better positioned to take on a farm sponsorship role."

Megan's gut seethed with anger, but she refused to open her mouth. Ophelia was good at twisting things around. It was her job. As Megan left, Ophelia called after her, voice as sweet as Bibi's lemon curd jam. "Don't forget to like us on Facebook!"

Ten

Megan looked up from her perch on the floor of the main greenhouse to see Denver standing in the doorway, a cooler in one hand and a basket in the other. He smiled warmly when she glanced his way.

"Bonnie told me you've been holed up here since you got home hours ago. She said you're in a mood." His smile broadened. "Is that right? Are ye in a mood, Megs?"

Megan returned to weeding the area around her delicate spinach shoots. "She said that, huh?"

"A bit more directly." He put down his packages, slipped off his jacket, and joined her by the bed. "So what are we doing?"

"Weeding."

"Aye. Got that. What is a weed and what is a plant?"

Megan showed him the slender spinach stalks. "Don't pull these."

They worked quietly, side by side, for a quarter of an hour. Curiosity finally won out and Megan asked him, "What's in the cooler?"

"Dinner."

"Oh yeah? What kind of dinner?"

"The kind we can eat that does not require a stove." He pushed a strand of thick auburn hair away from his eyes. Megan resisted the urge to wipe away the streak of mud left behind by dirt-covered fingers. He looked adorable sitting there—out of his element and trying so hard. He said, "I have enough for Bonnie too."

"She has bingo tonight."

"Well, I guess we'll share with Sadie and Gunther."

Megan smiled. Her first real smile since leaving Ophelia. "Dinner sounds nice. I just need to wash up."

"You look fine." He glanced at her hands, muddy from the vegetable beds. "Okay, maybe your hands."

"I need a shower. Give me fifteen? And yes, I am that fast."

They closed up the greenhouse and washed up in the sink in the barn. Megan ran back to the house for a quick shower, leaving Denver wandering around the barn yard with Gunther and Sadie. When she went back outside, Denver was waiting for her. He wore a backpack and carried a flashlight.

"It's so warm today. I thought we could hike up to Potter Hill and watch the sunset." He lifted the flashlight. "We can use this on the way back down, if we need it." He smiled. "I know you know the way with your eyes closed."

Megan hadn't been back up to Potter Hill since she found the chair. Her first reaction was to say no—the thought of someone up there, watching her, still gave her the creeps. But she hadn't told Denver about her watcher, and she wasn't about to now.

"Let me grab my jacket."

The route to Potter Hill took them forty minutes. They walked in companionable silence, Gunther and Sadie trotting along happily ahead. A cool breeze had settled in, and although the setting sun still lit their way, Megan could feel the chill night air descending.

It was only when they reached the top that Megan realized she'd been clenching her jaw. When she glanced around, there was no chair, nothing to suggest someone had been there recently. She let out her breath, feeling the tension in her body release as well.

Denver spread a blanket near the top of the hill, in front of a tall pine. He pulled a bottle of white wine—chilled—from inside, two plastic wineglasses, a loaf of rustic French bread, and an assortment of cheeses and fruit.

"I hope this is okay," he said, placing the food and some paper plates on the blanket. "I don't cook much."

Megan was well aware of Denver's lack of cooking skill. Their first date had been over canned soup. She smiled. "This is so thoughtful. Thank you."

As with the walk to the hill, they ate quietly, without much conversation. Megan felt her mood improving. She tossed bread and cheese to the dogs, who sat next to one another on the grassy patch beside the blanket, waiting patiently for a handout. The sun was sinking low in the horizon, and bands of orange and pink highlighted the dark tree line below. The farm was spread before them, clearly visible from their perch—only fifty feet from where Megan had found the chair. It seemed like ages ago though, and being here with Denver and the dogs made the discovery feel inconsequential.

After they ate, Denver and Megan cleaned up the remnants, careful not to leave food behind for the black bears that occasionally roamed this area. The dogs took off, chasing each other over and around the hill.

"I guess we should head back down," Denver said. "It's getting dark."

"This was nice." Megan hugged him. He tilted his face down toward her and she kissed his lips, lightly at first, then harder. Pulling away, she said, "I'll fetch the mutts." At the edge of the woods, Megan turned to call for Sadie and Gunther. Walking backwards, she tripped, falling on her side.

She quickly stood. "What the hell?"

Denver sprinted over. "Ye okay, Megs?"

"I'm fine." She pointed to a small ring of stones encircling blackened logs. "Didn't even see it."

"'Cause it's tucked out of the way, not meant to be seen." He bent down. "Hikers aren't supposed to be camping up here. Must've been trying to hide the evidence." He touched the wood. "By the looks of it, it's pretty fresh. A few days, maybe. You might want to let King know. Don't want any fires starting, not now while the woods are so dry."

Megan nodded. She wasn't sure she'd tell King, not after his earlier reaction. Denver headed into the woods to fetch the dogs and Megan knelt down by the fire ring. Night was falling fast, and it was hard to see much other than the cold gray of Pennsylvania stones melding with the cloudy night sky. Where was the full harvest moon when she needed it?

"Ready?" Denver called. He was standing by the path, holding the flashlight before him and keeping the dogs in line.

"Coming!"

As Denver turned, the flashlight beam moved with him. Something shiny a few feet from the fire ring, under a tree, caught Megan's attention. She crawled over, feeling along the spot with her hand. Nothing. She used the flashlight on her phone to scour the grassy area under the oak. Within seconds a flash of blue and rust glinted from the darkness.

It was a tiny object, no more than four inches by an inch.

"Megs?" Denver called from the path.

"Sorry—be right there."

Megan stared at the object in her hand. It appeared to be a butterfly knife. A very small butterfly knife.

Carefully, she separated the blade from its holder. The handle was a kaleidoscope of swirling blues and silvers and reds—quite lovely, actually. Megan tucked it into her pocket. Someone *had* been here. First the chair, then the fire. The knife seemed more decorative than weapon-like, a collector's item. What did that say about her stalker?

It didn't seem to be much of a clue. But it was a start.

Denver said goodnight with a warm hug outside of her house. Bibi was back from bingo, and Denver had an early morning surgery, so he needed to get home. Megan thanked him and headed inside. She found Bibi in the sitting room watching television, feet propped on an ottoman and thick white circulation socks covering her ankles and calves. She smiled when she saw Megan, although her smile still lacked its normal spark.

"Are you feeling okay?" Megan asked. She sank into the chair opposite her grandmother and curled her legs under her.

"Just the day catching up with me." Bibi picked up the remote and shut off the television. "Did you enjoy your time with Dr. Finn?" There was a sudden and mischievous glint in her eye. "He is a handsome man. And he knows his way around a scalpel."

Megan laughed, happy just to see a flash of Bibi's spirit. "Is that an attribute I should be looking for in a man?"

Bibi smiled. "There are worse attributes. Did you have fun?"

"We did, thank you. We picnicked on Potter Hill."

Bibi nodded approvingly. Slowly, she pulled each leg down off the ottoman and pushed herself up off the chair. "It's no good to stay put," she mumbled. "What's the saying? A body in motion..."

"Stays in motion."

Bibi nodded. "Stay in motion, Megan. Because once you stop...well, you know." Bibi hobbled to the doorway, pulling herself straighter with each step. At the threshold, she turned slightly and said, "Your Mick was a good guy."

"The best."

"I liked him from the day I met him, sitting there at my kitchen table, eating blueberry scones and talking about baseball and inner-city kids. Strong, courageous, gentle. A rare mix in a boy that age—and in a man." She lowered her voice so that it was quiet but firm. "That Dr. Finn is another good man. Mick would want you to be happy."

Before Megan could respond, Bibi disappeared into the hallway.

Megan sat back against the couch. Sadie, well trained in recognizing melancholy, hopped onto the furniture next to her. Curled around Megan's legs, she placed her head on Megan's lap and looked up at her with adoring brown eyes.

"You like Dr. Finn?"

The dog wagged her tail.

"Do you like root canals?"

Another tail thump.

"You're no help whatsoever."

Sadie's paw shot out and rested on Megan's arm. Megan sank down, scratching Sadie's chest just like the dog liked it. She was rewarded with a yawn and more tail wagging.

"If only people were so easy to please," Megan muttered. "Right, girl?"

Only Sadie was already asleep. Still, her tail waved slowly, back and forth, as trustworthy an indicator as any.

At eleven, Megan wiped the sleep from her own eyes and disentangled herself from Sadie. Gunther was outside with the goats. She called him and, with the dog at her side, made a last check of the farm. With all in order, she headed back to the house and let the bigger dog inside for the night.

In the kitchen, Megan heard a buzzing. She looked around for the sound and finally identified her grandmother's new phone, ringing away on the kitchen counter. By the time she got to it, the call had stopped. A check of the ID told her it had been Eddie, Megan's father. Typical of him to forget the time difference and call his eighty-four-year-old mother at eleven thirty at night. He'd left no message, and Megan didn't have the energy to call him back.

She was about to put the phone down when she remembered her grandmother's difficulties calling 911. Her grandmother often hit the camera button by accident, so on a hunch, Megan opened the photos section of the computer. She saw four fuzzy pictures from the day Otto died. Megan couldn't identify much: the edge of a solar panel, two blurred shots of the back of Otto's neck and torso, and the tree line beyond the solar farm.

Disappointed, she clicked off the phone. She patted her pocket, remembering the knife. She'd put that in a safe place for further investigation and get to bed.

*   *   *

Megan awakened with a start at two thirty in the morning. It took her a moment to remember where she was—in her bed, in her home. Her subconscious had been working overtime in her sleep, and her dreams had revolved around the Vance family. The solar farm. Otto's death. Bibi's camera.

Something about the pictures was off, and now she thought she knew what it was. She sat up in bed, still physically drained but suddenly alert.

Downstairs, she flicked on the kitchen light and picked up Bibi's phone. She opened the photos from the day of Otto's death and flipped through them until she got to the ones of his torso. That was it. While the photos only showed a blurry streak of his body, it was enough to see what he was wearing: a white button-down shirt, smeared with streaks of blood.

No gray vest.

Megan pictured Otto the morning of his accident. She'd been surprised by the vest, thinking he looked unusually formal, even for a man so careful about his clothing. And now the vest was gone.

Bibi might not have picked up on that because she wouldn't have seen him the morning he died. She'd been working in the kitchen. Nor would the police. Lana might have, if she was paying attention—but she was grieving, so a lack of attention to detail might make sense. And that's *if* she'd seen his corpse. Because it was so clearly Otto Vance, the police may not have asked her to identify his body. And if they had, they would have removed his clothes or covered his body.

Megan downloaded the photos onto her laptop. By themselves, they weren't much to go on. Maybe there was a logical explanation—the vest had already been found in his car, or he'd returned home to change his clothes before heading out again. But if not, it could mean someone had removed an article of his clothing. Perhaps because it showed evidence of a struggle. Or because it contained their DNA.

Eleven

Megan didn't have to seek out Bobby King. The police chief wandered into the café right before lunchtime, just as Alvaro was testing out the chili he planned to serve at Oktoberfest.

"Chili doesn't sound very German," King said.

"It's a chili cook-off. No one said it has to be German," Alvaro snapped back. "Besides, I add beer. German beer."

Bobby looked at Megan with a sympathetic grin. He accepted the small cup and the grin morphed into a genuine smile. "Why isn't that on the menu, Alvaro? It's delicious."

"It'll be on the menu the week of Oktoberfest."

King held out his cup. "I may need to sample a little more."

"You can have more the week of Oktoberfest."

King shook his head. "Clearly Megan didn't hire you for your customer-service skills."

Alvaro mumbled something along the lines of, "You want to eat, I serve you food. That's customer service."

"What can we help you with?" Megan asked.

"I thought I'd pick up a sandwich to go."

Megan handed him an order form and a pencil. "Bibi's back there. She can have it ready in a few minutes. Do you want some coffee while you wait?"

"That would be nice."

Megan gave King's order form—a tuna sandwich on rye and smoked mozzarella pasta salad—to Bibi and poured the police chief a cup of coffee. She placed the coffee on one of the smaller tables, away from the few other patrons, and settled in across from him, her laptop in front of her. Clover, who had been ringing up customers at the front of the store, started to walk in their direction. King held up a hand to hold her off.

King peered at Megan over the rim of his mug. "Are you still angry with me?"

"I wasn't angry."

"You sure looked angry."

"I was hurt and upset. You know me better than to think I would give in to paranoia and rash judgments. Something's going on. After all we've been through, you could have given me the benefit of the doubt—without the condescension."

"I'm sorry. I really am." King pointed at the computer. "I assume you're not just going to show me pictures of the farm?"

Megan hesitated, unwilling to start another disagreement with King. Finally she said, "When you searched Otto's car, did you come across a sweater vest?"

"A sweater vest? Megan, the coroner is going to rule this an accident. The autopsy showed cause of death to be due to trauma—"

"Head trauma. I get that, Bobby, but just hear me out." Megan lowered her voice. "I'm a lawyer and a businesswoman, not some hysterical bored onlooker. And I have legitimate concerns about Otto's death."

"Because he passed by Porter on his way to the solar field."

"That and other reasons."

"Ted Kuhl."

"Among others."

King crossed his arms. "Lana got to you."

Surprised, Megan said, "She told you?"

"About Ophelia? Yes. She accused Ophelia of being an adulteress." King leaned in. "But screwing around with someone's husband isn't a crime, Megan. Nor is leaving your home to get away and think."

"But Ted left his bank information with Emily. Doesn't that make you wonder why? Some of these things add up."

"Zero plus zero is still zero."

Megan pushed the computer toward him. "Just take a look, Bobby."

"What am I looking at?"

Megan explained Bibi's malfunction with the phone. "I don't even think she knew she took any pictures, but she's done this before."

Bobby glanced up, brow creased. "We took photos of the scene. And besides, these are blurry."

"It's not about the pictures. It's about what's not in the pictures." Megan honed in on Otto's torso. "When I saw him earlier that day, he was wearing a gray sweater vest. I hadn't seen him wear it before, so I took notice. When Bibi found him, the vest was gone—only the shirt he had been wearing underneath was still on him."

"He could have taken it off earlier because he was too warm."

"It was a warm day, maybe too warm for a coat, but not *that* warm. Why take off the vest?"

"Maybe he'd gotten it dirty. Or he didn't like it. People change clothes all the time." Bobby shook his head. "Maybe Otto knew he looked overly fussy and wanted to ditch the vest."

"Was it in his car?"

King sighed. "I'd have to check, but I don't think so." He ran a hand through sandy blond hair and shook his head in a gesture of frustration. "Again, Megan, he could have gone home and changed."

"The timing seems pretty tight for that. But you could check with Lana."

"Even if we find out that the vest is missing, so what? What does that prove?"

"It could be evidence of a conflict."

King thought for a moment. "You're again suggesting this wasn't an accident? Otto and someone had a fight, the vest contained evidence, and someone pulled it off him before fleeing the scene."

"That's exactly what I'm suggesting."

"It's a longshot." King frowned. "You're not going to let this go until I check, are you?"

Megan smiled.

Alvaro gave a shout from behind the lunch counter: "Your sandwich is ready."

King stood.

"You know, if you're right, the timing is bad."

Was the timing ever right? "Because it will put a damper on Oktoberfest?"

"Because we could have a killer in our midst. Again." King placed his palms on the table between them and bent over. In a hissed whisper, he said, "Only this time, we'd also have several thousand strangers watching the drama unfold."

Aunt Sarah's words rang in Megan's ears: you didn't create the problem, so don't feel responsible for other people's actions.

"It's better to be ahead of things than wish you'd acted sooner," Megan said.

"I guess. I just wish we had big-city resources. If you're right, my force will go from thin to sheer."

Megan pulled into the farm at 2:10, leaving the café after the lunch crowd had dispersed, and got right to work helping Clay and Porter. Alvaro had sent over his café order earlier, and when Megan found her manager and farm hand in the barn, they were staring at a crinkled piece of notepaper containing a paragraph of hard-to-read scribblings.

"Do we even have two hundred pounds of potatoes to spare?" Porter was asking.

They both looked up when Megan came in. The barn—a huge multi-roomed building that dated back to Pennsylvania's Colonial roots—housed their farm office, a washing and prep station, the Cool-Bot where they kept their veggies and eggs, and most of the farm tools. It lacked good lighting and comfortable seating though, and both men were standing under a bare bulb, brows furrowed in frustration.

"That man is nuts if he thinks we can give him this stuff," Porter said. He handed Megan the list. "I don't think we can grow that amount of arugula between now and then. And the beets? We have a lot in storage, but his request will wipe out the entire cellar."

Clay nodded. "Do you know what he intends to do with all of those potatoes?"

"Potato pancakes." Megan handed the list to Clay. "He's cooking things we can mostly make ahead and sell in large quantities. Chili, vegetarian chili, latkes with sour cream, quinoa salad with roasted beets and local goat cheese. Mini funnel cakes with fruit compote made from local berries. Street food with a twist."

"I guess that makes sense." Clay still looked skeptical.

"Well, let's start scouting out what we have—and what we'll need. If we have large quantities of something in storage, Alvaro may be able to alter the menu."

"We have a lot of celeriac," Porter said. "But what do you do with that?"

"Knowing Alvaro, something good," Clay said. Alvaro had been the cook on the commune where Clover and Clay grew up. If anyone had an appreciation for the man's culinary skills, it was Clay. "Celery root and apple soup, for example."

"Not a bad idea. Celeriac and apples," Megan said, pulling on her gloves. "Winsome has plenty of both."

"Do you think that many people will come?" Porter asked. "Their estimates seem high."

Clay said, "I think we'll have a good-sized crowd. Ophelia Dilworth has done a great job getting the word out there. Whatever your thoughts about her, she's a hard worker."

Megan didn't say anything. She was thinking of yesterday's conversation with Ophelia and the impact of crowds—and the need to control them—on Winsome.

"There was an article about Otto's death in the paper today,"

Porter said. He spoke slowly, as though weighing his words. "An op ed piece about the safety of solar. The author said his accident proves that fields should be secured. Not a lot of moving parts, but sharp edges represent danger. I say that's a load of crap." He stared defiantly at Megan. "And who's to say that Otto's death was an accident?"

Megan shot him a questioning look.

"Why do you say that?"

"Otto sped by me when I had that flat, before you or Dr. Finn arrived. I did some work for Otto. He used to give me odd jobs around the brewery when I was having trouble making ends meet."

"So?" Clay had stopped what he was doing to listen. "What does that have to do with his death?"

Porter rubbed his eyes. "I don't know. But sometimes you get a feeling about someone, right? And I got a feeling about Otto. He was distracted and in a hurry, otherwise he would have stopped. Then he winds up dead." His gaze turned to Megan. "People are talking, wondering what happened and why he was there. They don't know I hear them, but I do. And they know you've been talking to Bobby, Megan."

"So?" Clay said again.

Another shrug. "So people make connections—right or not. Megan comes back to Winsome and things happen. People talk."

As they headed deeper into the barn to go through the root cellar, Clay pulled her aside. "Don't listen to Brian," he said. "He means well, but he doesn't always think. People aren't talking about you."

Megan struggled not to let the hurt show on her face. "I don't know about that. Porter was just being honest."

"If people are talking about you, it's because of all the good things you're bringing to Winsome."

This time, her stoic veneer cracked.

"Am I though?" she said finally. "I'm not so sure."

* * *

King called at ten o'clock that night. Bibi was taking a bath, and Megan was in the kitchen drawing up plans for the layout of a new greenhouse. Clay and Porter had cleared the brush in a section of the property between Washington Acres Farm and the old abandoned Marshall house next door, and they were going to begin construction of a new heated greenhouse after Oktoberfest. Megan had her sights set on buying the Marshall property—someday, when she had the funds. In the meantime, she figured she could distinguish herself from Sauer and some of the other local large farms by offering more greens and other fresh vegetables year-round. She could also sell to farm-to-table restaurants in the Philly area. The farm was creeping toward the black, but as a small operation offering organically grown produce, she needed to diversify her revenue sources. And everyone appreciated fresh vegetables in the dead of winter. But which ones would prove to sell best?

So when the phone rang, Megan, deep in thought, jumped. "Hello," she said, assuming it was Denver or her father.

"Megan, it's Bobby King. Do you have a moment?"

She tensed. "Of course."

"That sweater vest Otto Vance was wearing the morning he died, can you describe it?"

"Uh, sure...let me think." Megan closed her eyes, picturing Vance at the table with the other members of the Breakfast Club. "Charcoal grey, probably Merino wool, pockets—"

"Can you describe the front in more detail?"

"Button-down, two slash pockets on the bottom."

"The button detail?"

"The buttons? Large, round, kind of a pewter look." She concentrated on her visual image, honing in on Otto as he'd appeared that morning—a trick she'd taught witnesses when preparing them for trial for the firm. She could *see* Otto in that vest, could picture the minute details of the garment. "They had x's in the center and a thick ring around the outside. The buttons were distinctive and almost retro." She paused. "Why?"

"No vest in the car, and Lana said he hadn't returned home that morning. We went back and searched the area again before dark." King hesitated. "We located a button that matches your description at the solar farm. Not far from where Otto's body was found. I'll need you to take a look, just to be sure."

Megan ran through the implications of the police discovery. Could mean a conflict, just as she'd predicted. Which meant a second person had been involved.

"I'm afraid this also means we need Bonnie's phone. And we'll need to talk with her again."

"But she already told you what she found when she arrived at the field. Can't we leave her out of this?"

"You know the drill, Megan. This could be a game changer, and Bonnie was the first on the scene."

Megan was familiar with the drill, all right. More so than she'd like to be.

Twelve

Winsome's police headquarters consisted of four rooms and a holding cell about two miles from the historic downtown center. The building was a glass-fronted concrete rectangle, a slave to utility rather than style. When Megan and Bibi pulled into the lot the next day, Bobby King stood outside speaking with a linebacker-sized man in a tailored suit.

"That's Jenner," Bibi hissed. "I know those shoulders anywhere."

"Made sense that they'd pull him in. He does own the solar field."

"Bet he's as angry as a bull on castration day," Bibi said. "Hasn't lived in Winsome for thirty years. The last thing he'll want is trouble on the one piece of property he still owns."

Megan was well aware of Jenner's reputation. He owned the solar farm and a number of other real estate holdings within fifty miles of Winsome, but his real money maker was his investment firm. Mostly he stayed out of Winsome business, coming up occasionally to check on his investments or visit his mother who lived in a retirement home in the next town over.

Megan said, "May actually be better for him if it wasn't an accident, at least from a liability perspective."

"Spoken like a lawyer," Bibi said. She squeezed Megan's arm. "Don't lose that aspect of yourself, Megan. You worked hard for your law degree."

King and Jenner parted with a curt nod. King spotted Megan and Bibi and walked briskly in their direction.

"Looks like I get to use that aspect of myself now. Ready?"

"I'm always ready."

Megan smiled. Bonnie Birch *was* always ready—something else Megan loved about her grandmother. "Have your phone?"

Bibi held up a plastic sandwich bag with her cell phone inside. A small label identified her name and the date.

"I think they bag the evidence, Bibi—not you."

"I'm giving them a hand," she said. "Sometimes these younger folks need a lesson in efficiency."

"That is the button I saw on Otto's sweater," Megan said.

Bobby pushed the object closer. "You're sure?"

"Positive."

They were in a windowed conference room that smelled of stale perfume and even staler coffee. Megan and Bibi sat on one side of the table, King on the other, next to a freckle-faced woman in uniform.

King sat back, rubbed his face with his hands. "Thank you." He didn't sound at all like he meant it.

Megan said, "I assume you checked the button for prints or blood."

"Yep on both counts—nothing."

"Did Lana Vance have any insight?"

"She was surprised he'd worn the vest. Said she bought it for him years ago and he let it sit in the back of his closet. Didn't remember seeing him in it that morning, but she admitted he left before she was out of bed." King asked, "Do you recall what time he left the café that morning?"

"He was still there when I left. Bibi arrived at the café later. He may have already gone." She turned to her grandmother. "I think he'd already left. Is that right?"

"Let me see. I got to the café about eleven thirty. I was going to bake, but instead I helped Alvaro make potato leek soup for lunch because he'd run out of his tomato bisque. It's so good, Bobby—try it if you haven't already. I wasn't paying too much attention to the customers—you know how Alvaro can be about uniformity when it comes to dicing vegetables." She met King's gaze. "Alvaro likes everything to be exactly the same size. He's very particular."

King smiled. "Otto, Bonnie."

"Oh, yes. I never saw him. He must have been gone already."

Megan turned to King. "Which makes sense. Bibi received the call from Otto at the café shortly before Denver and I arrived to help Porter. He had been waiting there a while. Even so, if there's a gap, it's a short one."

King turned to the uniformed officer. "We'll need to construct a timeline."

Megan said, "You know he didn't arrive at the solar farm until after his call to the café to report Porter's flat. In the interim, Denver and I helped Porter. We heard the sirens. The solar farm is right up the road. That means either he took a detour after seeing Porter or he was at the park or solar field for a fairly long time. Bibi left the café to pick up Porter and happened by the solar farm, which is when she saw Otto's body. You know what time her 911 call came in. That part should be easy to piece together."

Bobby was jotting down notes. "We pieced most of that together, and there is a gap. I agree. Either Otto made a detour before going to Jenner's field, or he was there longer than we'd originally thought."

"So what was Otto doing between the time he left the café and when he arrived at the solar farm?" Bibi said. She sat back, thinking. "Have you checked his phone?"

"We have, Bonnie."

"How about his calendar."

King looked amused. "Yes, of course."

"And?"

"And nothing so far." King dismissed the officer with instructions to send him the timeline. When the officer was gone, he said, "Anything else, ladies? And here I thought I brought you in so I could ask the questions."

Megan knew he was trying to be funny for Bonnie's sake, but she didn't feel like playing along. Not after the hard time he had given her. Instead she said, "There's still no sign of Kuhl?"

"No. Nothing." He seemed to weigh how much to divulge. Finally he settled on, "We've spoken with Emily, have been by the tap room, even talked to some of the men he breakfasts with regularly. Nothing. It's as though he simply disappeared."

"Is Emily still worried he's done something to hurt himself?"

"I don't think she knows what to think."

They sat in silence until Bibi asked, "Is Teddy your chief suspect?"

King turned to her in surprise. "Frankly, Bonnie, we don't know if we even have a crime. We've just reopened the investigation." He tapped his fingers against the table top. "The medical examiner found Otto's wounds to be consistent with the fall, but the button and the vest call into question whether we missed signs of a struggle. You heard him arguing with Ted, Megan. So at this point, Ted's a person of interest."

Megan wasn't surprised—and it was the right thing for the police to do. It didn't mean she felt good about it.

Bibi, who'd been mostly quiet up until now, asked, "Do you need anything else from us, Bobby? I'm tired and would like to go home."

"I need to take a statement from Megan about what she heard at the café. But you don't need to be here for that."

"And then what?" Bibi asked.

"For the police? The real fun begins. For you? You get to go back to the farm."

When they were finished with their statements, Bibi headed to the restroom. Megan took that as her chance to talk with King alone. She pulled the chief aside and showed him the knife she found at

Potter Hill. "There was a fire too. Well, the remnants of a campfire."

He stared at the knife for a moment. Took it from her, turned it over, and opened it. "Beautiful work." He handed it back.

"You don't want it?"

"You've touched it. Any prints will be worthless." He rubbed his temples with beefy fingers. "Look, Megan, I know you may have been right about Otto, and I admit I should have believed you from the beginning. But Potter Hill is public domain. Whoever was up there shouldn't have stayed overnight—if they even did—but I don't have a name, anything. There's been no real crime."

Megan said the thing that had been plaguing her. "What if they're related?"

"Otto's death and your hiker?"

"Yes."

"What would make you think that whoever tussled with Otto has it out for you too?" He narrowed his eyes. "Are you hiding something?"

"No," Megan said firmly. "I'm just looking for patterns. And I don't like the idea of someone up there, especially at night, possibly spying on the farm."

"You don't know that's what they were doing. It's a lookout point. Could've been a couple of kids seeking privacy. Could have been someone who is interested in farms. Could have been leaf peepers. It's that time of year."

Or it could have been someone interested in the treasure a farm may hold, Megan thought. She said, "But the chair. Someone went to a lot of trouble to drag a chair up there. And that knife seems expensive. Whoever left it may have bolted in a rush."

"I will admit there are some oddities, but short of setting up surveillance, there's nothing we can do. And we have no basis for that kind of capital expenditure, human or otherwise." He took the knife from Megan, rubbed a calloused thumb over the smooth metalwork again, thinking. "Do you know Molly and Mort Herr?"

"No."

"They live about six miles down Curly Hill Road, on the edge of the park, well past the solar farm. They have a shop about a mile farther down. They're knife makers and sellers." He held out the knife and Megan took it. "Talk to them. Maybe they can tell you something about the owner."

Her interest piqued, Megan nodded. "Maybe I will."

King put a hand on Megan's shoulder. "If you hear anything else at the café, let me know. But please, if you and Bonnie could keep this quiet, I'd appreciate it. I don't want the committee or that Ophelia woman blaming me for ruining Oktoberfest."

Megan agreed.

King said, "Plus, if there was a fight and it resulted in Otto's death, it was likely over a personal issue." He looked out toward the small lobby where Bibi was chatting with the receptionist. "Nothing for anyone else in Winsome to worry about. At least I hope so."

Megan nodded her assent, although the weight of that knife in her hand caused her to wonder.

Bibi was quiet on the way back to the farm. She responded to Megan's questions with one-word answers and nods, her attention on other things. When they arrived home, Bibi headed for the kitchen. Without a word, she took out a large pot and filled it with water. To this she added the carcass of a roasted chicken she pulled from the freezer and placed the pot on the gas stove. She reached for an onion and started peeling it on the worn wooden butcher block.

Megan stood in the doorway watching her. Bibi had on a "Winsome Proud" t-shirt with a rainbow across the front. Megan wasn't sure if Bibi knew her father had made them for Gay Pride week, but she didn't think Bibi would care. In fact, she figured her grandmother would embrace the idea. Her spirit was one of the things Megan loved most about the woman who'd raised her. So this recent bout of reserve—if that was even the right word—had Megan worried.

"Don't you have a farm to tend to?" Bibi asked.

She tossed an onion in the pot and wiped her eyes with the back of her hand.

"Are you crying, Bibi?"

"It's the darn onions. I should peel them under water, but I always forget."

Megan sat down on the chair, signaling to her grandmother that she wasn't going anywhere. "Something's clearly been bothering you. You've been off ever since Otto's fall."

"You mean murder."

"We don't know that. It still could have been an accident."

Bibi peeled another onion—no running water again—and lowered it in the pot. She added celery stalks and tops and two unpeeled cloves of garlic. Megan was waiting through the addition of peppercorns when impatience got the best of her.

"So you're upset about Otto's death, Bibi. That's understandable."

Her grandmother stirred her pot. "I'm not upset. I'm disgusted." She looked at Megan, a deep frown etched on her face. "First Simon Duvall last spring, and now this. At the risk of sounding every one of my eighty-four years, what is the world coming to?"

"We don't know what *this* even is."

Bibi shook her head. "Something's not right—I knew it the moment I laid eyes on poor Otto. Only I didn't know it was Otto." She stirred the pot with a violent twist of her wrist. "Otto was a good man. But I've known Teddy Kuhl his whole life. When Marcia died, he was heartbroken. He had to reinvent himself, and he did that—through his brewery and by taking on his daughter and granddaughter after Emily's divorce. Why would he risk everything in his life that mattered because he was angry he didn't get sponsorship at a stupid town celebration?" Bibi let out a huff. "Chili cook-off? That's not even German."

"Emily told me Ted had money issues."

Bibi spun around, her face red with anger. "*This farm* had money issues. Did *you* kill someone because of them?"

"Of course not."

Bibi lowered herself into a chair. Sadie and Gunther, who'd been hovering near the stove, sensed her distress. Gunther put his great head in her lap. She put a hand on it but sat there, still.

"You're angry at me," Megan said with dawning realization. "You think I should have kept my mouth shut about what I heard transpire between Ted and Otto."

Bibi slouched down in her chair. "I'm not angry, Megan. You did what you thought was right. That's what any grandparent wants to see."

"But?"

"But nothing. Ted is a grown man. If he did something dumb, he should be called in to account for it." She twirled her fingers around the long tufts of hair on Gunther's head, using the dog to steady her arm. "Oh, heck. Otto's life is over. Lana's life will never be the same. Even if Teddy is completely innocent, once Merry Chance and her band of blithering idiots gets hold of the story, his life will be in tatters too. I just hate to see another family affected when it won't bring Otto back."

"Maybe it wasn't Ted."

"We served Ted up on a silver platter. I've seen enough of those cop shows to understand that motive plus opportunity equals guilt."

"Not always."

Bibi sighed. "You're not thinking like King."

Her grandmother was right. King wouldn't want the media nightmare of a murder in this quintessential American town—not right before Oktoberfest and not six months after another murder occurred on Winsome soil. If Kuhl was guilty, Otto became the victim of a grudge match, nothing more. Winsome could go back to being a safe little all-American town.

Megan stood. Despite Bibi's words, she knew Bibi was annoyed at her for sticking her nose in where perhaps it didn't belong, but she also knew Bibi would want the truth exposed—and justice for Otto—as much as anyone.

"You're heading out?" her grandmother asked.

"Maybe I can help set things straight."

"It may be too late for that. What's done is done."

Megan glanced at her grandmother's tiny frame against the backdrop of this big problem. "I can try," she said. "And I will."

Thirteen

Emily wasn't home. Megan knocked and waited, thinking perhaps she was tending to Lily. Both the driveway and street were empty of Emily's old Pontiac Grand Prix, so after a few minutes, Megan gave up.

She knew of one other place Emily—or Ted—could be.

Megan pulled into the parking lot of the industrial complex off Towers Drive nine minutes later. She wound her way through machine shops, printing operations, and blade-sharpening businesses until she got to a squat-looking building fronted by two garage doors. A simple sign over the garage door on the right read "Road Master Brewing Co." in thick red letters. No cars sat out front.

Megan got out of her truck and walked around the small property. She'd been here twice: once when it first opened and a second time a few months later with Denver. On warm-weather weekends, Ted would open the garage doors and serve beer at the tap room, offering flights of his three varietals and sometimes bringing in a local band. It was always BYOF—bring your own food. She had to admit, the beer was significantly better than what Vance served, even if the operation was tied together with gossamer strings.

Megan knocked on each of the garage doors. No answer. She peeked inside, but the interior was dark. She turned to go. Out of the corner of her eye, she caught the metal glint of the small mailbox attached outside of one of the doors. She opened it and peered inside. It seemed to be stuffed with bills and circulars—enough material to suggest Ted hadn't been here in some time.

Megan ran back to the truck and grabbed a notebook from the glove compartment. She scribbled a quick note asking Ted or Emily to contact her and placed it in the box. The police could get a warrant and search the box, she knew. But they wouldn't know when she'd put it there—or why.

Megan took a wrong turn while leaving the industrial park. She meandered through the unrelenting sameness of now-deserted buildings, watching for the deer that moved in from the outlying woods. It was dusk when she finally pulled out onto the road. Her stomach grumbled, but she knew even Bibi's chicken soup wouldn't satisfy this raw feeling gnawing at her insides.

Saturday morning came and went, and with it Megan's next opportunity to visit the knife shop Chief King had mentioned. Megan kept the knife wrapped in a linen shawl in a dresser drawer. Although she didn't mention the stalker to Bibi, she asked her grandmother to be vigilant based on recent Winsome events. She also kept Gunther with Bibi—inside or outside—and had the massive dog doing extra rounds of the farm each evening. She knew Denver would tell her to keep him outside all night—he was a sheepdog after all, meant to guard—but she felt safer with him close by, and she hated the idea of him sleeping in the cold. He'd proven his fierceness and loyalty last spring. He'd do it again if required, she was sure.

By two o'clock Saturday afternoon, Megan felt worn out and her arms ached from pushing the tiller. They'd planted cover crops on most outdoor beds in September, and now they were turning the last of the pumpkin beds with a large roto-tiller. She could feel the vibrations from the machine up through her shoulders, and her hands felt numb. Clay was also tilling, and Porter had the unenviable task of turning the compost piles, pungent and hot from bacterial breakdown—and chock-full of fat earthworms.

Finished with the last row of one large bed, she turned off her machine and pulled it onto the surrounding grass. She tugged at a water bottle hooked into a belt around her waist and guzzled a long drink of lemon water. The sun was high and warm today. The leaves, still flaming around her, rustled in a gentle October wind. The wintery feeling of a few days ago had passed, and now Megan smelled the earthy autumn scents of decaying plants and burning wood.

"Want to call it a day?" Clay asked from behind her. A sheen of perspiration covered his tanned face and the bare skin of his sinewy arms. He wore a gray t-shirt and jeans, and his hair was pulled into a neat ponytail. "You look beat and I feel it."

Megan surveyed the fields. Pennsylvania weather was tricky. They could go an entire winter without snow, or the white stuff could start falling as early as October. They had one more bed to turn, and then they could plant clover. The clover crop may or may not take before winter depending on the temperatures, but any nitrogen she could add back to the soil would be a boon for next year's vegetables.

"Let's push through and finish," she said. "If you can stay another hour or so."

"Sure thing," Clay said. He took the handle of Megan's roto-tiller and started pulling it toward the last bed. "You start from one side, me the other?"

"That works."

Before Megan could get through half of her side, she saw Gunther barking down by the house, and then watched as a silver BMW five series fishtailed up the driveway.

"That must be Ophelia, the PR lady," Clay said. He'd turned off his machine and was wiping sweat from his brow with the back of his hand. "She said she might stop by."

"I know very well who Ophelia is," Megan said, sounding more snappish than she'd intended. "Why is she here?"

"She had an idea for showcasing the farm. I told her I thought it sounded like a good opportunity."

Megan glared at her farm manager. "I don't want anything to do with Ophelia or her ideas."

"It's for Oktoberfest." He turned his head, following Ophelia's progress out of the car and onto the stone driveway. "Just have an open mind, okay?"

Megan didn't answer. Ophelia was wearing a tailored red pencil skirt, a low-cut matching fitted jacket, and black stilettos. Watching her navigate the bumpy pavement was entertaining. Watching her race walk away from the dogs was downright hysterical.

"Can you call off the white one?" Ophelia yelled. She was holding her purse in front of her like a shield.

Gunther was sniffing Ophelia—*all* of Ophelia—quite intensely.

"Gunther, come," Clay called. He glanced at Megan in exasperation. "He only listens to you," he hissed under his breath. "Do something."

Megan let him continue sniffing for a few more seconds, then she called him off. He stayed by the intruder's side though, one eye on Ophelia and another on Megan. Good boy, Megan thought. She and Clay headed down by the barn where Ophelia was waiting. While Megan would have loved nothing more than to see Ophelia struggle through the fields in those preposterous shoes, she didn't want her twisting an ankle on the farm.

"Megan, hopefully Clay mentioned the discussion he and I had yesterday," Ophelia said. Her hair looked perfect, her makeup flawless, but now a streak of mud colored the hosiery of one calf. "We had such a great talk."

Megan looked at Clay, eyebrows raised. He suddenly found something in the direction of the goat pen very interesting.

Megan should have invited Ophelia in. She should have politely invited discussion about her idea. But she was cross with Clay and cross with Ophelia and she really wanted to finish the last vegetable bed before dinnertime. So all that came out of her mouth was, "What do you want, Ophelia?"

"Ah, yes." Ophelia smiled. Always the media-savvy

professional. "This farm is gorgeous. With the views of the mountains and the fields and the beautiful old building," she pointed to the barn, "tourists would love to understand what you do here. What you grow in the greenhouses, how you maintain crops without chemicals—"

"We still use chemicals occasionally, they're just approved for organic produce. Natural derivatives."

"Yes, well, people will find that interesting, I'm sure." Although the glazed look in her eyes said she found it anything but interesting. "And Clay says you have animals." Her glance at Clay, on the other hand, was full of interest. Like a wolf eyeing an injured bison calf.

Clay said, "Just a few. Chickens, mostly. And two dogs. And the goats—"

But there was no need to finish that sentence. Unbeknownst to all of them, Heidi and Dimples had snuck out of their pen. Curious by nature, they'd walked up behind the newcomer. Dimples was sniffing Ophelia's shoes, and Heidi, her perpetually naughty sister, had the peplum of Ophelia's skirt in her mouth.

"Ah!" Ophelia yelled. She jumped, tripped, and landed on her derriere in the grass.

"Oh," Megan muttered.

Clay helped Ophelia up. "I guess you've met the goats."

Ophelia's shiny armor was beginning to wear. "I guess I did." A forced smile wormed its way onto Ophelia's face. "Goats...they're cute."

She said "cute" the same way you might say "fetid"—with a disgusted expression.

Megan squatted down and took Heidi into her arms. The tiny goat pulled again toward Ophelia.

"Maybe they should go in their pen," Clay said.

"Good idea," Megan agreed.

Clay picked up Dimples and carted her toward the goat enclosure.

"You really don't like me," Ophelia said when Clay was out of earshot, all pretense of being polite gone. "What have I done to make you feel this way?"

Once again startled by Ophelia's directness, Megan said, "It's what you haven't done."

"Sauer again."

"It's not Sauer. It's your lack of explanation."

"Maybe I can make that up to you. When Clay and I chatted, he mentioned your future plans for a CSA and a pizza farm. It got me thinking. Why not take the first step and have an open house the first day of Oktoberfest? You may not be able to cook here yet, but your café could cater the event. Introduce people to the farm. Let them *really* see what Winsome is all about."

Ophelia was right—they did have plans for a community supported agriculture arrangement and a pizza farm someday, but that wasn't for public consumption. The CSA meant that local people would buy shares before the farming season, thereby reserving their portion of the harvest. The farm received the proceeds ahead of planting, and in return, customers got fresh vegetables each week, whatever was in season. It was a pre-pay arrangement and a win/win for the consumer and the farm. With that and a pizza farm—a wood-fired pizza kitchen open in the barn on weekends—the farm could afford to buy the neighboring Marshall property and expand. But these were just pipe dreams. For now.

Clay ran back and scooped up Heidi. He gave Megan a baleful look over his shoulder as he trotted away. Megan watched Clay leave before turning her attention back to Ophelia. Was she for real?

"You're saying you think people will love small and local, yet you chose our biggest, least local farm to represent Winsome. Do you know what Sauer produces? Genetically modified corn and soy—which he ships off to other parts of the country for animal consumption. And beef—from cattle too crammed in their pens to turn around." Megan could barely spit out the words. She was sure Sauer had his own economic reasons for farming his huge amount of acreage the way he did, but if Ophelia wanted to draw attention to a farm that produced for the local population, Sauer's was not it.

"All the better reason to get Washington Acres involved. Show the people who visit Winsome that small farms that do things the old way—"

"We don't necessarily do things the old way," Clay said. He was back and barely out of breath from running back and forth with the goats. "Organic farming isn't anti-progress or anti-science. In fact, innovation is very important. We just prefer to do it in a sustainable manner that nurtures—rather than destroys—our ecosystem and the eco-balance on the farm."

"Well said." Ophelia clapped as though she'd won the battle. "And something people should hear. So you'll do it? Next Saturday? Maybe some tours, a stand with food from the café. Hay rides would be nice. Music?"

"I didn't say yes."

Clay stared at Megan. She glared back.

"Oktoberfest starts Saturday. We will publish this in the brochure and you'll get the attention you're seeking."

"This isn't about attention—"

Ophelia smiled knowingly. "Perfect then. Saturday morning at Washington Acres." She turned to Clay and her smile broadened. "Thank you, Clay. I hope Megan knows what a catch she has here."

Clay actually blushed. Disgusted, Megan trudged back toward the roto-tiller, the ache in her head now matching the ache in her arms.

Poor Lana didn't realize what she'd been up against.

Sunday brought the kind of thunderstorms that had everyone holed up in their homes, thinking about the long nights and short days ahead. Megan and Bibi worked side by side in the kitchen, making soups from the farm's fall vegetable harvest—butternut squash bisque, potato leek, harvest vegetable—that they would freeze for the leaner months. Normally an activity that invoked the intimacy of family and warm memories of youth, this time it felt strained and tense. Bibi maintained her reserve, talking only when making suggestions or asking a question. She wasn't curt or grouchy—the bite of anger would have given Megan something to latch onto—just quiet.

Rain pelted the windows and wind blew the old shutters. The chickens stayed warm in their chicken tractors, and the goats seemed for once content to be in their pens. Megan watched streams of water run against glass, the sky beyond bruised and battered, and thought about Denver. He was working; she wished he was here.

At four thirty in the afternoon, Megan slipped on her galoshes and rain coat. She'd have rather stayed in where it was warm, but she needed to lock up the animals and check on the greenhouses. Stronger winds were expected that evening, and anything blowing about now would lose its footing by morning. Sadie stayed with Bibi by the warmth of the stove, but Gunther waited by the door, anxious to accompany her. She didn't welcome the thought of a wet dog in the house, but he seemed insistent, and he was easy company. Woman and dog headed into the twilight.

The air outside was heavy but warm. Rain pelted Megan from an angle, and she fought against the gusts of winds that barreled through the valley and swirled between the house and barn. Gunther wagged his tail furiously, leading the way first to the goats and then out toward the chicken tractors, happy to be outside.

The chickens seemed restless, little harbingers of harsher storms ahead. Megan was locking up the final tractor when she felt Gunther stirring beside her, his body suddenly tense. The chickens weren't far from the wooded edge of the property, and the trees were blowing madly. Megan chalked the dog's reaction to the sound of waving branches.

But as she began the descent toward the house, he stiffened again, and growled—a deep throaty growl that she'd only heard once before, when a killer was on her property. Heart strumming against her windpipe, she forced herself to stop and listen. The woods were dark, but Potter Hill was semi-visible, shrouded in a veil of rain and mist. Megan squinted, looking up. Suddenly a noise behind her startled her, and then Gunther went running toward the woods, his bark sharp against the rumblings of distant thunder.

"Gunther," she called. "Gunther!"

She called him again. And again. Alone now, she felt someone's gaze on her. Imagination? She didn't know. She pulled a pocket knife from her jacket and switched open the blade. She couldn't wait for the dog any longer. Her hairs rose on her neck, her blood pulsed in her ears.

"Gunther, come!" she called again as she walked slowly toward the house. She kept the knife close.

A burst of motion from her left caused her heart to plummet into her stomach. It was the dog, wet and mud-covered from the nearby creek. He ran to her and pressed his dirty body against her leg, clearly pleased with a job well done. She jogged the rest of the way toward the house with him at her side. It had been a rabbit, she told herself while she bathed the caked mud and twigs from his fur. Or a deer.

Only she knew Gunther wouldn't leave her side for a rabbit or a deer.

There'd been someone in the woods, watching her. If only she could figure out who.

Fourteen

Megan and Clay spent Monday morning shuttling root vegetables to the café so Bibi and Alvaro could start making vegetarian chili and meat chili for the Oktoberfest celebration. The café had deep freezers, which would come in handy for storing backup quantities. When they arrived before eight, Bibi was sitting on a stool by the prep counters, chopping onion and garlic in amounts big enough to make a giant cry. Alvaro was standing by the stove, browning meat and telling Bibi she was chopping all wrong.

"Why don't you tell someone who cares," Bibi snapped back. She looked up, saw Megan and Clay, and smiled wanly. "We work well together, don't you think?"

Megan smiled back. "Better than anyone else works with Alvaro."

The chef huffed out a sigh, but he looked pleased. "Do you have my potatoes?"

"Clay is bringing them in through the back. One hundred sixty-eight pounds."

"I asked for two hundred."

"You're going to clear us out. We harvested a thousand pounds, but they need to last through the winter."

Alvaro shook his head in disgust. Clearly the farm had failed him.

Megan peeked into the pans on the stove. There were four, all the size of large lobster pots. Two contained a savory concoction of ground beef and neatly chopped vegetables, and the other two sat empty, a coating of olive oil on the bottom, waiting for the onions and garlic.

"Looks good," Megan said.

"Would look better with two hundred pounds of potatoes in my pantry," Alvaro grumbled.

Megan gave his shoulder a quick squeeze. "We love you too."

She met Clay outside and they climbed back in the truck. "That should do it for now," Megan said. "Although we may want to bring Alvaro another thirty or so pounds of potatoes so he stops grumbling."

"He'll never let that go. Alvaro forgets nothing. And if we bring him more potatoes, he'll just find something else to grumble about."

The storm had taken its toll, and after their trip to the café, they concentrated on tidying up the farm. Megan couldn't bring herself to talk about the upcoming open house—she was still annoyed at Clay for going behind her back and herself for caving—but she made a mental note of the things they would need. She dreaded bringing the topic up with Alvaro. Maybe they could serve something simple, like Bibi's fall breads and apple cider. They still had twenty or thirty loaves of zucchini bread, carrot-apple loaf, and pumpkin bread in the freezer. Less work for Alvaro, more room for storage. Megan made a mental note to double check their supplies.

At ten, Porter arrived with Sarge, his German Shepherd, running along beside him, to Gunther and Sadie's delight. Porter was late, but his cargo shorts and sweatshirt looked clean and his face, covered in stubble, was freshly scrubbed. Megan was always on alert for a relapse with Porter. She'd promised Denver she'd watch out for the young man, and she intended to stick by her word.

"Sorry. Odd amount of traffic on Smyth Pike," Porter said. "Construction out by Sauer farm."

Megan nodded. When Porter first started, he showed up when he wanted and rarely made conversation. A post-traumatic stress sufferer from his time serving in Afghanistan, Porter liked to drink and hang out with Sarge—and that was about it. People had always been an annoyance he avoided. Denver, who saw echoes of himself in Porter, had asked Megan to find work for him on the farm. Megan didn't need too much arm twisting. Not only did she respect Denver, but after losing Mick to the same war on terrorism, Megan had felt obliged to help. After five months, Porter was still pretty antisocial, but now he had the wherewithal to apologize when he was late. Definitely an improvement.

Megan handed Porter a rake. "Help Clay clean up, please," she said. She patted Sarge, who responded by darting toward the goat pen. "Then the two of you can start clearing out the main section of the barn." She told him about Ophelia's idea for the open house to kick off Oktoberfest. "That gives us less than a week to get ready. We need hay bales for the hay rides." Megan turned to Porter and explained, "I want organic hay for the ride so we can use it afterward as mulch." When his expression remained blank, she said, "Treated hay often contains persistent herbicides that stay in the soil and can affect certain types of plants."

"Like brassicas?"

Megan smiled at Porter, impressed. "Yes. You've been paying attention."

A sly smile crossed his face. "Give me some credit."

"I think Diamond Farm has extra hay," Clay said.

"Then that's where I'll go," Megan said.

"Need help?" Clay's expression was apologetic. "That's a lot of hay to haul into the back of your truck."

"I'll be fine. Besides, Mark will help me." Mark Gregario, the farmer who owned Diamond Farm, had become a friend over the past year. Farming was a tough existence, and small farmers often stuck together. He'd become her go-to person for the things Washington Acres didn't produce on its own.

"I could go with you."

"I'll be fine. You stay here and work with Porter. I have a few other things to do get done."

She felt Clay watching her as she left. The open house

continued to be the elephant lounging between them. The event was a good idea—but she didn't like feeling ganged up on, and she especially didn't like that Clay had spoken to Ophelia before talking with her. He knew Ophelia was offering the event to placate Megan. Or if he didn't, it was because Winsome's new PR expert had clouded his very male vision.

The knife shop existed in a small strip mall off the side of the road, between an ice cream shack and a gun shop. The parking lot was wide and shallow. The ice cream shack was closed for the season, and only two other vehicles sat in the lot—a beat-up Ford pickup and a brand new Honda Civic. Megan parked next to the truck.

The knife shop was empty save for an older woman with frizzy gray hair and a high oily forehead. She stood behind the counter talking with a thin pimply boy of around nineteen who was staring into a display case. When Megan walked in, the boy ignored her. The woman looked up.

"What can I do ya for?" she asked.

Megan approached the counter, knife in hand. "Are you Molly?"

"One and the same." She squinted. "Who's asking?"

Megan introduced herself.

"Eddie's girl! I should have known. You have his eyes."

"You know my father?"

"Mort grew up in Allentown, but I've lived near Winsome my whole life. In fact, I knew—" Her face colored ruby red. "Oh, dear, I'm rambling. What can I help you with? You in the market for a new knife?"

Megan figured she was about to mention her mother. She wanted badly to quiz her, but wasn't sure she could take the look of pity now plastered on Molly Herr's features. Megan knew that look all too well. She'd endured it for all the years she lived in Winsome as a child. Instead of mentioning her mother, Megan got right to the point. She laid the knife on the counter.

"What can you tell me about this?"

Molly picked up the knife and opened it. She ran a stained stub-nailed finger over the handle.

"Nice piece of craftsmanship." She glanced up. "What do you want to know?"

"I was hoping you knew who bought it."

Molly shook her head. "Sorry, love. This isn't one we sold. Custom job."

"Might you know who made it?"

Molly frowned. "Hold on." She ran into the rear of the shop and came back with a binder full of catalogs and brochures. After a few minutes of paging through, she shook her head. "See these patterns?" She pointed to the intricate inner handle. "They look vaguely familiar. But I can't place the knife maker."

The boy wandered over and looked at the knife. Megan gave him a few seconds to admire it before packing it up in the linen wrap and placing it back in her bag.

"Why you asking, anyway?" Molly asked. "Looking to buy another?"

"Not exactly. I found this and want to return it to the owner."

The boy spoke, his stutter so thick it took Megan a moment to understand what he was saying. "Pr—rr—oww—st De—ee—signs," he said.

Molly snapped her fingers. "You're right, Craig! That's it." Molly wrote something on a piece of paper. "Jacob Proust Designs," it said.

"He's over in Quakertown. May not talk to you, but he does nice work."

The boy looked longingly at the knife. "Ni-ice stu-u-ff."

"Tell you what," Megan said to him. "If I can't find the owner, it's yours."

Megan's next stop was Diamond Farm, the smallish operation run by Mark Gregario and Ann West, two relative newcomers to

Winsome. They'd been living on the land on the outskirts of Winsome next to the quarry for over a decade, and the farm was on its sixth year. Megan drove down the short driveway, shoving the truck's five-speed transmission into park in front of the couple's modular home. Fruit trees—mostly apple, with a few cherry and peach trees—dotted the front few acres of the farm. Behind that, horse pastures and rows and rows of raspberry, blueberry, and blackberry bushes spread out on either side. To the right of the fruit trees, the owners had cordoned off two areas for pasture. A handful of chickens pecked alongside a dozen sheep. A small garden sat behind the house, more for personal use than commerce. Diamond Farm specialized in therapy horses, sheep milk cheeses, and organic fruit—plus organic free-range chicken. Fruit was tough to grow without pesticides and Megan was in awe of their talent and resolve.

She knocked on the door. A moment later, Ann opened it. She wore a denim skirt that brushed her ankles, a jade green turtleneck sweater, and red Crocs. Her tight black curls were pulled in a bun with wisps floating around her round face. A small fat infant hugged her hip, and a two-year-old girl dressed only in her underwear peeked out behind her right leg. Ann and Mark had seven kids. How they did it, Megan had no idea.

Ann smiled broadly when she saw Megan. "Here for chicken? If so, I'm afraid we're completely out." She adjusted the baby so he was on the other hip. "We have apples though. Lots of apples."

"Actually, I'm here for hay. Do you have some I can purchase?"

"Mark's around back. He should be able to help you."

Megan found Mark in the raspberry beds raking soil around the bushes. Two little girls were "helping" him. One was playing with a small Tonka truck in the dirt along the side of the raspberries. The older one had her own rake and was mimicking her father's movement. Mark said a gruff but friendly "hello" to Megan, finished with the bush he was working on, and then placed his rake up against a fence.

"Megan, good to see you. Need apples, chicken, or cheese?"

"None of the above. In any case, I hear you're already out of chicken."

"And we just processed them in September. Fastest sale ever."

Megan laughed. "I'm here for hay—whatever you can spare."

Mark helped her fill the truck bed with hay bales. He was a thin, short man with wiry muscles, a thick neck, and a full salt and pepper beard. Used to hard labor and efficient motions, he made short work of the process.

While they loaded, Megan watched the horses, who were enjoying some afternoon sun in their pasture. If it weren't for the noise of the nearby quarry, this would be a perfect spot. Mark seemed oblivious to the current rumblings from his closest neighbor.

"Shame about Oktoberfest," Mark said.

"What do you mean?"

"Sauer. Ann and I weren't surprised when we didn't win the sponsorship. Figured we have some good competition with Washington Acres and some of the other farms." He nodded in the general direction of Sauer's farm. "But we didn't think Sauer was even qualified to be part of the lottery."

"Nor did I." Megan stopped what she was doing. "Did you challenge their decision, Mark?"

"Nah, who has time for that? Besides, that Ophelia Dilworth did an article on our farm, and they bought the berries for the pie-eating contest from us."

Another consolation prize.

When the truck bed was as full as it could be, Megan paid Mark and thanked him for the hay. He nodded. His daughters had migrated from the berry bushes to the sheep pasture and were busily fawning over two sheep—who looked less than excited for the attention. He called his daughters over.

"I'll be back for apples." Megan told him about the open house she was hosting. "Bibi may want to make some more baked goods. I want to keep everything, cider included, local."

"Yeah, that's kind of the point, isn't it?" He squinted up into the sun. "You can have whatever we can spare. Alvaro already bought a few bushels for soup he's making."

"He has a whole menu planned. The café is included as one of the street vendors for a few of the events." Megan swung a leg up into the truck. "Bet he's the one who relieved you of your chicken supply. He's been waiting for fresh free-range chicken."

"Nah, it was Sauer."

"Sauer? For what? They have their own chickens." Crowded into one large dark barn, with no room to roam, Megan thought— but she kept that part to herself.

"I guess they didn't raise enough this year. Said he needed them for Oktoberfest." Mark smiled. "Wasn't going to argue. He paid a nice premium."

Wonder what that was all about, Megan mused as she pulled away. Sauer gets the Oktoberfest slot because he's big enough to supply meat for the event—but he has to buy the chicken from Mark? Strange.

But being strange didn't make it relevant.

Suddenly Megan wanted to talk through everything with someone. Normally she'd ping Clay, but he was busy, and she still didn't feel like confiding in him. Clover was too close to King, and she didn't want to talk with King until she knew more. Bibi had been burdened enough. Megan picked up the phone and called Denver. They could have dinner at the farm and then chat over a glass of wine or a good bottle of beer.

Denver picked up right away. "Megan. Glad ye called. I was just going to ring ye. It's like you have a sixth sense or something."

Megan felt herself smile at the sound of his voice. She invited him over for dinner. "Bibi's playing bridge at the church tonight, but I can make whatever you feel like eating."

"I wish I could join you. That sounds like a much better offer than what I have going. But I'm afraid I'm meeting with Ophelia."

Megan felt her shoulders tense. "Oh?"

"Something about doing a photo journal of the life of a country vet for Oktoberfest."

He sounded pleased, even if he was trying not to let on. "You're a regular James Herriot," Megan said.

"Or I will be when she's done with me. She's a force to be reckoned with."

"So I hear."

Denver remained quiet for a moment. "Are you sore about this, Megs? I can cancel if you need me."

Yes. "No, no," Megan said quickly. "Go."

"I don't know how late we'll finish, but I can try to stop by afterwards."

"That's okay. We'll talk another time. Have fun."

"I think you're doing that woman thing where you tell me one thing, but it's the opposite of what you're feeling."

Megan laughed despite herself. "I don't trust Ophelia. Something smells in this town, and it seems to lead back to her."

"Aye, it's that bloody perfume she wears. Stinks like the cosmetic section of Macy's. I'll take her through the dog pens at the clinic. That should help do the trick."

Thinking of Clay's reaction to Ophelia, she said, "Just don't fall for her charms. I've seen other men, stronger than you, succumb."

"Someone in Winsome is stronger than me?"

"It's good to have competition, Doctor. Keeps you sharp."

Denver laughed. "I'll call you tomorrow, then?"

Tomorrow. A lot could happen between now and tomorrow. But Megan said "Sure" as though tomorrow was just fine.

Fifteen

The evening dragged on. Knowing Denver was with Ophelia didn't help, nor did Megan's sense of isolation. After a dinner of butternut squash bisque, bread, and salad, Megan opened her laptop and started searching for Proust, the knife maker. It didn't take long to find his website. Just as Molly had said, he lived in Quakertown, not too far from Megan's farm. His website was bare bones though, and other than a few photographs of his work and a phone number, Megan had little to go by. No address—only a PO Box. And no email address.

She called the number listed and it went to voicemail. Megan left her name and return number.

She followed up with a few other searches: "Proust" and "customer reviews" (hoping someone would post a photo of the knife she'd found), and Proust on Facebook, Twitter, and other social media sites. Other than an old Facebook page that hadn't been updated since knives were invented, there wasn't much she could find on the knife maker. She sent a message through Facebook and switched to researching Ophelia Dilworth.

By eight thirty, she knew three things about Ophelia. One, she was only twenty-nine. Two, she'd gone to Yale. And three, her current employer was a firm called Ledbecker LLC.

Make that four: she was still out with Denver.

Megan was just closing up her laptop when her phone rang. Megan glanced at the screen. Unknown number. It was awfully late for Bibi to still be out, and a quick chill twisted its way down her spine. She switched on the outside light and answered the call.

"Is this Megan?" a soft voice asked.

"It is. Who is this?"

"Emily. Ted's daughter." Emily's voice sounded thick and husky, as though she'd been crying.

"Are you okay?"

"Yes, yes. Lily's just asleep—finally—and I'm trying not to wake her. I was hoping we could talk." She paused. "I found your note at the brewery." Another pause, this one more prolonged. Megan heard the distant horn of a train. No train trekked through Winsome, which meant Emily wasn't home. "Tomorrow?" Emily said finally. "At the brewery. Say eight o'clock?"

Megan ran through her to-do list. There was no good time tomorrow, so eight would have to work. She agreed to meet her at Road Master in the industrial park.

"Don't tell anyone, okay?" Emily said. "I just want to talk."

It seemed like an odd request, but then, this had been an odd few weeks.

"Fine," Megan responded. She hung up, wondering where her grandmother was and why Emily Kuhl was staying somewhere other than her home.

There was no sleeping in on a farm. At Washington Acres, the sun would peek its way over the eastern horizon around seven fifteen, but Megan was up well before that, feeding the chickens and cleaning out the goat enclosure. Dimples and Heidi were in a rare mood Tuesday morning. They greeted Megan with head butts and sloppy goat kisses, and even seemed happy to see Gunther, whom they normally taunted with childlike glee.

Megan took a few minutes to play with them, relishing the brisk morning air and thinking about the day before her. Bibi had gotten home after ten—very late for her—but she seemed more animated, which was a relief. She'd told Megan that her bridge group knew Ted was missing, and that he was wanted for questioning in Otto's death.

News *did* travel fast.

But Bibi had been able to address the gossip head on, which had made her grandmother happy. "I told them that there was nothing but circumstantial evidence pointing to Ted. After that, Merry said she'd heard Lana did it as retribution for an affair. And Dee Stalk said she'd heard that Otto's lover pushed him during a fit of passion and he'd hit his head." Bibi had looked at Megan, eyes shining with laughter. "Both plausible explanations, by the way. I had some torrid times in my marriage. These things can happen. Sex can be dangerous."

Megan, amused, had remained silent about Emily's phone call. It too was merely circumstantial, as Bibi put it.

But this morning, in the darkness before dawn when everything seemed gloomier, Megan reconsidered all of those explanations. Could it have been Lana? And had Otto had an affair with Ophelia? He was a handsome man, true—strong and tall with a chiseled face that harkened back to the Hollywood stars of yesteryear. But would an up-and-coming PR specialist from the city be interested in a man like Otto? More importantly, would a family man like Otto risk everything for a fling with a woman like Ophelia? Megan saw how Ophelia operated. She was a flirt and a tease, perhaps—but an adulteress? It wasn't hard to picture, but somehow the whole situation didn't sit right.

If Megan assumed Merry or Dee was right and this was a love triangle issue, then what about Ted Kuhl? Was his daughter correct? Had Ted fled because his business was failing? Was he a danger to himself—and only himself?

Circumstantial evidence, Bibi had said. Wasn't all of this—an overheard conversation, strange behavior, a popped button, a missing sweater vest—circumstantial? And were the chair and the campsite at the top of Potter Hill related?

Maybe King was right, Megan thought, and I've let the events of last spring get to me.

Megan had just started watering plants in the large greenhouse when she heard tires on gravel. She looked outside, surprised to see Denver's 4Runner. Gunther was greeting the vet as though he was a long-lost best friend.

Megan waved from the greenhouse door. A moment later, Denver was inside. He wore jeans and a brown plaid flannel shirt. A wool cap sat atop his thick auburn waves. He smiled broadly, flexing dimples that made her melt.

"Morning."

She smiled. "Good morning to you too. What brings you here so early?"

"Sauer."

"Glen Sauer? I thought you didn't go there anymore."

"Aye, you're right. But he had a cow in trouble and didn't have time to get his usual doctor. I felt bad for the cow, so I agreed. And I guess seeing me was better than losing an asset." Denver frowned. "Make no mistake, his cows are nothing to him but assets."

"Try telling that to Ophelia and her Oktoberfest committee."

Denver smiled. "I did."

"You did?"

"Aye. Last night. During my photoshoot." He flashed a comical sultry pose. They both laughed.

"Did she listen?"

"As they say in my home country, 'A nod's as guid as a wink tae a blind horse.'"

"Translation?"

"A nod's as good as a wink to a blind horse."

Megan nodded. "That was my impression too. She has a thing about Sauer and there's no changing her view." Megan sat against the potting table she'd placed at the back of the greenhouse. "Did it look like Sauer was preparing for the festivities?"

"If by preparing ye mean casting a thick cloud of gloom over all he touches, sure."

"Seriously."

"Seriously? Who can tell? The barns are still rundown, there are still old cars parked by the house. I got in and out as fast as that poor sick cow would allow."

Megan thought about her conversation with Mark Gregario the day before.

"Did you know Sauer bought Mark's chicken? I mean the meat. All of it."

"Seems out of character."

"Did Sauer stop raising chickens?"

Denver considered the question. "Not that I know of. But then, the wee things are stashed tightly in a barn, not outside, so I can't really say."

"Maybe he wanted to pass off Mark's organic chicken as his own. For Oktoberfest."

"That sounds like Glen Sauer." Denver pulled himself up on the potting table next to Megan. "One thing *was* odd about today's visit."

"What was that?" Megan scooted nearer to Denver. He put his arm around her, pulling her close. He smelled of Old Spice and damp hay—an interesting combination. She put her head on his shoulder, happy he'd stopped by.

"The missus."

"Irene?"

"Aye. She was downright friendly. Even at four in the morning. I didn't know what to make of it." Denver pulled off his cap and pushed his longish hair away from his face. "Come to think of it, I don't think I've ever seen the woman smile. Until today."

Irene Sauer was a sour-faced woman who mostly kept to herself. Thick, tall, and stocky, with thin brown bobbed hair and broad shoulders, she rarely had anything nice to say to anyone. Megan had always felt sorry for her. Glen was no peach, and farm life could be grueling, but Irene wasn't from Winsome and she let everyone know it at every opportunity—a habit Megan found tiresome. And then there was her attitude toward the animals in her care. Anyone who could condone the mistreatment of dogs was not someone Megan wanted to be acquainted with.

"That is odd. Maybe she's happy about the sponsorship. Sees it as her ticket to financial freedom."

Denver laughed. "Need I remind you it's only a little festival in a wee little town, Megs? No one is getting rich off the Winsome Oktoberfest celebration. Not even Glen Sauer. No matter what manure Ophelia tries to feed everyone."

"Tell that to Ted Kuhl." *Ted Kuhl.* Megan remembered her appointment with Emily. She needed to get going soon.

"Sauer asked about you," Denver said. "Knows you have Gunther."

Megan tensed.

"Don't worry. He seems to have his hands full these days—he wasn't asking to get that dog back. Even if he did, he has no right to him."

"Why was he asking about me, then?"

"Wanted to know how the farm was coming along, whether you'd tired of country life, that sort of thing."

"He's waiting for me to fail."

"Aye, maybe. I kept all your secrets though."

Megan stood and gave Denver a playful jab. "What secrets do I have?"

"For starters, that you have a thing for the local country vet. A very dashing young man who is about to be made famous by a stunning photo journal of his very interesting country vet life."

"Is that so? You're not that far from Philadelphia, Dr. Finn. I wouldn't call Winsome *terribly* country. This is no Darrowby."

"Oh yeah?" Denver joked. "Tell that to Mrs. Kennedy." He glanced at his watch and stood up, placing the cap back on his head. "I am just now making a house call to check on her cat's new litter of kittens, after which she—that's Mrs. Kennedy, not her cat—has invited me to stay for a breakfast of bacon, sausage, and eggs. Wasn't Dr. Herriot always eating fat-back with his clients?" He smiled. "So there you go, wee lassie. I am quite the country vet."

Megan laughed. "I should be worried, then."

"Aye, very worried indeed."

Sixteen

Megan raised a fist to knock on the door of Road Master Brewery, but before her hand connected, the door swung open and Emily Kuhl pulled her inside. The interior of the building was dark. Emily flipped on a flashlight, and Megan could make out Lily sleeping in a car seat in the corner atop a sheepskin rug.

"The electric company turned off the power for nonpayment," Emily said. "That means all of Dad's beer...ruined." She shook her head. "I thought it couldn't get any worse, and then...and then I found some stuff in his safe deposit box."

"Are you okay?"

"It depends on what you mean by okay." Emily pulled two chairs from the corner and set them up next to one another. She lifted a battery-powered lantern and flipped it on. A soft glow illuminated the center of the cavernous space, casting the rest of the room in shadows. Megan got a better look at Emily in the dim light. Deep bags hollowed out her angular face. Blue spa scrubs hung off her thin frame.

"Sit," Emily said. "And I'll explain."

Megan took a seat across from Emily. She looked around the interior, recognizing the large vats for beer, the cold metal hardware of the brewing business, and the long scarred bar that doubled as a work space for Ted. The bathroom door was ajar, and Megan nodded toward it.

"Have you looked around for intruders?"

"First thing I did."

Megan swallowed a growing sense of trepidation. "So what's going on?"

Emily pulled her phone out of her purse. She fooled with it a moment before handing it to Megan. It only took Megan a few seconds to realize what she was seeing.

"Trolls." She handed the phone back to Emily. "That's all they are. Sad, lonely people with nothing better to do than leave mean reviews and comments online. The web allows strangers to bask in the safety of cowardly anonymity. Hurtful, Emily—but not meaningful."

"Only Dad didn't think they were strangers." Emily rose and went behind the bar. She pulled out a laptop and scrolled to a page. With a deep breath, she said, "Look at this first."

It was a series of emails between Ted's business account and someone named TheJoker777. In each one, The Joker poked fun at Road Master Brewery, calling it subpar, uninspired, and the beer rancid. Ted's responses began as dismissive, moved to cordial, and ended with irate.

"This person contacted your father through the brewery's website?"

Emily nodded.

"Why didn't he simply ignore this jerk?"

"Good question." Emily switched to a different view. "Maybe this will explain why."

Megan was looking at another string of emails. This time they were between Ted and someone she recognized—Otto Vance.

"Your dad thought Otto was TheJoker777?" Megan asked. "Why would Otto do something like that?"

"I don't know. But Dad sure thought he had."

It looked like Ted had spent quite a bit of time accusing Otto of trolling him online and sending the brewery mean emails. But why would Otto do that? And what made Ted come to that conclusion?

"This just doesn't make sense."

"Unless my dad is paranoid. I told you he was desperate to make this business work. He wanted nothing more than to prove himself. When Mom died, I think a lot of people thought he'd failed her."

"I'm sure no one thought that, Emily."

She snorted. "Had he made more money, had health insurance, she could have had better treatment options. He always felt like people were looking at him with pity, even scorn. My mom was the one they loved. Dad? He was the quiet loner who let her down." She smiled, but it evoked only sadness. "A small town can be a great place to live...until it isn't."

Megan stared at the screen, at the exchanges between Otto and Ted. She reread the last four. They were short and hardly sweet, but telling.

"Emily, I don't think in the end your father thought Otto was the one trolling him."

"I don't know what you mean." She bent closer to the screen. "He says, 'this needs to stop' to Otto. And he accuses him of being complicit."

"Complicit implies something larger than one person."

"A conspiracy?"

"Maybe. Something illegal—something involving more than just Otto." Megan pointed to a line in the last email. It seemed innocuous at first glance. "See here?"

Emily read the sentence aloud: "'You must have figured it out by now.'" Emily looked at her questioningly. "Figured what out?"

"I don't know—I guess that's the question. Are there any other exchanges between Otto and your dad?"

With a glance at her sleeping daughter, Emily pushed the computer closer to Megan. "I saw these and was afraid to look further. Go for it. Please."

Megan spent the next half hour reading through Ted's emails, feeling very much like a snoop. She skipped everything personal, looking for more information on what transpired between Otto and Kuhl. While there was no smoking gun, there was evidence that they planned to meet—and talk.

"Here." Megan moved back so Emily could get closer to the

laptop. "It looks like your dad and Otto met the day before Otto died." The same day they were arguing at my café, Megan thought.

Emily read the email. It was an innocuous exchange between the two men with the subject line "Oktoberfest," but it mentioned meeting at the café to discuss the matter further.

"Only your father knows what went down between them."

"And I have no idea where he is." Emily rubbed her eyes. "This doesn't look good for him, does it?"

Megan thought about the events: nasty online reviews, emails, allegations that Otto—his only real Winsome competitor—was part of it, the arguments at the café, Otto's death, and then Ted's disappearance. No, it didn't look good.

"Do I have to turn this over to the police?" Emily asked.

"Not if they haven't asked. There's nothing in there to suggest guilt. But you shouldn't erase or destroy anything in case they do get a warrant. That could be obstruction of justice."

Emily nodded. "I don't feel safe at home," she said after a long minute. "Not with the baby and all." She looked down at her scrubs. "Last night we slept in my office."

"You're welcome to stay at the farm. We have a guest room."

Emily's face shone with gratitude.

"Oh, thank you, Megan. We'll be okay. My dad still has Grandma's old property across town. The house is rundown, but the plumbing works. I'll stay there for a few days, get my head straight."

Megan nodded. "If you change your mind, call." She paused, listening to the sound of trucks idling at a nearby business. The brewery smelled stuffy, mildewy. No place for a baby. "And if you do get wind of something more, or if you hear from your dad, please call the police. You can contact Chief Bobby King directly."

Emily agreed, although her expression remained noncommittal.

"Let's leave together," Megan said. "I'd feel better if I knew you and your daughter were safely in your car."

They walked outside. Emily had taken her father's business

laptop with her. She had the baby under one arm and the laptop and papers under the other. Megan helped her into her car.

"Are you sure you'll be all right?" Megan asked, hearing the lameness of the question even as it left her lips.

Emily answered through the open window. "How can I be? Either my father is guilty of hurting someone and he's now dead or on the lam, which is unthinkable, or he is in danger, running from someone who wants to hurt him and his business. In either case, I'm terrified."

Softly, Megan said, "You really need to have this conversation with King. Show him what you found."

"How can I go to the police? I wouldn't know what to say. All I have that's real is a father who left and a bunch of emails that don't tell us much at all."

"You're feeling unsafe. That's something."

Emily glanced back at Lily, still sleeping despite her mother's angst. "I will feel safest at my grandmother's old house." She sighed. "If I go to King, he's liable to jump to the conclusion that my dad is guilty. If there are other suspects, he'll be focused on Dad instead of them. Leaving Dad in danger."

Megan nodded. She had a point.

Emily started the car. "I'll go looking for Dad again after work. He's the one person who can clear things up."

Megan pulled out onto Smythe Road a minute after Emily. She'd been listening to the two voicemails from Clover begging her to stop by the café. Alvaro was upset about the quality of the neighboring farm's goat cheese, and the café had a slew of customers, the first of the tourists arriving for the Oktoberfest celebration and leaf peeping their way around the region.

Megan approached the first and only stoplight between the brewery and the main part of town and slowed to a stop. She saw Emily's car go through the yellow light. A gray Honda Accord with Jersey plates was behind her, and it too sped up to get through the light. Megan waited and watched, thinking about Emily. Mother deceased, father gone, recently divorced. Now it was her and her daughter against the world. Would be nice if she could at least count on the folks in her hometown. But would they come through?

The light turned green. Smythe Road was straight and flat. Megan was accelerating through the intersection, past a construction crew, when she noticed Emily turn onto a street ahead of her into a neighborhood area. The Honda turned too. Megan pressed harder on the gas pedal, but by the time she reached the spot where Emily had turned, there was no sign of either car and too many avenues down which either could have gone.

Megan pulled over and noted what she could remember about the Honda in her phone. Couldn't hurt to have the information.

Just in case.

Seventeen

By Wednesday afternoon, Porter and Clay had the barn cleaned out and ready for tables. The yard was mowed and raked, weeds whacked, and most of the remaining beds had been turned over and planted with cover crops or mulched. Three Port-o-Potties were expected to arrive the next morning, and Bibi had purchased bags of Halloween candy and treats for the kids—despite Megan's admonishments about too much sugar. They each had their assigned roles. Clover would give walking tours, Clay would drive the hay truck, Porter would play security guard, Bibi would see to sales of baked goods, and Megan would sell and manage the vegetables. And the goats and dogs would do what they did best: be adorable.

Despite her trailing annoyance at Ophelia, Megan had to admit things had come together quite nicely. Clay had been pushing for a wood-fired pizza oven in the big barn and a family pizza farm night during the summer. Maybe that wasn't such a bad idea. Perhaps next year.

She caught Clay in one of the smaller greenhouses, pulling weeds. He smiled when he saw her. She told him her thoughts on the pizza farm and that smile broadened.

"Clover will be excited. We had one at the commune. Alvaro makes amazing wood-fired pizza—if you can convince him to do it." He stood, wiping hair out of his eyes with the back of a gloved hand. "Speaking of Alvaro, who will be manning the store and café on Saturday while we're here?"

"I gave Alvaro the morning off. I'm closing the café."

"The Breakfast Club won't be happy."

"I don't think we've seen much of that crowd. Not since Otto."

Clay cocked his head. "I guess that makes sense. Must be tough on them." He shook his head. "Speaking of Otto, Lana stopped by to see you yesterday. You weren't here. I thought maybe she called you afterward."

"No, I haven't heard from her. Did she say what she wanted?"

"Only that it was important."

"Hmm. Okay, thanks." Megan turned to leave, but thought better of it. She decided to share with Clay the discovery of the knife on Potter Hill and her concern that someone had been watching her from the woods again the other night. As she expected, he was angry.

"Dammit, Megan." His hands balled into fists, his face turned the color of beets. "Did you tell King?"

"I did."

"And?"

"What can the police do? It's not illegal to hike."

"So he didn't take it seriously."

Megan didn't respond.

Clay gritted his teeth. "I don't like this."

"What would constitute 'this'?"

"All of it. None of it. Otto. The person on Potter Hill."

Megan weighed what to tell him. She decided to share her concerns about Kuhl and her conversations with Emily. It would help to get another perspective.

Megan told him everything in one big jumble, relieved to be sharing this burden with someone else. She explained the conversation she'd overheard at the café, the missing sweater vest, and the found button. She added Emily's concerns and the email exchanges between Otto and Kuhl. The red slowly drained from Clay's face, replaced with a sickly gray.

"Are you okay?" Megan asked him.

Clay looked around the greenhouse. His eyes rested on the

doorway. With a resigned sigh, he said, "I need to show you something."

Megan didn't like the sudden look of distress on Clay's face. "What?"

"I may be able to fill in one of the missing puzzle pieces."

It took Clay twenty minutes to find what he wanted to show her, and that twenty minutes involved sorting through three large garbage bags' worth of farm detritus from the open house cleanup initiative. He finally pulled a plastic Walmart bag out of the bottom of one of them. It was wet and muddy. He looked inside, grimaced, and opened it for her to see.

She knew immediately what it was. Gray wool material sat balled up the bottom, along with some sodden paper towels. The vest Otto had been wearing the morning he died.

"Where did you find it?"

"In the creek bed. The bag had snagged on a rock."

The creek bed was tucked inside the woods on the edge of their property. Thinking of the hiker/stalker, Megan said, "So you don't think someone placed it there purposefully?"

Clay closed the bag. They were by the barn, and Gunther and Sadie were sniffing madly at the garbage bag Clay had just rummaged through. Gunther turned his attention to the Walmart bag. Clay held it up higher, out of the dog's reach.

"If I had to guess, I'd say no. I think someone tossed it into the creek farther up, where it's deeper, and it came downstream and caught on the rock." His frown deepened. "But clearly someone was trying to get rid of it."

Megan pulled her cell out of her pocket. She started dialing. King answered immediately. And she told him what Clay had found.

"Is the button missing?" he asked

"It's compressed and wet in a bag, so I can't tell. Do you want us to touch it?"

"No. I was hoping it was plainly visible."

"It's not. And neither is blood. At least from what I can see."

"Vance had bled profusely. That could mean it was removed before Vance hit his head. Or maybe you just can't see the blood—the stream may have washed it out." King paused and said something to someone in the room with him. When he came back, he barked, "Sit tight, Megan. We'll be there soon."

King and the red-haired officer arrived at Washington Acres in record time. King took possession of the bag. Donning gloves, he opened it and laid the vest out on a plastic sheet in the back of his car. As suspected, a button was missing. The right pocket was also ripped. Otherwise, it looked clean of blood, but Megan knew it would be sent to the lab to test for any trace evidence. She also knew the police would have to determine whether a crime had been committed on the farm property, or whether evidence had simply arrived at the farm via the creek.

Megan shared Clay's theory that the bag had floated downstream and snagged on a boulder in the creek.

"Sounds about right," King said. "But I'd feel better if we take a look around. We'll need Clay to show us exactly where he found the bag." He glanced at Clay. "Can you do that?"

"Sure can."

The police were done nearly an hour later.

"Nothing," King said to Megan. She wasn't surprised. "A forensics team is on the way, just to be sure we didn't miss something, but I think Clay's theory is correct. Someone tried to dispose of this by tossing it in the water."

Megan said, "The fact that the button is gone, the pocket is ripped, and that you found the missing button at the solar farm says Otto likely didn't discard the sweater himself."

"That's right." The police chief looked pained.

"We're not going to say anything, if that's what you're worried about. To the media, I mean."

"I'm thinking about Kuhl. Given what you overheard, I think we need to put extra effort into finding him."

Guilt nagged at Megan. She didn't want to be the one to tell King about the emails Emily had shared, but nor did she want to mislead the police by staying silent. Besides, those emails could show that Ted was innocent, and that he'd stumbled upon something more sinister. And if he'd done something wrong? Justice was the only right course of action.

"I think you should talk to Ted's daughter," Megan said. She told him about their discussion earlier that week.

"You should have come to me then."

"Why? So you could have told me I was being paranoid and overly sensitive?"

King had the decency to blush. "Things have changed since then."

Megan folded her arms across her chest. "And *now* I'm telling you."

"Fair enough."

Clay and the red-haired officer ambled over. Gunther was following the policeman closely, a wary eye on this new visitor.

"Gunther, down," Megan said. The dog sat at full attention, waiting for a new command.

"He's quite a dog," King said. "Can't believe it's the same mutt old man Sauer had."

"Amazing what can happen when you don't neglect an animal."

King looked at Megan sideways. "Still bitter?"

Megan's eyes widened. "Wouldn't you be?"

"Suppose so."

They stood there for a few seconds by the unmarked car. Megan figured she'd come clean about everything she'd noticed recently. She told King about the Honda that had been driving behind Emily. And about Gunther's chase in the woods a few nights before.

King shook his head and opened his mouth to say something

when Megan put up a hand. "I'm telling you what I observed. Now you can't accuse me of holding back. Take it or leave it—that's your choice."

"The dog was spooked? I guess I need to trust your instincts at this point. Gunther's too."

"You should have been trusting them all along," Clay piped in.

"I'll have someone check out Potter Hill again." King shook his head. "An older gray Honda, huh?"

Megan read him the notes from her phone.

"We certainly have a bunch of disparate facts and no cohesive theory."

"Oktoberfest," Clay said. "I would start there."

Megan nodded. "Sure feels like that's the connection."

"I wonder if we should cancel it," the uniformed officer murmured.

"And suffer the wrath of Ophelia and the committee?" King said jokingly. But Megan could tell he didn't find this the least bit funny. It was a terrible choice to make—and she didn't envy him the decision.

Eighteen

It was decided the next day that Oktoberfest would go on. King met with the committee and they agreed to increase security, hiring extra guards for the week of the celebrations. A visit to Potter Hill had turned up nothing, and the Honda seemed to be a dead end. The police, deciding that Ted Kuhl was their prime suspect, expressed hope that whatever had occurred was between two people, and that no further issues should occur during the seven days' worth of festivities.

Megan wished she shared their optimism.

Friday came and went quickly. Megan, Clay, and Porter set up tables in the barn and hung paper lanterns from the rafters. Bibi's sweet quick breads and other baked goods were defrosted at the café, and Bibi and Clover arranged them on decorative trays. Alvaro brewed spiced apple cider in large batches. The goat pen was cleaned, the dogs endured the grooming table, and baskets and bushels of vegetables, including greens from the greenhouses, were made ready for public sale. Even Denver lent a hand, helping Clay put together an outdoor pen for Heidi and Dimples, who would be making their first public appearance the next day.

By seven o'clock that night, Megan fell, exhausted, into a chair in the living room. Denver, Clay, and Porter had stayed for dinner, and Bibi—energized by the commotion at the farm—had whipped up a supper of grilled local cheddar on sourdough and homemade minestrone soup.

"Your grandmother could probably make even mushrooms taste good," Denver said. "I appreciate her touch in the kitchen."

"We all do," Megan said. "How did your photo journal turn out?"

"Haven't seen it yet. Ophelia called me twice today though."

Megan's eyebrows shot up. "Oh?"

"She's a nosy lassie, that one. I tried to avoid her, but my receptionist put her through late this afternoon." He smiled. "Not sure she was happy with my response."

"What do you mean?"

"I told her I had my hand up a dog's arse and maybe now would not be such a great time to talk."

Megan pictured Ophelia's uptight smile twisted into a shocked frown. She laughed.

"I'm sure she loved that."

"Aye. Just kept on yapping though." Denver rubbed Megan's arm with one long-fingered hand. He reached for her palm, turned it over, and began massaging the kinks from the base. Megan felt the tension release.

"A bit o' stress in your hands, Megs," he said. "You're twisted into knots."

"It's just this open house tomorrow."

Bibi was listening to blues in the kitchen. The distinctive sound of Freddy King could be heard through the walls.

"Maybe that's why Ophelia kept asking me about you."

Megan sat up straighter, pulling her hand away from Denver's. "She was asking about me? Why?"

"Not sure, really. Wanted to know if you were ready for the open house, was quite gung ho for the whole affair. A little too gung ho, if you're askin'."

"That was it?"

Like that, the music stopped. Megan heard the back door open, then close. Bibi must be looking for Gunther, Megan thought. He'd been out prowling the grounds and didn't want to come in earlier.

"Asked me if you liked Winsome, whether the farm was doing well. That kind of stuff."

"Out of concern for us, I'm sure."

"No doubt." Denver took Megan's hand again and resumed the massage. "I told her to ask you herself."

"Good."

"Aye, she's a scunner, that one. Not sure where the committee found her."

"Scunner?"

"Nuisance."

"She went to Yale, you know."

"Lot of good it did her."

"And she's beautiful."

"She's too clean for my taste." Denver leaned in and kissed Megan on the cheek. "I like a lassie with some dirt under her fingernails. Someone who really knows how to roll around in the muck."

Megan laughed. "Do you now?"

"I do."

They kissed again. By the third kiss, Megan had forgotten about Ophelia Dilworth. And tomorrow's open house.

A bit later, they flipped on the television and settled for the last half of *Sleepless in Seattle*. At ten after ten, Denver rose to leave. "I'd best get home to the dogs. And you need your rest for tomorrow."

"Are you coming?"

"Wouldn't miss it. Will do my morning appointments—Mrs. Kennedy and her bacon, I mean kittens, again—and then I'll be by. Call me if you need me to bring anything."

"Well, I won't be calling for candy. Bibi bought enough for the entire Commonwealth."

Bibi. Speaking of her grandmother, Megan hadn't heard her in the kitchen. She bounced off the couch and ran through the hall, calling Bibi's name.

No answer. No Gunther either.

"I don't know if she ever came back in," Megan said to Denver. They were both slipping on their shoes and grabbing their coats. Megan's heart was racing. She was glad Denver was a doctor. Who knew what had befallen her grandmother. At eighty-four, anything could have happened. A fall. A slip. A stroke.

A stalker.

Get yourself together, Megan told herself. But she'd been there with Denver, enjoying herself. While her grandmother was...where?

"Come on," Denver said. He grabbed two flashlights from the shelf on the porch and ran outside. Megan and Sadie sprinted after him.

Bibi wasn't in the yard outside the house. Neither was Gunther.

"Bibi!" Megan called.

"Bonnie!" Denver yelled.

The night air was cool but not cold. Beyond the flood lights near the main house, the farm was bathed in a wash of eerie darkness. Trees rustled in the wind, making it hard to hear. Megan strained to listen for her grandmother, her eyes all the while scanning for movement.

"Could she be in the barn?"

"Maybe. You check the woods and I'll check the barn."

"We stay together, Megan."

His tone was clear: if Bibi had fallen victim to something besides natural causes, that something could be out there still. A lump formed in Megan's throat. She nodded.

They ran to the barn and opened the door. The place was dark, the interior set up just as it had been when they closed up more than four hours before. Denver nodded and they went in together, echoes of a similar situation weighing, Megan was sure, on both of them.

Only this time the barn was blessedly empty.

They were about to leave and call the police when Denver put a hand on Megan's arm. "Shh. Listen."

Megan couldn't hear over the sounds of her own ragged breathing and thumping heart. "What is it?"

"Music." He tilted his head. "In the goat pen."

They trotted quickly from the barn to the goat enclosure. The music became louder as they approached.

"There she is," Denver whispered.

And indeed, there she was.

Bibi lay fast asleep on the fresh hay bales, her fleece coat wrapped snuggly around her diminutive body. Gunther lay by her side, on the floor. His tail wagged furiously when he caught sight of Megan and Denver, but he stayed by his charge. Heidi was curled at the end of the hay bale, and Dimples was on the floor a few feet from Gunther. A CD player poured the sounds of Arlo Guthrie into the small space.

Megan felt hot tears of relief track down her face. Denver grabbed her hand.

"What is she doing out here?" Denver wondered aloud. "Poor woman is knackered."

Megan placed a hand on Bibi's back and roused her gently. It took her grandmother a moment to wake up. She stirred, stretched, and sat up with some difficulty. Looking around at Megan, Denver, and the animals, she said, "Oh my, I must have dozed off. I'm going to pay for this tomorrow."

Megan sat on the floor in front of her grandmother. She wanted to pick her up and squeeze her tightly, crushing the terrifying images of her in the hands of some faceless intruder. Instead she said, "What are you doing out here, Bibi?"

"I heard something outside. Thought maybe it was Clay or Porter, that they'd forgotten something for tomorrow. Remembered Gunther was still outside and went looking for him." She smiled. "He was up here by the goats. Clay had brought the CD player for tomorrow, and I thought I'd listen to some music. It's quite peaceful out here. And you kids needed some time alone."

"We don't need time alone, Bibi. We can get that at Denver's house if we really want it. You gave us quite a scare," Megan said.

"I'm sorry. I didn't mean to frighten you."

"We're just glad you're okay," Denver replied. He knelt down by Gunther and gave the dog a pat.

Bibi closed her eyes and smiled again. "Your grandfather and I used to sneak up to the barn when you were little, Megan. We'd play some music and dance. He liked to dance." She opened her eyes. "I bet you didn't know that about him."

"No, I didn't."

"There is a lot you didn't know. He wasn't always such a hard man."

Megan thought about her discussion with Aunt Sarah, the suggestion that her mother had been forced into marriage. Not the moment for questions, but it made her wonder whether her grandparents were capable of making such a demanding ultimatum. A conversation for another time.

Megan said, "Let's get you back to the house, Bibi."

Denver squeezed Megan's hand. "Why don't we all sit out here for a few minutes? Give Bonnie a moment to wake up. The music and breeze are nice."

They sat in silence for a quarter of an hour, listening to Arlo and watching the animals sleep the sleep of the just.

Eventually Megan said, "What was the noise you heard? The one that originally brought you outside."

Bonnie waved a hand dismissively.

"It was nothing."

"What did you think it was?" Denver asked.

"Footsteps. On the porch," Bibi said. "Turned out to be just an old woman's imagination."

On the way back down to the house, Denver pulled Megan aside. "I don't think it was your grandmother's imagination."

"Why is that?"

Denver pulled something from his pocket. It was a man's nylon glove, dark gray, with tooth marks along the thumb. "It was lying by Gunther."

Megan's heart beat wildly against her ribcage. She struggled to keep her face neutral. "He could have just found it. It doesn't mean someone was here."

Even in the faint glow of the outdoor lights, Megan could see the disbelief on Denver's face. "Someone was here, Megs. Someone Gunther chased away."

Nineteen

In the brilliant sunlight of Saturday morning's kickoff event, the prior night's problems seemed far away. Mother Nature had graced Winsome with a perfect fall day. The leaves still displayed their brightest kaleidoscope of reds, yellows, and oranges, the muddy browns of late autumn decay a few weeks away. Sun poured through the treetops, dappling the farm yard with a lacework of greens and warming the air to a comfortable fifty degrees. The sky, lapis lazuli blue, domed overhead, a backdrop to crows and hawks soaring through the air. Even the goats cooperated, allowing small hands to pet their necks and gently taking the oats offered on tiny outstretched hands.

"*This* is what Winsome is all about," Ophelia beamed. She breathed in, exhaled, and smiled. "Aren't you glad you agreed to do the open house?"

"If this is what Winsome is about, then why isn't Washington Acres the farm sponsor?" Bibi asked. She had been handing out slices of her homemade pumpkin loaf and small cups of spiced apple cider, but now they had a lull at the treat table. She shook her head. "The committee should be ashamed of itself, choosing the Sauers' farm. What were the lot of you thinking?"

But Ophelia didn't bat a single heavily mascaraed eyelash. She simply clapped her hands, smiled more broadly, and said, "Mrs. Birch, you make the *best* pumpkin loaf," and walked away toward Clover and the tour line.

"How would you know?" Bibi called after her. "You haven't eaten any!"

Megan stifled a laugh. She was selling produce at the table next to Bibi, and she handed a customer change and their bag of veggies—baby spinach and lettuce from the greenhouse and two butternut squash from the fall harvest—before reaching under the table for her thermos of coffee. They'd had a steady stream of visitors since the open house started at nine, and they were almost out of everything, including candy. Bibi, wearing a "Fall for Winsome" sweatshirt embroidered with tiny gold and red leaves, another leftover from Megan's father's old store, was restocking the last of the breads on the trays. After that, they were down to some sugar cookies and a tray of cinnamon scones.

When the last vegetable customer had walked away, Megan said, "I have to hand it to Ophelia. She's unflappable." Not many people could ignore Bonnie Birch's infrequent but biting comments—but Ophelia managed.

"She's a puppet," Bibi said. "But whose?"

Megan glanced at her grandmother. It seemed an odd but insightful thing for Bibi to say. Megan didn't have time to follow up on Bibi's statement before both of them received a new queue of customers, but her comment gave her pause. Ophelia had gone to Yale, and she was good at her job. But her job—public relations—meant putting a good face on everything. Creating and protecting an image by carefully constructing a story. But whose interests was she representing? Winsome's?

Or someone else's?

By noon, the last of the visitors were finishing their walking tour. Clover returned with seventeen people in tow—twelve adults and five children. Megan sold the last of her greens and a few more squash and other root vegetables to the adults while Bibi plied the children with cookies and cider. The kids loved Bibi—but not as much as they loved the goats. Megan knew that Heidi and Dimples had stolen/been given more than their fair share of baked goods, despite the signs asking that they not be fed human food. She wouldn't be surprised if the services of the good Dr. Finn were needed later to calm the bloated bellies of two little Pygmy goats.

Speaking of Denver, where was he? Megan wondered. She figured he'd gotten caught up in an emergency and couldn't make it. Or he'd fallen into conversation over Mrs. Kennedy's bacon and egg breakfast. She'd check her phone once the last guests were gone.

"Lovely farm," one of the customers said to her, a slender woman in her thirties with long straight dark brown hair and almond-shaped green eyes. The woman wore a fitted designer coat, and her calfskin ankle boots screamed "money" in Italian. Her accent said New York City. The woman's daughter, a sweet-faced child wearing head-to-toe leopard print, nodded.

"I like the goats," the girl said. "They're funny."

"And I'm sure they loved you," Megan replied, eyeing the girl's half-eaten sugar cookie. Megan was pretty sure where the other half now resided.

"Beautiful area." The mother looked around. "Amazing scenery. Old-world community feel."

Megan nodded. "I grew up here."

"I bet it's as safe as you can get on the East Coast."

Not recently, Megan thought. Luckily she was saved from having to respond by the appearance of the woman's husband. He was a few inches shorter than his wife, and he had a bald pate and a runner's restless body. His smile emanated warmth and intelligence. Like his wife, his clothes looked custom. He reached a hand out and Megan shook it, self-conscious of her grimy fingers from handling the produce all morning.

"Nice place," the man said. "That house. A hundred and fifty years old?"

"Dates back to before the Revolutionary War," Megan said. "George Washington was rumored to have stayed here."

"Really." The man took his wife's hand. "I heard the town of

Winsome has several connections to Washington." He turned to his wife. "Someday there will even be a museum celebrating the town's history."

His wife smiled. "We're looking forward to the Oktoberfest celebration."

Megan asked, "Did you come in for the week?"

"We don't live that far away. Jersey." The man's eyes darted around while he spoke to Megan, finally settling on the goats. "Figured we'd drive in today and then maybe next weekend too. My daughter would like to do the apple picking at the other farm. Good for her to get some fresh air and a taste of country living."

Megan nodded. "Well, make sure to stop by the Washington Acres Café food stand next Friday if you come in for the chili cook-off. We use primarily local ingredients and pesticide-free produce from our farm."

The woman smiled. "We certainly will. That sounds great."

The family trailed off toward their car. Megan watched the daughter tug on her father's hand for one last "goodbye" to the goats.

"Cute family," Clover said. She'd come up behind Megan and was watching the last of the cars pull out of the makeshift lot. Porter had set up cones at noon, blocking new arrivals, and now he was removing them to let the final customers leave. "Money. But I guess that's what the committee was hoping to bring in."

"Seem like nice people."

Megan turned to Clover and Bibi, who had two sugar cookies in her hand and one in her mouth.

"Bibi, your cholesterol."

"The heck with my cholesterol," Bibi said. "I've been waiting all morning to have some of these cookies."

Megan shook her head. She knew very well the cookies would be followed by a thick slab of bread with real butter and a cup of tea with a shot of whiskey. And maybe a handful of whatever Halloween candy Bibi had stashed away in a drawer. But there was no arguing with Bonnie Birch when it came to food. And at eighty-four, her grandmother was clearly doing something right—so Megan usually just let it go.

"Clover, do you have the Oktoberfest schedule?"

"I have a pamphlet right here. Why?"

"Can I see it?"

Megan skimmed the brightly colored pamphlet. In the midst of a collage of disparate photos—the German flag, Winsome's Canal Street, a bushel of apples, and the sign at the entrance of the Sauers' farm—her suspicions were confirmed.

"What's up?" Clover asked, peeking over her shoulder.

"The kick-off event is here, at the farm. Tomorrow is the Picnic on the Canal and craft show. During the week there are specials at Otto's Brew Pub, the concert on the green, and some other events. Friday is the chili cook-off in town, and it all wraps up with apple picking at Diamond Farm next weekend, right before Halloween."

"So?"

"What's on the front of this brochure?"

Clover stared at the cover. "Oktoberfest."

"Sponsored by..."

"Sauer Farms and Otto's Brew Pub." Bibi had joined them by the produce table. There was an edge to her voice. "But none of the events are being held at Glen's place."

Megan looked at her grandmother. "Exactly."

"But Glen is supplying beef for the Winsome Historical Society's chili stand, frozen corn for the church's fundraiser on Wednesday, and the chicken and hot dogs for the Picnic by the Canal." Clover shook her head. "I don't see what the big deal is."

"Frankly, I'm not sure myself. But I heard you earlier, Bibi, when you said Ophelia is somebody's puppet. Otto's Brew Pub makes sense. The beer isn't great, but tourists have a place to go where they can drink and eat—and Oktoberfest was Otto's brain child. Eating isn't possible at Ted's brewery. Same with Glen Sauer. He could have supplied the meat without being the sponsor, especially if he wasn't going to host events. We're supplying food too, as is Diamond and a few other farms."

"Plus, they bookended Oktoberfest with the two nicest local farms—at least from a touristy perspective," Bibi said.

"True." Megan hadn't thought about that. "Tourists come to Winsome expecting to see the canal, the leaves, abundant orchards, and quaint farms with old stone houses. We have the quaint farm and Mark and Ann have the orchards. And on the two busiest days—the first and last—that's what Ophelia is giving them."

"So why Sauer? Money?" Clover asked.

"I don't know." Megan reached for her phone. "But I intend to find out." She glanced at the home screen and frowned. "Looks like Denver's been trying to reach me."

Megan dialed his number. No answer. Just then, Porter jogged up the driveway and stopped where they were standing. Resting one hand on a knee while he caught his breath, he pointed to a blue Chevrolet parked along the road by the cones.

"Bobby King's here, Megan. He wants to talk to you."

What now? Megan thought. "Did he say why?"

"Nope."

Clover said, "We'll start cleaning up. Do what you need to do." She looked worried. "Brian can help us."

Megan walked down to King's car, head spinning with possibilities. He was inside the vehicle, on the phone, but when he saw Megan he ended the call and climbed out.

"Afternoon," he said.

Megan nodded. "What's going on?"

"I'm afraid I have some news."

Megan flashed to Denver's calls. "Is Denver okay?"

King looked momentarily confused. "Dr. Finn? Yes, of course...he's fine. It's not him, although he was involved."

"Bobby, get to the point."

"Ted Kuhl is dead."

Megan stared at him. "Dead?"

King nodded. "I'm afraid so."

"Did he...did he take his own life?"

"We're not sure what happened." King paused. "I may need

some help with his daughter, Emily. She's beside herself. Asked for you."

"Of course. I'll do what I can." Megan glanced up toward the barn. She could see Clover, Bibi, Clay, and Porter all staring down, no doubt wondering what was going on. "Can you please tell me what happened?"

"Dr. Finn was tending to Mrs. Kennedy's cats when she complained of an odd smell in the field behind her house. He investigated for her and there he was."

"In the field, just in the open?"

"Not quite."

"Can you be more specific?"

Bobby King, looking suddenly young and inexperienced, sighed. "Dr. Finn found Ted Kuhl in Marilyn Kennedy's tool shed. The exact cause of death is under investigation, but it appears to be asphyxiation. Indicators point to intoxication at the time of death."

Megan was horrified. "So he choked on his own vomit?"

"No, I don't think so."

"What then? Bobby, this is quite frustrating—"

"He suffered a reaction from a peanut allergy. His windpipe closed. At least's that what we think. We're waiting for the coroner's report. It will take some time to know for sure."

"Anaphylactic shock?" Megan shook her head. "You mean to tell me Ted crawled into the tool shed, drunk, and knowingly consumed a food he was deathly allergic to? I don't think so."

"Could have been an accident."

Megan simply stared at him.

King said, "It fits with suicidal intent."

"It fits with a frame-up too."

"If someone wanted to kill Ted, I can think of easier ways to get the job done."

"And I can think of better ways to commit suicide." Megan's voice was creeping up in octave, and she took a deep breath to control it. "Bobby, what would it take for someone to force him to eat peanuts? Or feed him something that contained peanuts, something he would never expect? Otto was supposed to look like an accident and so is this."

King nodded, but he didn't look convinced.

"You don't want it to be murder. None of us do. But all of these disparate facts are starting to add up. Ted knew something, and he shared it with Otto. Whatever it was, it got them both killed."

"We'll see what the coroner finds in Ted's stomach. That may tell us something—whether he was given peanuts unknowingly, or whether he ingested them outright."

Megan nodded. "The killer made one mistake," she said.

Bobby took off his cap and pushed back his blond hair. He looked pale and uncomfortable, and a pang of sympathy coursed through Megan. Their police chief was having to grow up fast.

"What's that, Megan?"

"Think about it for a moment."

Understanding flashed across King's face. "Peanuts. A medical condition—"

"That only someone who knew Ted would know about," Megan finished. "Chances are, you're not dealing with a stranger, Bobby."

"He wore one of those medical bracelets."

"Not always."

"Oh, damn," King said. "How many rotten apples do we have here in Winsome?"

"Very few," Megan said. "But you'd never know it by the smell."

Twenty

Miriam Dorfman Kuhl's property stood on the outskirts of Winsome, not far from the Jo-Mar strip mall, Tally's Creamy Freeze, and Sauer's two-hundred-plus-acre farm. The property, formerly owned by Ted's mother, consisted of a hodgepodge of buildings on about ten acres. Just yards from the road sat the main house, a once stately stone Cape Cod that had declined into something sagging and in need of repair since Miriam's death. About a hundred yards behind the Cape Cod sat a derelict trailer, its windows busted and the door hanging crookedly from a twisted frame. A second trailer had been parked in the field on the edge of the woods. This one was smaller and rundown, but the windows and door were intact. The fields were in dire need of a mow, and the hedges and flower beds were overgrown to the point of earning jungle status.

Megan pointed toward the trailer. "Is that where Emily is staying?"

King shook his head. "She's at her grandmother's house. The last renter left a few weeks ago, and Ted had been getting it ready for new tenants. The power is still on." He glanced at Megan. "Look, I know it's unorthodox, but I have some questions for Emily and I would like you to be there. She seems to trust you. Is that okay?"

Megan nodded.

They approached the door and knocked. Emily, accompanied by a uniformed female officer, opened the door. When she saw Megan, Emily started to cry.

"I'm sorry to drag you in," she said between sobs. "But you've been there since the beginning...and I...thought...you could explain that this was no accident. Dad always carried his EpiPen. Always. And the police said it wasn't even with him."

"I already told Chief King that I thought this could be intentional, Emily."

This seemed to calm Emily somewhat. She gulped air, and then wiped her eyes with the back of one long arm.

"Come in," Emily said. "Please."

Megan followed King and Emily into the cramped house. The downstairs consisted of three rooms: a small outdated kitchen, a floral-wallpapered dining room, and a square living room devoid of furniture. Emily led them into the dining room where Lily was lying awake in a playpen. They sat in folding chairs around a folding table. Tubs of latex paint perched on sawhorses on the beige-carpeted floor. Rags and paintbrushes had been left in a pile in the corner. Boxes were stacked here and there with no apparent order.

Emily followed Megan's gaze. "Dad was trying to rent this house. Figured if he fixed it up, he could get more money."

After a few minutes of idle chitchat aimed at putting Emily at ease, King asked gently, "You say it was no accident, but do you know why someone might have wanted to harm your father?"

Emily shook her head. Her gaze darted to Megan.

"She can stay," King said. "If that's what you want."

"I'd prefer it."

After a pause, King continued. "Do you think it's possible that your dad was blackmailing someone?"

Emily stared at the police chief, startled. "Blackmail? Over what?"

"We're just exploring all options."

The idea of blackmail was news to Megan, but she had to admit it made a certain sense. Had Ted learned something, something that killed Otto, one way to deal with it *and* solve his financial problems would be blackmail. But blackmail was a dangerous game—as Ted would have learned.

"No, absolutely not," Emily said. "No way."

"How about Ophelia Dilworth? Does that name ring a bell?"

"The woman organizing Oktoberfest."

"That's right." King crossed one leg over another. Mr. Casual. "Is it possible she and your father were having an affair?"

The look of incredulity on Emily's face seemed genuine. "Seriously? She's like thirty and Dad was in his sixties. I don't think so."

"Is it possible?"

"No, I don't think so. Dad was devoted to the memory of my mom. If he had been seeing someone, I would have known." She shook her head again. "He would never do that."

Megan knew King was thinking of two potential scenarios. A love triangle—two men after the same woman, and the deaths were related to a lovers' quarrel. Or Ted was blackmailing Ophelia or Otto over an illicit affair—ending in two deaths.

"You never heard your father talk about Ophelia?" King pressed.

"Only in the context of Oktoberfest."

"And then because..."

"Because he was damn bitter that he wasn't chosen as the sponsoring brewery. He saw it as his ticket to success here in Winsome, something he desperately needed." Emily held the Chief's gaze. "And deserved."

King and the uniformed officer exchanged a look.

"Assuming this wasn't his own doing—and to be clear, we haven't ruled that out—do you have any idea whether a customer may have wanted to do him harm? Or maybe someone he was doing business with?"

"No." Emily let out a long, low sob. "No one who knew him would want to hurt him."

"Emily, we will need more access to your father's things. At your residence, here, and at the brewery. Will that be a problem? I've asked for a warrant, but it would make things easier if you give permission."

Emily nodded. "Whatever you need." Megan handed her a tissue, which she used to dab her eyes and blow her nose. "Just find who did this."

"Will you be staying here? We need to know where to find you." King's voice was soft. "But I don't think you should be alone."

"I guess I—we—can stay with my ex."

"She'll stay with us," Megan said quickly. "There's room at the farm." There was no way she'd let Emily and her daughter return to her ex, not if the rumors of his bullying behavior were true. And of course King was right. She shouldn't be alone.

Emily nodded gratefully.

"It's settled then. I'll have more questions, so if you go anywhere else, call me." King stood, the signal to go. He stopped short of the door. "Emily, is it possible your ex did something to your father? Maybe over anger that he took you and your daughter in?"

"No. My former husband is in Ohio. And he doesn't have the money to hire someone. Besides, his anger is at me, not my dad." She stood, drawing in an audible breath. "Don't waste time looking at Kent. Or me. Find my dad's killer. Because I know in my heart that my father was murdered."

"Peanuts." Denver sighed. "I have now officially seen everything."

"It must have been awful. Finding Ted the way you did."

"Aye." A shadow fell across Denver's face. "But worse for Mrs. Kennedy. I'm afraid she could not hold down her bacon or her sausages."

They were at Denver's home, sitting out back with the dogs. His Great Dane brought Megan a tennis ball. She threw it, and the dog stood there, watching it fly.

"He only likes to see you work, that silly beast." Denver reached over and petted the dog behind the ears absentmindedly. "Doesn't actually fetch anything. Will sit here while you run across the yard and get that bloody ball yourself."

Megan smiled. All of Denver's dogs—all five—were rescues. And a motley crew, at that.

"Emily's convinced it was murder. What's your medical opinion?"

"He died from an allergic reaction, that much seemed apparent. The question is whether the poor laddie was moved, and whether he was fed something with peanuts—forcibly or through trickery." Denver frowned. "I suppose it could have been an accident. He had clearly been drinking. The smell of liquor in that shed was strong."

Megan walked the length of the fenced-in yard, retrieved the tennis ball, and threw it to Denver's Golden Retriever, who seemed much happier to actually fetch the toy than the Great Dane had. Back at the deck, she reached over her head, stretching her sore back.

She said, "The police are treating Ted's death as suspicious, which is the right call, I think. I'm anxious to see if that changes once the scene of his death has been analyzed."

"Aye, they called me in again to ask some questions. They want me to stay mum on the topic, should the media, or anyone, ask. Official reason is asphyxiation due to allergic shock. That is all I am to say."

"Same here. King didn't even want me to tell Bibi, but with Emily coming to stay, I had to tell my grandmother." Megan threw the ball for the Golden again. "King said yes. What else could he do?"

Denver's gaze followed the dog as she raced across the yard. He looked troubled. "How are things with Emily, poor lassie?"

"She's only been there since yesterday. Bibi has taken to the baby like a child with a puppy, and I think my grandmother's presence has had a calming effect on Emily." Megan smiled wistfully. "Bibi is like that. She cares, and people know it."

"Aye, that's true. Is Emily getting on? I know you said last night that she was mostly moping around her room."

Megan considered his question. "She helped with the chickens this morning. And she offered to accompany Clover and Alvaro to this afternoon's Picnic on the Canal. She just learned of her dad's death, but I think she's been expecting it. She wants to get out of the house, be busy."

"Are you going to the picnic?"

"I think I need to."

Megan tossed the Golden the ball one last time. She needed to head out. In fact, she'd just stopped by to say "hello" to Denver and check on him after Saturday's calamity. Doctor or no, finding a second body in the super-safe Winsome had to have been a shock.

"Maybe we can go to the picnic together?" Denver asked. "I'd be happy to help."

"The café is making funnel cake and donuts. Feel like spending some time with hot grease and powdered sugar?"

"Sounds better than many of my afternoons."

"Okay, then. Say three o'clock? I can swing by and pick you up."

Denver shook his head. "I forgot. I promised to check on one of Mark Gregario's horses. It took a tumble and now it's acting lame. How about if I meet you in town?"

"That works. By the café's booth, on the south side of the square."

Denver looked up. The sky, like Saturday's, was clear blue, the temperature a bit warmer. Unseasonable for October, but perfect for a fall picnic.

Denver stood. His broad chest and narrow waist were accentuated by the sweater he'd chosen, and Megan's mind switched unwittingly to the day Porter was stranded—to seeing Denver without a shirt by the side of the road. Which inevitably made her think of the solar field and Otto Vance. And Lana Vance. Lana had stopped by to see Megan, and had since also called, but Megan had forgotten in the midst of everything else. She wondered now what Otto's widow had wanted.

Megan glanced at her watch. If she stopped by to see Lana now, she could still get changed in time to help Clover and Alvaro set up for the picnic. She stood on tippy-toe and gave Denver a kiss.

"You're off then?"

"I am. I'll see you this afternoon?"

"Aye." He hugged her, and she sank into his embrace. "Do ye want to come back here afterwards, Meg?"

She knew what he meant, and she did want to. She really did. "I shouldn't leave Bibi home alone with Emily and the baby. Not with everything—"

Denver put two fingers on Megan's lips to quiet her. He leaned down for another kiss, this one heavier, more demanding.

"It's okay," he said. There was a husky undertone to his voice that quickened Megan's breath. "Another time."

Twenty-One

Megan started with the Vance Brew Pub. A sign on the wooden door of the tavern read "Oktoberfest Special: Any Vance Brew on Tap $3." Inside, the place felt packed. Every bar seat, every table was taken. The Rolling Stones' "Start Me Up" blared from overhead speakers. The air smelled of wood smoke from the corner fireplace, fried foods, and beer. And bodies. Lots of chatting, laughing bodies.

A petite blond with a full chest and sunny smile stood behind the bar. It took Megan a moment to recognize Vance's youngest daughter, Hedy. Megan greeted her, and once Hedy was free from serving customers, asked whether Lana was there.

"Afraid not. Mom's not been herself since Dad passed. She's likely home. Sleeping."

"She was looking for me late last week. Thought I'd stop by to check on her."

The young woman nodded. "That's really nice of you. Maybe try the house?"

"I will."

"The café did such a nice job at Dad's funeral," Hedy said. "Dad would have loved it."

"Thank you. We tried to do something he would have appreciated."

Hedy glanced around, then lowered her voice. "It was just a shame *she* came."

Surprised, and not wanting to betray Lana's confidences, Megan said, "Who would that be?"

"Ophelia. You know, She Who Must Not Be Named."

Uncomfortable talking about this with Otto's daughter, Megan simply nodded. "I'm sure this has all been very hard on your mother."

Hedy shook her blond tresses. "That's an understatement. Mom pretends to be stoic, but it's killing her. She's supposed to be running this place, but she can't even step inside. We're managing it through Oktoberfest, my brother and me. Then what? I don't know."

"I'm really sorry to hear how much your family's going through."

Hedy Vance sighed. "I know you mean it, Megan. I really do. But until you're in a situation like this—losing someone you love and then realizing they were never the person you thought they were—you have no idea how hard it is. None at all."

Megan drove up Baker Street, past The Village Diner and out past Ray Lottie's small woodshop and farmstead. "Barn Sale" was advertised in big wooden letters across the barn's bright red exterior. At Weeping Willow Lane, Megan turned left. On the right were Sauer's back fields, and Megan could see two dozen steer standing in a crowded holding pen behind a rundown barn. No surprise that Sauer wasn't hosting any of the events, Megan thought. Probably best he was sticking to meat and corn. His place was as welcoming as the gallows.

Megan's phone rang. She glanced at the caller ID and, seeing it was Aunt Sarah, hit the off button. Sarah had left two messages this week, but Megan had no desire to talk to her. Not now. Not after their last conversation.

At Pine Road, Megan made another left. She passed the turnoff for Emily's grandmother's property and, beyond that, a small Baptist church. Past the church was the Vance estate. Megan pulled her pickup next to Lana's black Acura sedan. She climbed out and went to the door. She rang the bell. It took a minute before

Lana showed up at the entryway. Her hair was disheveled. Her mascara had left tracks over sharp cheekbones and under the pale hollows of her jawline. She wore a blue robe that looked as though it hadn't seen a washing machine in weeks.

"Megan," she said flatly.

"Lana, I'm so sorry. I know you called, but some things happened, and this was my first chance to—"

"No need to apologize." Lana stayed in the doorway, her body angled to block the view of the interior. Megan smelled stale smoke and despair.

"Can I come in?"

"Now's not a good time."

"I thought we could talk. About things that have happened."

Lana shook her head. Her eyes widened, her pupils looked dilated. "I'm fine. Really."

"The police are investigating Otto's death. They probably told you already. I thought you should know."

"They told me. It's not necessary. He died accidentally. And we know how." Lana started to close the door. "It is what it is, as they say."

"But what if that's not the case? What if there's more? Things that would make this easier to deal with? That would let you know that Otto wasn't doing the things you suspected?" *That he'd been faithful.*

As Megan spoke, she heard the echoes of her own life, of her questions to Aunt Sarah just weeks before. *What if you could make this horrible thing make sense?* She wanted to ask Lana. *Wouldn't you do it? I would.*

Only Lana arranged her face into a mask of indifference. "And what if what they find is worse than what I think? I am on a precipice, Megan. Teetering off is not unthinkable nor improbable. That may just be the push."

"You should talk to someone, Lana. Someone who can help you deal with your grief."

"There is no help for what ails me."

With that, Lana slammed the door.

Megan stared at it a moment, wondering about the shift in Lana's demeanor and attitude since the funeral. Then she'd seemed vulnerable, wounded but open. Now? A different person. Rage could do that.

Megan left, feeling more hurt than she believed she had a right to. Lana never did tell her what she'd wanted. Megan wanted to help Lana. But maybe Lana was beyond help.

Twenty-Two

It was hard to reconcile the deaths of two of Winsome's sons with the joviality of Oktoberfest week. Sunday's Picnic by the Canal was, in everyone's estimation, a great success. Fourteen hundred tourists showed up for the event. Megan watched from the café's food booth as families rode bikes, navigated canoes and kayaks through the canal, and strolled along the canal path. There were three-legged races, water balloon tosses, carnival rides for tots, a band in Austrian garb, and food and beer. So much food and beer.

Including the café's contribution: Alvaro's donuts and funnel cakes. The treats were provided by the café, and the profits went to Winsome's Historical Society. Alvaro worked tirelessly, pouring donut batter into hot oil and handing the goods to Emily, who sprinkled powdered sugar on the fried dough. Clover handled the money. Bibi was home, watching Lily. She'd offered happily, and Emily had accepted gratefully. Megan was just thrilled to see her grandmother content.

Megan didn't see Lana Vance, nor did she spot Ophelia. She did, however, see Glen and Irene Sauer walking by the ticket tent. His hulking form shadowed her slightly smaller one. They huddled together, stalwarts of gloom against the cheerful façade of the picnic.

"What's that painting?" Clover whispered when she spotted them. "American Gothic?"

Megan snickered despite her distaste for their role in the event. The famous artwork was a decent rendition of the couple.

She followed the Sauers' progress as they checked in with Merry Chance at the ticket booth, then headed back toward Canal Street and their Ford Bronco.

"So much for a sponsorship role," Clover said.

"I guess engagement wasn't a condition."

Later Megan had a chance to meet Roger Becker while refilling the ice in the coolers of water, iced tea, and juice the café was selling. The Sauers still on her mind, Megan remembered what Merry Chance had said days ago: Roger would know who recommended Ophelia to the Oktoberfest committee.

"Megan," Roger said. "Happy to see the café has been such a success."

"Thanks. We're pleased. We owe it to Alvaro—he's an amazing cook."

"Well, the café has been just what Winsome needs." Roger looked around the makeshift fairground, a wide smile on his thin face. Roger was a skinny man, tall and narrow, with a long narrow face reminiscent of Ichabod Crane. He'd been a lifelong resident of the town, and despite what Megan often thought of as occasional overzealousness on his part, he generally meant well. "The Oktoberfest celebration too. I just wish Otto was here to see his idea come to fruition."

"Oktoberfest will definitely bring some attention to the small business owners here, which is what Otto wanted. Speaking of which—" Megan lowered her tone conspiratorially "—can you tell me who recommended Ophelia?"

Becker's jaw tightened. "Is this over Sauer?"

"No, actually."

"Then why do you ask?"

"She's done a bang-up job with Oktoberfest. I thought she might help advertise the farm."

"Really?" Becker looked at her, brow knit into a V. "She said you were annoyed over her choice to let Sauer be the farm sponsor."

"I was confused by the decision. It seemed the opposite of

every guiding principle the Oktoberfest committee set forth last year."

"Ah, but that was before Ophelia came along. She convinced us that our sponsors had to be big enough to meet our supply demands."

"So the farm had to meet the meat requirements."

"Absolutely. And you can't do that."

Megan chose not to point out that Sauer couldn't meet the vegetable requirements—he only produced soybeans and corn. She said, "That sounds like a stretch, Roger. You've known me and Bonnie for a long time. Tell me the truth."

Roger looked suddenly uncomfortable, just as Merry had before. Were they embarrassed to have handed Ophelia control—or was there more? Megan wished she knew.

Roger continued. "Look, I respect you and Bonnie, you know that, Megan. You've done an amazing job, as have Mark and Ann at Diamond Farm. But part of our agreement with Ophelia's firm was that we would take her direction as the expert. And this was her direction." He glanced down at his feet, shoulders hunched. "What do we know about running something this ambitious? That's why we hired her."

"So she is *so* good that she could call the terms despite the fact that the town's paying her?"

Roger looked like Megan had purposefully stepped on his sandcastle. "We got a Yale graduate from a big PR firm for a good price. We were pretty pleased with ourselves." His demeanor shifted. Suddenly he was looking at Megan like he was a school teacher and she was a naughty student. "And you can't see that because your business wasn't chosen."

"Oh, Roger, you know us better than that. It's just that small farms are disappearing, and I—we all—thought the point of this exercise was to highlight small farms and businesses."

"On a national scale, Sauer's still small."

Megan was ready to end this pissing match. It was going nowhere. She watched a family of four skip down a hill toward the canal and said, "Did Sauer recommend Ophelia's firm to the committee?"

Becker laughed. "Heavens no, Megan. That would have been a conflict of interest. Marty Jenner knows the head of the firm. It was he who suggested Ophelia."

Jenner? He wasn't even on the committee. Megan nodded and thanked Roger for the information. Clover would be wondering where the missing cooler was. She needed to get back to their tent.

"Let me know how it goes," Becker called after her.

"How what goes?"

"The PR for the farm. With Ophelia."

"Oh that. I sure will. Assuming we can afford her."

"Maybe you can work a deal," Becker said. "Free veggies for a year." He laughed, quite taken with his own humor. "If she likes Winsome enough, maybe she'll stay."

Oh, I hope not, Megan thought. But she kept on walking toward Alvaro and the line of tourists waiting for donuts and funnel cake.

It took Denver longer than anticipated to wrestle with and examine the agitated horse at Diamond Farm. He finally arrived at the Picnic on the Canal at six thirty, just as the afternoon event was winding down, distinctly *not* looking like a man who had spent the afternoon tussling with a mammal many times his size. He'd showered and changed, and his normally beard-shadowed face was clean shaven.

Megan smiled when she saw him approaching the tent. "Another photoshoot?"

Denver laughed. "This masterpiece is for you, not my adoring public."

Emily had long-since returned to the farm, but Alvaro and Clover were packing up the last of the supplies. Clay was due any moment with his truck, and they were going to cart the fryers, cookware, and coolers back to the café.

"We have a few minutes," Clover said. "Why don't you two go for a stroll?" She winked at Alvaro.

The cook made a pained face, rolling his eyes. "Go, go."

The setting sun reflected off the water in the canal, painting the downtown area in brush strokes of orange, red, and purple. Ducks had collected by the canal banks, and children were tossing them leftover bits of bread and funnel cake. Denver reached for Megan's hand.

"Watch it. The other single ladies in Winsome will be jealous."

"Aye, as they should be. How was the picnic?"

"Fine. Raised quite a bit for the historical society. Merry said it's earmarked for Simon Duvall's museum."

"How do you feel about that?" Denver didn't mention the secret they shared—a treasure buried somewhere on Washington Acres' property. A secret that would have been of interest to Simon, had he not been brutally murdered last spring.

"Feels like the right thing."

They'd come to an Oktoberfest Week display board attached to a sturdy wooden stand at the entrance of the canal walkway.

Denver said, "Speaking of raising money, how did Irene and Glen Sauer do? Being the sponsor and all."

"He didn't actually have a booth. His meats and chicken were prepared by the Historical Society, which sold hot dogs and grilled chicken sandwiches." She considered the crowds amassed around the food booths. "I guess it went well. I didn't ask."

"Ophelia must be proud. Looks like they had a big turnout."

"Never saw Ophelia. Come to think of it, you'd think she would have wanted to be here."

"She's probably getting ready for the next round of events."

"Perhaps."

Denver led Megan down the path and under a row of trees that bordered the canal. A few paddlers were still on the water, and Megan watched as a large canoe holding a couple and a young child floated by.

She told Denver about her conversation with Becker. "I'd been hoping the connection was Sauer, but it was Jenner. That seem odd?"

"Not really. He runs a business himself, so it's logical he'd need PR help. And he's connected to the area." Denver placed a hand over his eyes and squinted up toward the main thoroughfare, Canal Street. "I saw him here when I arrived. In fact, there he is now with his family."

Megan looked in the direction that Denver was pointing. She recognized the ruddy-faced thick-haired businessman. He wore pressed dark denim jeans and a tan field coat. A maroon scarf was draped in an elegant twist around his neck. A woman half his age held his arm, and in her arms perched an infant.

"I had no idea Jenner was a new father."

"I had no idea either. I think that's the new wife. I'd heard the last one left him when he decided one lassie wasn't enough, if ye know what I mean."

Megan did know exactly what he meant. Lana's allegations about Otto and Ophelia popped into her mind.

"Think maybe Ophelia had been the other woman?" Megan whispered.

"Don't know, don't much care. I have no time for cheaters." He squeezed Megan's hand. "It's all gossip in any case."

Only Megan didn't care about gossip. She wasn't thinking of the illicit nature of Jenner's affair, assuming he'd actually had one. She was thinking of motive and love triangles and murder.

And chicken.

"Well, look at that," Megan said. She pointed to the sign listing today's events. Under the culinary board, the offerings of each farm were listed. The notice said, "All-Beef Hot Dogs and Organic Chicken from Sauer Farm."

Denver's brow crinkled. "So?"

"So Glen Sauer doesn't raise organic chickens. But Mark Gregorio does."

"Still not following, Megs."

"The committee wanted sponsors who could meet product

demands. Yet Sauer provided Mark's chicken as his own, which he bought at a premium from Diamond Farm."

"Maybe he decided the organic label was important."

"Maybe," Megan said. "Or maybe I am smelling bullshit. And not from one of Sauer's bovines."

It was well after eight by the time Megan returned to the farm. Clay's truck was still there, and Megan saw a light on in the barn. Before going inside the house, she walked back to talk with her farm manager. She found him drawing something on a large sheet of white paper, which he had spread out on a wooden potting bench that was doubling as a drafting table. A large measuring tape lay on one side, and a scattering of other drafting tools were by Clay's left arm.

"Hey," Megan said. "What are you doing here so late?"

Clay looked up quickly, startled, then smiled when he realized it was Megan. Gunther was with him, and the big dog ran over to give Megan a very wet hello.

"The open house was such a success, I thought I would start to lay out plans for the pizza oven."

"You're really into that idea."

"I think locals would love it, and it would be another way to bring money into the farm."

Megan glanced down at the paper he was working on, which sat next to a hammer and a flashlight. She saw lines and figures and measurement numbers. A wave of affection ran through her.

"Looks good, Clay. The idea is growing on me," she said. "But you decided Sunday night at 8:36 after an exhausting weekend was the right time to pull together the plans?" Megan smiled. "Why are you really here?" She pointed to the hammer, a weapon in the hands of someone who knew just how to use it. Someone like Clay.

Clay sighed. He pulled the band out of his long hair, shook it free, then pulled it back again, securing it tightly. His handsome face looked wan and tired.

"I figured I'd stay until you got home."

"Because?"

"Because I didn't like the idea of leaving a grieving woman, a baby, and an eighty-four-year-old grandmother here alone."

Megan touched his arm. "We're always here alone."

"Not under these circumstances."

Megan gave him an inquisitive look.

Clay sighed again. He started putting his drafting tools away in a clear zippered case, turning away from Megan's stare. "Look, Emily seemed nervous so I had decided to stick around a while. I was in here, cleaning up, and Emily was outside with the baby when she saw something."

Megan thought of the glove Gunther had found before. "It was probably a deer," she said. Hollow words.

Clay stopped what he was doing long enough to meet Megan's gaze. "She saw a man by the barn. She screamed and he ran."

"She just lost her father. Perhaps she's imagining things."

Clay stared at her. He crossed his arms over his chest and leaned forward. "I came running outside. I saw him too, Megan. Gunther was in the house. By the time I made sure Emily and Lily were safe and ran after the man, he'd disappeared into the woods." Clay's eyes were round with worry. "I think it was your stalker. He's still here."

Megan could barely bring herself to speak. Finally she nodded. "Thank you." She told him about the sound in the woods, the footsteps Bibi had heard, and the glove Gunther found. "I didn't want to jump to conclusions. But we're not all hallucinating. Someone is watching this farm."

Clay nodded. "We should tell Bobby."

"He knows. He's been sending a patrol officer to the area on occasion."

"I'm not so sure a sporadic patrol will help. Someone could hide in these woods for months and never be found. They're dense. Beyond Potter Hill, they just keep going."

"Bobby has his hands full right now. They're short on

resources. Most of Winsome was at the Picnic on the Canal tonight. It's unlikely our visitor is connected to what happened to Otto." She said the words as much to convince herself as Clay. He didn't seem to buy it—and deep down neither did she.

Clay packed up the rest of his tools. As he was rolling the drafting paper into a tube shape, he said, "You're the one who found the chair on Potter Hill."

"I know. But I keep telling myself that was a coincidence."

Clay shook his head. "A human's ability to rationalize almost anything is well-documented. You keep telling yourself that, Megan. Just don't start believing it."

Twenty-Three

Clay's words were still ringing in Megan's ears the next morning. She knew she needed to reinforce their vulnerability with King, and she left the chief a message explaining what had transpired the night before. Before she left the farm, she patted her pocket to make sure she had the print-outs about Proust, the knife maker. Proust had responded to her Facebook message with a short note giving her the time and place of a knife show he'd be at in a neighboring town. If Megan finished her morning chores quickly enough, she could make it there before the show closed.

Monday was overcast. A heavy layer of fog had settled over the canal, misting the grass and smothering the downtown area in a wash of gray. Megan parked in front of the café and went inside, carrying two crates of fresh lettuce from the greenhouse for Alvaro's Monday special—a Cobb salad featuring the farm's produce and eggs. She was greeted with the shy smile of Judge Bernie Mason, one of the Breakfast Club members. The *Wall Street Journal* sat next to him, and his hand clutched a large mug of coffee.

"Here alone today, Bernie?" Megan said as she passed him.

He nodded. "Oktoberfest has everyone running."

In the kitchen, Alvaro was already chopping and sautéing for today's Oktoberfest specials. He'd refused to keep solely with the German theme, but had, after some heavy coaxing, agreed to one German-inspired meal each day. Today's was Kohlroulade, German cabbage rolls covered in a savory, rich gravy. Alvaro had made them ahead of time, and what he was cooking now smelled distinctly Mexican—not German.

"New Mexico chili," Alvaro said without being asked. "Posole, green chilies, grass-fed beef...try it." Alvaro started to scoop some in a bowl before Megan could respond. "Want me to make you some eggs too? And I have homemade corn tortillas. I brought them for my lunch. I could whip up some huevos rancheros."

Megan politely declined the eggs and tortilla. Although her stomach didn't feel up to a breakfast of chili, she took the bowl and tasted it. Layers of flavors and textures—the piquant heat of the chilies, the sweet chewiness of the hominy, the richness of beef and tomato—melded together beautifully.

"Are you adding this to the cook-off menu for Friday?"

"Depends. What do you think?"

"It's delicious."

Alvaro nodded. He didn't smile—he rarely smiled—but his eyes shone with pleasure. "I put some aside for Dr. Finn," he said gruffly.

Megan thanked him. "I see Bernie Mason out there, sitting alone. Have the other members of the crew been here much since Otto's passing?"

Alvaro shook his head. He had a full head of white hair, which contrasted strikingly with mocha-colored skin. His eyes, now coal-black and stormy, softened. "No, not much." He shrugged his broad shoulders. "I was just getting used to having them around."

Megan smiled. "Me too."

Alvaro nodded. "Yeah, well. This much tragedy makes you think. Appreciate what you got."

"By tragedy, you mean Otto and Ted's deaths?"

"And the erosion of trust." Alvaro stopped chopping. He placed his chef's knife down on the wooden chopping block and wiped his hands on his immaculate white apron. "For a town like this to work, people have to trust each other *and* the system. No trust, the heart of the town withers and dies." Alvaro struck his chest with his hand. "Something is not right. We have a traitor among us. I know it."

Megan knew Alvaro was speaking figuratively, and she was relieved Alvaro had sensed it too. He seemed to keep to himself. But in his role behind the counter, watching the comings and goings of Winsome's regulars, it made sense that he'd observe what other people missed.

"You need to go now," Alvaro said, his tone suddenly gruff again. "I have to finish the day's specials or customers will arrive and I'll be running around like a mad goat." He pointed to the large chili pot. "And this Oktoberfest? Never-ending. Now you like this chili too, so I have to make it as well." He shook his head as though her compliments on his newest chili had been an affront causing him even more work.

Megan smiled. She gave the cook a hug. To her surprise, he hugged her back.

New Hope sat on the west bank of the Delaware River, across from Lambertville, New Jersey. Another historic Bucks County town, its main drag was home to upscale stores, art boutiques, quaint inns, and high-end restaurants. Only Megan wasn't heading to one of New Hope's finer establishments. The address she had was an old school off of busy Route 202.

The address led to a large brick rectangle positioned well off the road. Cracked and pitted blacktop looped around the front and ended in a large parking lot in the back. The lot was almost full. Megan climbed out of her truck and walked to the main entrance. She opened the front doors and paused to let two heavily tattooed men out. Unsure what to expect, she made her way through a hall and into the main area—presumably once the school auditorium. The building still had an institutional feel.

Inside felt like a flea market. Proust hadn't said anything about where he'd be, and his website contained no photographs of the illusive artist. Megan hadn't expected this many vendors. Knife makers and other related craftsmen lined narrow pathways throughout the space, most cramming their wares on five-by-eight-foot tables. A few had set up elaborate display cases, and one craftsmen even had a small replica of his forge. What little light there was filtered through high grime-covered windows. That didn't seem to bother the customers, many of whom were carrying multiple packages. The smells of body odor, mildew, and acetone were strong.

"Ticket?" someone said.

To Megan's right, an older woman with curly white hair was selling tickets. Other than the flower tattooed on her right hand and a diamond stud nose piercing, she looked like someone's kindly conservative grandmother.

"Ticket?" the woman repeated.

"I'm just here to speak to someone."

"You still need a ticket."

Megan fumbled with her purse. She handed the woman a twenty and waited for her change. "Can you tell me which one is Proust?"

"Sorry. I come with the building, not the knife makers."

Someone else was waiting to enter and Megan shuffled her way inside. She started down one aisle, then zigzagged her way around the auditorium. She finally caught the attention of a young woman who pointed toward the stage when Megan asked about Proust.

There were two vendors wedged next to the front portion of the old auditorium: a middle-aged bald man wearing army fatigues and a youngish man in his late twenties wearing a button-down checked shirt and glasses. Megan put her money on Army Fatigues, but as soon as she got close to his table, she realized she was mistaken. Army Fatigue made switchblades and hunting knives. Her mark would make butterfly knives.

The younger man's display was meticulous. Three rows of knives, all in different sizes, sat on a bed of brown plush material. Two easels showcased photographs of his modest work space and his forge. The artist himself looked more like an accountant than a knife maker.

Megan waited until two other customers were finished talking with the man, then she stepped forward and introduced herself. "Proust?"

He nodded. "That's me. What do you need?"

He had an unnerving way of speaking. His words were clipped, and his eye contact was intense and never wavered. Megan looked away first.

"I messaged you on Facebook." She pulled the knife from her purse and separated it from its linen shroud. "I'm looking for the owner."

He took the knife from her and turned it over. "You found this?"

Megan nodded.

"I'm afraid I can't help you."

"It's not yours?"

"I made the knife. But someone altered it. Significantly."

"In what way?"

Proust frowned. He flipped the knife open and traced the blade with one finger, echoing what Molly Herr at the knife shop had done. If his clothes and demeanor screamed white collar, Proust's hands told a different story. They were strong and thick-knuckled, with small red scars and flat glossy burn spots along the digits and palms.

Proust handed the knife back to Megan.

"Everything's different. The blade. The coloring. This may have had two or three owners since I originally sold it."

"Do you remember who bought it from you? Maybe I can start there."

Proust looked over Megan's head toward the entrance way. Suddenly, he placed his hands on the table and leaned down so that his face was near Megan's.

"What do you want with this guy?" His vitriolic tone startled Megan.

"I told you. I want to return the knife to its rightful owner."

"Lady," Proust said in that same penetrating way, "I sold this knife for $425. That's cheap in my world. It's been altered, so it's likely worth even less now. You're going to an awful lot of trouble to return this to someone you don't know."

"I have my reasons."

He stood straight, said, "I have my reasons too," and turned away.

"So you won't help me?"

Megan continued to stand there, unsure what to do next. She'd come this far. To leave with nothing didn't seem like an option.

"Please," she said. "Anything you can tell me. Anything."

Megan's voice must have betrayed her desperation, because Proust turned toward her finally and said, "The original buyer was an old guy. Paid cash. That's all I remember." His gaze stabbed at her. "Really."

Twenty-Four

Emily was outside with Clay when Megan arrived back at the farm. The two were digging in one of the rear beds, planting garlic bulbs for the following spring. Lily was asleep in a stroller under a shade tree, her small body wrapped neatly in a pink fleece blanket. Sadie lay beside the stroller, looking happy to have a tiny playmate to watch over. The rain that threatened that morning never materialized, but the afternoon was chilly and cloudy. Megan pulled a hat from her jacket pocket and pulled it on over her ears.

"Need some help?" she asked.

They glanced at her at the same time, each clearly lost in his or her own thoughts. Gardening was good for that.

"We're okay," Clay said. "Besides, you had a visitor."

Megan looked at him, waiting for more.

"It's okay," Emily murmured. "Chief King. He had a few more questions about my dad."

"Am I supposed to call him?"

Clay nodded. "He asked that you give him a ring when you're back and he'll stop by." Clay looked like he wanted to say more, but with a glance at Emily, he walked away, toward the barn.

Emily watched him go.

"He's a good guy."

"Clay? The best."

"Just reinforces what a loser my ex is."

"Something good came out of your relationship." Megan went

over to the baby and gently adjusted the blanket, warming her against the chill.

Emily brightened. "That's true. I don't know what I would do without Lily. Now she's all I have."

Megan's chest hurt. She watched from the kitchen window as Emily lifted Lily and clutched the baby to her thin frame. The baby stirred, stretched, and then pulled at a strand of Emily's blond hair. Tiny fingers, tiny smile, and despite losing her father just days before, Emily's face was awash with affection.

Megan pulled open the drawer next to the rarely used utensils. It was Bibi's version of a junk drawer, and she kept everything from pens and calendars to photos and old school ribbons in there. Megan knew that buried underneath was a stack of old Polaroids, including a snapshot of her and her parents when she was just Lily's age. Age had worn away the colors' sharpness, and repeated handling had caused tears and smudges along the edges. Still, Megan stared at that picture, just as she had so many times over the years, willing her lovely young mother to tell her why she'd left.

The answers never came.

The front door slammed open and Emily and Lily entered the kitchen, rosy-cheeked from the cold. "Are you okay?" Emily asked, peering at Megan as she unwound the blanket from around her daughter. "You don't look well."

"I'm fine. Just catching up on some chores."

"When are you not catching up on chores?" She held Lily out. "Would you mind? Just for a moment."

The baby snuggled against Megan, her soft fingers and warm body stabbing reminders of what her mother had left behind. Thankfully, Emily didn't say "holding a baby suits you" or "it will be your turn soon" or any of the other things that would have made the moment harder to bear. Instead she simply took her daughter back with a grateful smile once her own coat was off.

"Did you call King?" Emily asked.

Megan had forgotten. "I'll do that now."

"You'll let me know if you hear something new?"

"Of course. Although I think King would have told you directly."

Emily nodded. "I guess." She started to head up the steps toward the guest room, but hesitated.

"Do you need anything, Emily?"

Emily looked like she wanted to say something. Her mouth opened and closed, and finally she managed, "I'll be up here for a nap if you need me."

"Okay."

Emily paused again, indecision playing out on her face. Lily cooed and tugged at her hair. This seemed to be the push Emily needed. She nodded at Megan and continued up the stairs.

"Does the name Pichu Rivera mean anything to you?"

"Not a thing. Should it?"

"I'm not sure. Maybe."

King was in the parlor. He'd stopped by on his way back to the station to talk with Megan, and he seemed in no rush to leave. Megan made him coffee, which he took black and drank in great heaving gulps that had Megan worried for the health of his throat. He'd said no to Bibi's lemon pound cake, which had Megan worried for his emotional well-being. King never turned down food.

"I came by to talk to you about three things. The first is Pichu Rivera, the name of the gentleman to whom a 2003 gray Honda Accord was registered. The aforementioned Accord was found just three country blocks from where Ted Kuhl died." King swallowed another mouthful of coffee. "Didn't you say you saw a gray Accord following Emily?"

"I did."

"And this was an older model, just as you described."

"Sounds that way."

"And someone had set it on fire."

Megan's eyes widened.

"On *fire*?"

"On fire."

They sat staring at one another in silence. People weren't murdered in Winsome. Cars were not torched like in a late-night episode of *CSI*. Surely they were living in an alternate universe. The world felt like it had turned upside down—and Megan wasn't sure how to right it.

"Fire," King repeated. "We believe whoever did this was trying to cover up evidence."

"Like the evidence one might find if one had moved a dead body in that car."

"Exactly." King banged the mug down on Bibi's antique table. "Oh, man, sorry."

Megan waved away his apology. "I assume the car had been reported stolen."

King nodded. "You assume correctly. It was reported two months ago."

So reporting it was unlikely to be a ruse, Megan thought. "Anything back from the coroner?"

"Just some preliminary findings. No peanuts were found in Ted's gut. They're running toxicology reports to see if there was something else in his system."

"How about the alcohol content of his blood? Denver said the shed smelled like a Sunday morning at a frat house."

"Waiting on that too, although preliminary tests showed he'd been drinking—but not enough to cause that smell. Looks like someone poured alcohol inside the shed."

"Perhaps to make it look like he'd been drunk and careless."

"That's one explanation. We're trying to keep an open mind."

Megan smiled. "Bobby, when you say 'we' you mean 'I,' correct?"

He laughed. "Yes." He shook his head, laughed again. "Wasn't small-town policing supposed to be easier?"

"One would think. But Bibi and I watched enough *Murder, She*

Wrote when I was little to know that the really bad stuff happens in the cutest, quaintest, littlest towns."

"Sure feels that way." King drained his cup. "Got results on Otto's vest too. The one Clay found in the creek."

"And?"

"Nothing. No blood, no DNA. Bummer." He lifted the mug. "Got any more of the good stuff?"

"I do. Back in a second."

When Megan returned, Bobby was looking at pictures on the mantel over the fireplace. His gaze had locked on to one of Bibi and Grandpa when they were first married. Without turning around, he said, "I didn't just come to talk to you about the Honda, Megan. I got your message. I told you I would have one of my men drive by the woods and walk up to Potter Hill."

"And I appreciate that. Yesterday upped the ante a bit though—don't you think?

King turned, picked up the coffee, and sat back down. His face looked haggard. "I do, and that's partly why I'm here. Someone has been up there. No chair, no fire, but one of my men spent time in the military and knows tracking. He said there were some flattened spots and other things indicating a warm body—or several—had spent time on that ridge."

"So now we know—"

"But here's the rub. There's no indication that whoever is up there is any more than some errant hiker. Sheesh, for all we know it's a troop of Boy Scouts. Nothing points to malicious intent, or anything else for that matter."

"But what about last night? The man Clay and Emily saw?"

King looked deeply apologetic, but he shook his head slowly back and forth. "Here's the third thing I wanted to talk to you about. See, I'm getting all sorts of crap from the Commissioner. They want these two cases closed, and quickly. It's bad press for Winsome and bad press for the county. I don't need to tell you the importance of tourism and New York commuters to the local economy."

"What are you trying to say?"

"I just don't have the resources to assign someone to Potter Hill or the farm. Not without more to go on."

"So we have to wait until something bad happens."

King's hands morphed into claws, his shoulders hunched. "Yes. No." He threw up a hand. "Look, I know we're both sitting here thinking about Simon Duvall and what happened last spring. For one, there are things you and Bonnie can do to protect yourselves. Get this old house wired for an alarm system."

"And two?" Megan knew Bibi would want nothing to do with an alarm system. She could hear her grandmother now: *The day I get an alarm in my own home, in my own town, is the day they can just dig my grave and bury me in the backyard.*

"I will personally keep you posted on what's happening."

Stunned, Megan said, "That's it?"

"Obviously there may be things I can't tell you, but I'll share what I can so you'll feel safe. Look, Megan, I feel awful about all of this. You tried to tell me early on that something was happening and I didn't listen. Now I have two dead bodies, two sets of suspicious circumstances, and a burned-out shell of a car belonging to someone named after a Pokémon character. If the only way I can help you and Bonnie feel safe is to keep you informed, then that's what I'll do. I trust you'll be discreet."

"As I have been."

"I know, and I appreciate it. Besides, if something happens to you, Clover will kill me." King stood up. "For what it's worth, I really don't think your Potter Hill hiker is related to what happened to Kuhl and Vance."

Megan thought of the knife. "I wish I could be so sure."

She opened the parlor door just in time to get a glimpse of a shadow slinking away. The only person home was Emily. Had she been listening outside the parlor? And if so, why?

Twenty-Five

Emily seemed off at dinner. She had made Hungarian Goulash and salad, which she served with thick slices of black Russian bread and butter. Winter food, and outside it felt like winter. Hard to comprehend that just twenty-four hours prior half the town was playing by the river, enjoying sun and a picnic near the canal. But that was Pennsylvania weather—as unpredictable as its politics. Emily picked at her dinner, swirling noodles around on her plate and staring sullenly at her glass. Her silence permeated the kitchen.

Finally, Bibi said, "Emily, why don't you head to bed early? Megan and I can watch Lily for you." She glanced at Megan, who was clearing the table. "Right, Megan?"

"Sure," Megan said.

"I'm fine. I'd rather stay up."

Bibi flexed her fingers, grimaced, and with a glance at Megan said, "Well, then I will let you two young ladies finish up in the kitchen." She stretched, grimaced again, and said, "Old bones."

Megan knew that was her cue to talk with Emily.

Once Bibi left, Emily's mood seemed to get even worse. She banged around the kitchen, putting away dishes and drying pots without a word. The baby, propped in a swing in the doorway, seemed to sense her mother's mood, and she whined and whimpered quietly to herself, laughing only when one of the dogs decided to sniff her face, up close and personal.

When the last dish was away and the counters were wiped down, Megan could stand it no longer. "Is there something in particular bothering you, Emily?" she asked. "Did Bonnie or I do something?"

"No." Emily shook her head. "Not at all. You both have been so generous."

"You seem upset tonight."

Eyes shifted away, toward the stove. "Just missing my dad."

That was understandable, although Megan didn't believe for second that was the only thing on her mind. There was more, and Megan had a feeling it related to whatever Emily thought she heard King talking about behind the parlor doors.

"If you want to talk about the investigation, we can."

Emily threw her rag down on the counter. She walked to Lily and started unstrapping her daughter from the swing. "You know, maybe I am really tired." She glanced over her shoulder at Megan. "I think I will head to bed early."

It was only 7:48.

"Suit yourself," Megan said. "Do you want us to take Lily so you can sleep?"

"No. Thank you. She's had a long day too."

Megan watched Emily run up the stairs, moving her legs like the devil himself was chasing her.

"What in heaven's name was that about?" Bibi asked. They were settled in the parlor and Bibi was watching the nightly news. "That girl looked like Atlas with the world on her shoulders. Which I suppose she has, in some ways."

"I don't know," Megan said. "Something is definitely on her mind."

"I heard King was here. Anything new?"

"Nothing really on Otto or Ted. They're still trying to piece things together. But I have to tell you about something else. It seems like someone has been watching the farm from atop Potter Hill."

Megan gave her grandmother bare bones details about their

stalker. She included the two times Gunther chased something in the woods, but left out the knife, the man, and the campfire.

"Surely it's related to whatever happened with Teddy and Otto."

"Bobby doesn't think so."

"Then maybe Bobby needs to reconsider his position." Bibi sat back in her armchair. "I don't know what is happening around here, Megan, but it's time this all comes to a close. Folks need to feel safe in their own homes."

"We could get an alarm system." Megan braced herself for the onslaught.

"We could, but we won't. I refuse to rely on some gizmo to tell me when someone is on my property. Then my ears and eyes will go soft. And what else do we have these dogs for?" At that, Sadie, who was fast asleep at Bibi's feet, opened one eye.

"It's just an extra precaution."

"Old Mrs. Kennedy has one and look at the good it did her. Teddy Kuhl in her tool shed." Bibi shook her head, just as agitated as Megan knew she would be. "And then there are the false alarms. Merry Chance had to pay twice for ambulance visits that were triggered by false alarms. No way." She crossed her arms over the "Winsome and Lose Some" motto on her navy-blue sweatshirt. "And that's the end of that."

"Only it's not the end of that, Bibi. Until we know what's going on, we need to take precautions."

"The *police* need to do something."

"Bobby said they're stretched thin, getting pressure to close things with Otto and Ted and lacking in manpower. He'll keep us posted on what's happening though."

"Good of him to care." Bibi sighed, the steam streaming out of her as quickly as it had inflated. "I know Bobby means well. And this is big, and he is young." She shook her head. "Ask Porter and Clay to hike up there once a day. They should take Gunther. If someone is watching the farm, they'll know we're on to them. We may not catch whoever it is, but they'll leave us alone." She reached down and stroked Gunther, whose head was in her lap. "But I wouldn't leave Gunther outside alone. Just in case whoever it is wants to remove the threat."

"An excellent idea. Clay and Porter are already keeping a lookout, but I will ask them to be extra vigilant."

"And we don't go out alone at night either."

Megan was thinking of Bibi's evening nap in the goat enclosure. She figured Bibi was thinking of Megan's nighttime patrols of the property. "Fine."

That seemed to satisfy her grandmother. "Now, how about that Dr. Finn? When is he coming over again?"

"In the middle of all of this, you're matchmaking again?"

"He's single. Likes animals. And doesn't mind a woman as smart as him who prefers getting dirty to keeping a house clean. I think you should nab him before someone else does." Bibi smiled to let Megan know she was kidding—mostly.

"You make me sound like such a catch."

"You're a handful, Megan Sawyer. Stubborn and independent-minded." Bibi closed her eyes, the conversation and the nightly news losing to the call of sleep. "In your own way, quite a handful. And Dr. Denver Finn would be darn lucky to have you."

With Bibi dozing in the parlor and Emily upstairs, Megan found herself with some rare free time. She considered working on the farm's books, but decided instead to do some online sleuthing of her own. In particular, she was curious about the connection between Ophelia Dilworth and Marty Jenner. What had caused Jenner to recommend Ophelia's firm? And what about the twenty-nine-year-old was so special that the Oktoberfest committee would allow her to run the show?

The firm Ophelia worked for seemed to be reputable. Its online presence was limited but positive, as one would expect from a PR firm. Ophelia's page on the firm's website was short and to the point—and nothing Megan hadn't seen before.

Yale graduate. Social-media expert. Event manager. She looked legitimate.

Yet all of this started with Oktoberfest, an idea Otto had set forth last year. He wanted to celebrate the town's German roots. He wanted to highlight its local businesses. And now he was dead.

Megan's head was swimming. She felt for Bobby King—so many seemingly disconnected details, including a torched Accord that had been owned by someone named...what? King had mentioned Pokémon. Pinchu? No, Pichu. Pichu Rivera.

Just as she was sure the police had done, Megan entered Rivera's name, even paying for an online criminal search. Rivera was a two-bit thug with a history of theft and assault. Only the car had been stolen from Rivera, so his background likely meant nothing—given that he'd reported it stolen two months before it turned up in Winsome. Even if they discovered forensic evidence, there may be no way to trace the car back to the driver. If only she'd gotten a glimpse of whoever had been behind the wheel that day.

The knife maker Proust had said the original purchaser of the small butterfly knife was an older man. Could it have been Jenner? Somehow she didn't see the accomplished businessman spending his evenings on Potter Hill. Not with a young wife and a new baby.

Out of curiosity, Megan started a search for Jenner and the new wife. She hit pay dirt within five minutes when she came across a two-year-old wedding announcement in the *Philadelphia Inquirer*. A September wedding. The bride had worn an exquisite Charlotte Balbier gown. The reception took place at the lavish Cescaphe Ballroom. Nine bridesmaids, nine groomsmen, all with blue-blood last names. Only the best for Mrs. Janice Jenner.

Mrs. Janice *Dilworth* Jenner.

Sisters? Megan kept scanning the article. And there she was, listed as the maid of honor—one Ophelia Dilworth, looking glorious in pale-peach chiffon.

So Jenner hadn't had an affair with Ophelia. She was his sister-in-law.

Had that connection been disclosed to the Oktoberfest

Committee? And did it matter—this was a small affair for a small town, after all. Jenner was doing Winsome a favor. As was Ophelia.

Megan went to bed that night thinking of strange bedfellows and weird alliances—and wondering whether any of this would ever make sense.

Twenty-Six

Megan was at Ophelia's headquarters before it opened, so she waited in the shade for the PR expert to arrive. At 8:46, Ophelia's sporty Miata pulled into the lot and screeched to a stop in front of the building. Megan accosted her at the door.

"Can we chat?" Megan asked sweetly.

Ophelia, dressed neatly in a long black skirt, ankle boots, and a deep plum sweater, gave Megan a cursory glance. "I have a nine o'clock meeting," she said.

"This won't take long."

Ophelia unlocked the front door as she said, "I don't want to rehash the Sauer farm."

"Nor do I."

Ophelia looked marginally relieved. "Fine. Five minutes."

When the door had closed behind them, Megan cut right to the core. "Marty Jenner."

Ophelia looked ready to protest, but she settled on, "What about him?"

"He's your brother-in-law."

"So?"

"So does the Oktoberfest committee know that?"

"Oh my lord, Megan, what is your problem? I have no idea what Marty may or may not have told your little backwoods committee, but does it really matter?" She spun around on her black high heels. "Seriously. They're getting my firm's reputation for a steal. They're getting *me* for a steal."

"How well did you know Otto?"

This seemed to stymie Ophelia. She looked sideways at Megan, then frowned. "What do you mean?"

"I mean how well did you know Otto? Friends? Business colleagues?" Megan knew she was on fragile ground here. These were prying questions, and under normal circumstances, none of her business. But these were not normal circumstances, and so she persisted.

"You sound like *her*," Ophelia said. "And I think you should leave."

Megan assumed *her* was Lana Vance. "It's a fair question, all things considered."

In almost a growl, Ophelia said, "Is it? A younger woman comes to town and suddenly no one can see past her age or the way she looks? Forget that I have an Ivy League degree. Never mind that I had offers from big firms all over the country. No, it's my status as an attractive single woman that everyone focuses on. You simply assume I would stoop to sleeping with another woman's husband." She shook her head. "You of all people should understand the harm in that way of thinking."

Megan stood there, chagrined. She was right, of course. Ophelia seemed to use her flirtatiousness to get what she wanted, but that was no excuse. Megan had engaged in just the type of stereotyping she hated.

"I'll let myself out," Megan said finally. She didn't wait to hear Ophelia's response.

"Come on now, Megs, ye are being a bit hard on yourself, don't ye think?"

No, Megan didn't think, and she said as much. "I saw heels and designer threads and a flirty personality and I assumed she was a man-eater."

Denver looked bemused. "She still may be." Denver lifted Megan's chin and smiled. They were at his aunt's house, outside with her horses. Denver was finishing up so they could head into town for tonight's Concert by the Canal. The café was serving Alvaro's caramel popcorn balls and hot apple cider to the concert-goers. "Look, the woman is a PR specialist. She excels at making bad things look good. She used her skills to turn your decency against you."

Now Megan felt even worse. Either she was a small-minded chauvinist or easily fooled. "Either way, I look like an idiot."

Denver laughed. "Just a poor detective, perhaps." He ran a brush down the length of one of his aunt's Palominos, a striking animal with a testy disposition. The horse stomped and brayed. Denver spoke to her, firmly but kindly. He turned his attention back to Megan. "Have you found out anything new?"

Megan shared what she'd found on the internet.

"Jenner's sister-in-law, huh? Feels like something that should have been disclosed."

"That's what I said. Ophelia didn't agree."

"Maybe Jenner told the committee and they didn't care."

Megan nodded. "I guess. Especially if they were getting a deal."

Megan picked up a brush and started grooming the other horse, a large male Quarter Horse with a white star on his muzzle. Unlike his companion, he was a gentle giant. He leaned in to the brush, clearly enjoying the attention.

"Why would Jenner care enough to bring in his high-paid sister-in-law?" Denver asked. "Doesn't strike me as the civic-minded type."

"I don't know. That's what bothers me too."

"Maybe he's just being kind."

"Perhaps." Megan frowned. "Honestly, I don't know him that well. My guess is that he's trying to win some political points with the town."

"Or maybe Ophelia isn't the catch she pretends to be." Denver stopped brushing and turned around. "Maybe Jenner was doing his wife a favor by finding some work for her sister."

Megan hadn't thought of that angle. Yale grad, big firm? But you never knew. Perhaps Ophelia was having trouble drumming up business. Megan remembered her own days at the law firm. It wasn't enough to work hard and well. To move up, you needed to make rain. And if Ophelia really wasn't that great an employee, then her demand to have Sauer sponsor the event could have simply constituted bad judgment on her part. Nothing more.

The Palomino pushed at Denver's back with her nose. Denver caught her face gently with his hand. "Now, now, we'll have none of that," he said to the horse. The Palomino gave him a look of brazen disregard.

"She doesn't care what you have to say," Megan said with a smile. She reached out to pet the Palomino. The horse closed her eyes, then flicked her head.

"She likes you. Here—you can brush her." Denver handed the grooming brush to Megan. "Just watch out. She looks sweet, but she kicks." He leaned back against the fence rail and took a long sip of water from a bottle. "Ye know, Megs, there's another explanation as well. One that is less pleasant to consider."

"I'm all ears."

"Maybe Ophelia is a spy."

"I think this girl kicked *you* in the head."

"Hear me out. Not the international intrigue sort of spy. What if Jenner planted her here for a reason?"

"What reason could Jenner possibly have to plant a spy?"

"Figure that out and maybe you have your motive."

"Easier said than done."

Denver smiled. "You're the detective, Megs. I'm just the dashing country vet."

Twenty-Seven

Night came early to Winsome, or at least that's how it seemed. The streetlights had been dimmed for the concert, which was taking place on the green near the canal. The committee had set up a makeshift stage with seating for about a hundred guests who required something other than a grassy hill. The rest of the concert-goers were sitting on blankets on the lawn.

Driving down Canal Street, Megan saw that the downtown area had been transformed. Volunteers were selling Alvaro's popcorn balls, soda, water, and apple cider from small carts. The Historical Society was hawking hot dogs—donated by Sauer Farms—from a small booth on the south side of the lawn. Carmine Roy and the Revelers were playing cover tunes from the '70s, '80s, and '90s, and a dance floor had been set up under a large tent strewn with lights near the new statue of George Washington. At ten, there would be fireworks.

Parking was tight, but Megan crammed the truck in the alley behind the café. She and Denver helped Alvaro and Clay load the remainder of the popcorn balls and apple cider on two carts. Because volunteers were handling tonight's event, Clover would be able to enjoy the rest of the concert. They'd decided to close the store early, and the café had stopped serving at noon. Still, Clover waited until the carts were on their way down to the green before gathering her belongings to leave.

"Bobby meeting you?" Megan asked Clover.

"He's here already, keeping an eye on things down there." She pointed to the concert area. A shadow fell across her pretty features.

Clover was wearing an ankle-skimming brown sarong, boots, and a white blouse. A leather jacket hugged her curves. She looked beautiful and Megan told her so.

Clover beamed. "Hoping to distract Bobby a little tonight. He's been so stressed."

"Understandable."

Megan had no doubt Clover would succeed in distracting King. She and Denver watched the younger woman weave through the crowd on the way to the stage.

"How about you, Alvaro?" Denver said. "Sticking around for some music?"

"Ah, I don't listen to this stuff." Alvaro waved a gnarled hand toward the throngs of revelers. It was a school night, and there were fewer people than on the weekends. But still, Megan was shocked by the numbers. "I'm going to get some sleep."

"You've been a trooper," Megan said. "I know it's been a ton of work. We appreciate it."

Alvaro grunted something unintelligible. Then, "The kitchen's clean. Keep it like that."

"We will," Megan said.

Alvaro eyed Denver up and down. "Make sure you lock up. So many people here this week." He grunted again. "Strangers."

"Yes, sir," Denver said without an ounce of condescension.

Alvaro studied him for a moment longer. He nodded to Megan and touched Denver's arm before leaving.

"Quite a character," Denver said when Alvaro had left. "You lucked out."

"Don't I know it? He's the best thing that could've happened for the café."

Denver pulled Megan close. "Shall we go down and see what the fuss is all about?"

"Sure."

But before Megan could turn the key in the lock on their way out of the café, Denver's cell phone rang. "Hold on," he said. He walked back inside to take the call. When he came back out, his brow was creased with worry. "I'm sorry, Megan. That was Mark Gregario. That horse is worse. I'm afraid I need to make a house call."

Megan tried to flash a smile that said understanding, but she was afraid it came off as anything but. She'd been looking forward to a night with Denver—and she knew he had too. "No problem. Let me grab the truck. I'll take you over."

"No need. Ann's here with some of their kids. She's driving me to the farm." He kissed Megan. "Stay. Try to relax. Have a Vance Big Time Ale and think about something other than what's been plaguing ye." He glanced toward the green. Below him, at the bottom of the grassy hill, the band was warming up. The sound of the Beach Boys drowned out the collective voices of the crowd and made it hard to hear. "If all goes well, we'll be back in an hour."

Megan nodded.

"The life of a country vet."

"Aye, you're right." He gave her that dimpled smile and then he was off.

Megan wandered down toward the green. Bibi, worried about Emily, had opted to stay home, and Clay had taken a well-deserved night off. The air was dry and chilly, and a cool breeze blew through Winsome's center. Around her, families huddled on blankets, eating popcorn and hot dogs and drinking hot spiced cider from small paper cups. Children chased one another, playing tag or simply being kids, noisy and energetic. Megan recognized only a fraction of the faces. She climbed back up to Canal Street and sat on a sidewalk bench—an addition paid for by the Historical Society's Beautification Board. The crowds amplified a sudden and overwhelming feeling of loneliness.

At seven thirty, Megan decided to get some paperwork finished back at the store. She didn't feel much like partying alone. She was hurrying down the sidewalk, coat pulled tight against the creeping cold, when her own phone rang. She paused by Nel's Hair

Salon to pull her cell from her pocket. It was Bibi. Emily needed a box of the baby's things from Emily's grandmother's house.

"I don't think she should go over there herself," Bibi whispered. "Can you and Denver go on your way home from the concert?"

"Of course. Does she need the stuff right away?"

"I think it contains extra bottles and clothes and things. So probably not a rush." She explained to Megan where the key and the box could be found. "Later should be okay."

Only Bibi didn't sound like later would be okay, and Megan didn't have the heart to tell her Denver was gone. Megan glanced at her watch; paperwork could wait.

"No worries, Bibi. I'll grab what she needs. Everything else okay there?"

"I guess."

"You can't talk?"

"Correct."

"Emily still seem off?"

"Correct again."

"Okay. Hang tight. I'll see you in a bit."

"Be careful," Bibi said. "Lots of Oktoberfest concert-goers means lots of beer. Be alert on the roads."

"Of course."

Megan clicked off her phone. She pushed her dark hair back from her face and glanced around. Maybe Clover would want to go with her. But she sighted Clover by the hot dog booth with Bobby. They were laughing, arms wrapped around one another's waists. Winsome's police chief seemed to be having a good time. Deciding she was being paranoid again, Megan decided to go alone.

She walked back through the café, relocking the front and back doors, and climbed into her truck. She was just pulling out onto Canal when a figure emerged from the shadows.

It took Megan a moment to realize it was her Aunt Sarah. She was accompanied by Merry Chance. Both women wore heavy black coats and jeans, but Sarah had a bright pink and orange scarf wrapped around her neck. Her long thick braid made her easy to recognize.

Megan rolled her window down and greeted the women. "Heading to the concert?"

"We are," Merry said. "We'll be attending to the hot dog booth. Little will people know a famous novelist is serving their food." Merry looked quite thrilled at the prospect of deception.

"Are you leaving?" Aunt Sarah asked, ignoring Merry's comments.

"For a little while. I have to run an errand."

With a quick glance at her companion, Sarah said, "We need to talk."

"Tonight's not good, Aunt Sarah."

"I've called you twice."

"I've been busy."

"How about tomorrow?"

Megan figured Sarah wanted to continue the conversation about her mother. While she wanted to know more, she really didn't have the heart or stomach for confronting that particular issue. Soon...maybe. But not right now.

"We have a lot to do around the farm. Maybe in a few weeks when the harvest is completely over and we have the beds ready for winter—"

"It can't wait," Sarah said.

"It'll have to." Megan started rolling up her window. Sarah looked like she wanted to stop her. Whatever else she had to say would have to wait until another day. Megan accelerated away from the curb. She'd stop by the Kuhl property, grab the baby's stuff, and then give Denver a call. She was feeling tired. If he was going to be working much later, perhaps she'd just go home and go to bed.

Emily's grandmother's house was dark, illuminated only by the moon and the feeble milky light thrown by Megan's phone. Megan kept a flashlight in the back of the truck and she went to dig it out.

Bibi had explained where the key was hidden—within a fake rock in the unkempt flower bed—and Megan found it quickly.

She fumbled with the front door, heart a pounding jackhammer in her chest. The property was deserted, the two trailers just ghostly sentinels in the shadows, and the small Cape seemed anything but inviting this October evening. After the third try, the door finally opened. Megan held the flashlight out in front of her, sweeping the light back and forth against the blackness. It took her a moment to find a light switch. She flipped it on and nothing happened. She made her way through the hallway and into the kitchen, relieved when that overhead light worked.

It was only 8:08, but it felt like the Witching Hour. Perhaps it was the dark—or knowing that most of Winsome was a few miles away at the concert. Whatever the reason, Megan wanted to get in and out quickly.

She located the boxes just where Emily said they would be, in the living room. Three cardboard containers sat stacked one on top of the other. There was no light in the living room, so Megan held the flashlight under one arm while she struggled with the large boxes, pulling each onto the floor and undoing the taped tops. The second one held what she was looking for: baby clothes, bottles, diapers, and toys. She taped it back up, returned the others to a neat pile, and pushed the box toward the entrance.

Feeling only slightly calmer, Megan left the box by the front door so she could turn off the kitchen light. The sudden darkness felt oppressive.

A sound stopped her. Scratching, scurrying...just a mouse in the cabinets. Megan let out her breath, only just realizing she'd been holding it. She hustled toward the front door. There, she lifted the box and went back outside, locking the door behind her. She'd keep the key. She didn't relish the idea of spending more time hunting around the yard.

The box tucked neatly in the truck bed, Megan was walking around to the driver's side door when a new sound stopped her. Something was in the bushes by the nicer of the trailers. Megan whipped her flashlight around, aiming it toward the sound. She heard a growl in the distance.

"Who's there?"

A sweep of the area caught movement in the rear field. Someone or something was running across the high grass, toward the Sauer property across the road.

"Stop!" Megan called. She still had the knife she'd found in the woods, and she sprinted to the truck and pulled the knife from her purse. She was debating whether to get in the truck or chase down whoever was out there when the stream of light from her flashlight caught the shape of a dog in the road.

"Damn," Megan muttered under her breath. She locked the truck door and grabbed a rope from the truck bed. She was halfway to the road when motion again caught her eye. Her flashlight passed back and forth across the field. Nothing.

The dog was still in the road.

Megan called to it. It looked at her, then ran the rest of the way into the Sauers' property. The back section of the Sauer farm was largely pasture dedicated to grazing. Beyond that were the chicken and turkey barns and then barns for the cows. The house, a large Dutch Colonial with a long rambling tail of mismatched additions, sat toward the front of the two hundred plus acres, close to another road. The dog ran around the fenced pasture, toward the chicken barn. Megan pursued it, aware that the Sauers had barbed wire and electric fencing around their enclosures.

"Here, pup," she called. She glanced over her shoulder. No one there. "Come on, baby."

The dog ran farther into the darkened farm. Megan followed the thin band of land that hugged the pasture and led toward the front of the property. She was afraid the dog—scared as it was— would get tangled in the wire or shocked by the fencing, and pursuing it might only make it more likely to get hurt. If Glen found it though—well, she didn't trust him to do anything to help the dog find its owner. Megan glanced at the Sauers' house. She wondered whether they were at the concert. She was trespassing, and knew

Glen would be angry if he found her. She stood, indecision rooting her to her spot.

The glow from the flashlight dimmed. She couldn't stand there forever.

There was a sharp yelp, followed by a long whine. The hair on the back of Megan's neck bristled. The pup was hurt. She followed the whine past the inner pasture, toward the chicken barn. Shining the dying beam on the outside of the barn, she searched until she found the dog. It was huddled against the building, its foot caught in a band of barbed wire. It whined again.

Megan approached it carefully, low and hand out, palm down. It looked like a Beagle mix of some sort—small and muscular with a boxy face—but right now that face was twisted into a doggy grimace of pain. It growled.

Megan crawled close enough to reach the dog. Gently, carefully, she tied the rope to its collar. Then she unwound the wire from its leg. It growled twice more, but let her do it. When the wire was off, the dog pulled against the rope, trying to run. Thwarted, it stood and looked at Megan, teeth bared. She reached out again and this time the dog let her pet her. Her tail wagged from between her legs, tentatively at first and then with more vigor.

"Come on, sweetheart," Megan crooned. "Let's get you out of here."

Megan stood, the beam from the flashlight all but dead. She listened, trying to get her bearings. She pressed a palm against the barn door. It gave way. She stumbled and nearly fell into the Sauers' chicken barn.

Only there were no chickens. Megan couldn't see much past the entranceway, but the smell—musty and sour—and the complete lack of sound told her the entire structure was empty. Weird, she thought. The reason the Sauers bought Mark's organic chicken? Megan wondered if the turkeys were gone too. No time to look now. She needed to get the dog off the property and into Denver's hands so he could look at that leg. And she had to do it before the flashlight batteries were completely drained.

It took five minutes to return to the road and another minute to cross to her car. She loaded the dog into the passenger side of the truck, and then walked around to the driver's side. She looked around once more before climbing in. The Kuhl house remained dark, as did the trailers. The long grassy fields blew in the wind, but other than the moan of the breeze in the trees, silence shrouded the lot.

Still, Megan shuddered.

She couldn't shake the feeling that someone or something was watching her.

Twenty-Eight

"I'd say she's about six years old. Beagle mix, perhaps. Someone has cared well for the wee lassie." Denver straightened up, giving the dog a pat on the head. "Wish we had a name or something. In any case, that leg will heal just fine. A few deep scratches is all."

They were in the barn, where Megan had set up a home for the dog. They had no idea whether she was vaccinated, and until Denver had a chance to examine her, Megan didn't want to expose the other dogs or Lily.

"Can you vaccinate her?"

"Aye. I will give her the normal shots, the ones that won't hurt her if she's had them already—although I suspect she's up to date." He looked up. "Keep her isolated for a few days. And I wouldn't let her near the baby. Your dogs are vaccinated, but we should keep an eye on this one until we know she's healthy."

Megan watched him work with the dog, gentle but confident. The pup remained skittish, although she seemed more relaxed in the vet's presence. He'd come in response to Megan's frantic call, no questions asked. But now that the dog seemed to be settling down, she could see Denver's agitation increasing. Once Sammy—which they'd taken to calling the dog—was curled on a fleece blanket in the corner of her penned-in area, Denver leaned against the workbench, arms across his chest.

"Are ye going to tell me why ye went there alone tonight, Megan?"

Megan bristled. She was a grown woman who didn't feel the

need to explain her actions to Denver, Bibi, or anyone else, for that matter. She said as much.

"I'm not asking because I want to reprimand ye. King told me about the stalker up on the hill." Denver looked pained. He shook his head, ran a hand through unruly auburn hair. The shadow of a beard hugged the sharp planes of his face. The scar between his eyes seemed more pronounced in the artificial light of the barn, making him look sexy and slightly dangerous. "Oh hell, Megan. I'm just worried. Too many bad things happening around here, and knowing that ye put yourself in harm's way makes me—"

"Angry."

"Aye. A little." His face softened. "I care about ye."

"I know, and I'm sorry. I really am. I didn't want to worry you. I didn't want you to treat me—us—as though we are helpless, being here alone." Megan felt herself soften too. She'd be angry at him, and in retrospect it wasn't the smartest of ideas to go to the Kuhl place alone. Plus, she should have been truthful with Denver about Potter Hill from the start. But like Bibi, Megan resented having to curb her behavior in her own town. She should be able to feel safe. They all should.

"Ye need to have faith in me, Megan. If this," he waved his hand in the space between them, "if this is going to work."

Megan nodded slowly. He was right. "I called King on my way back to the farm. He's sending a crew over to check on the Kuhl property."

"Ye think someone's been staying there?"

"I don't know. I heard something and felt eyes watching me. And then she turned up," Megan said, pointing to Sammy. "But maybe it was just Sammy all along." Megan rubbed her arms, still feeling the goose pimples she'd experienced earlier.

"I guess we'll see."

Megan told him about the Sauers' farm and the empty chicken barn. "Why would his barns be empty?"

Denver frowned. "I don't know. Maybe they dispatched the whole flock for Oktoberfest?"

"But they were selling Mark's organic chicken."

"That's right, they were." Denver shook his head. "Either they had some disease wipe out their flock or they're getting out of the chicken business."

The Sauer family had been running that farm ever since Megan could remember. Before Glen started selling his poultry to big-box stores and national brands and distributors, the Sauer farm was the source of most local chicken and turkey. Growing up, every non-farming family ate a Sauer turkey for Thanksgiving, and people from surrounding towns placed orders directly with Michael Sauer, Glen's dad. Megan could remember driving into the Sauer farm with her grandfather as a young girl to buy chicks for their own flock. The hens roamed free, and many roosted in the trees that surrounded the Sauer house, watched over by a pair of matted gregarious Great Pyrenees. No more. Now it felt like a joyless place. At least at ten at night.

Megan glanced at her watch. It was nearly midnight, and they weren't going to solve this puzzle now. "You should go," she said to Denver. "You've had a long day. Bibi's waiting for me up at the house." And she will have a thing or two to say about this adventure as well, Megan thought. No need to fan those flames again.

"I could stay. My aunt can run over and let the dogs out."

Megan smiled her thanks. She'd love him to stay—but not that way, and not for that reason. "We'll be fine. Perhaps another time? Under better circumstances."

Denver moved closer. He smelled of spicy aftershave and wood smoke from Diamond Farm.

"I would like that."

While Denver gathered his things, Megan gave the dog a last pat for the night. She was a sweet little thing, and she wagged her tail gratefully when Megan sat beside her. Who are you? Megan wondered. And who is sitting up worried about you tonight?

But there was no time for further contemplation. Bibi showed up at the barn looking cross. "King is on the line up in the kitchen. He tried your cell, but you didn't answer," she said. Her eyes fell on

Denver; she avoided Megan's gaze. "He wants to talk to you, Megan."

Here we go, Megan thought, and followed Bibi's agitated form into the house.

"Someone's been living in that trailer. Not the one that's falling apart. The other one." King sounded out of breath and annoyed. "Bastard got away."

"Any clue as to who?"

"We're working on that. Whoever it was left in a hurry, but they mostly cleared the place out. I say mostly because they left behind some garbage and other sundry items. It's at the lab now."

"How about dog stuff?"

"Come to think of it, there was a bag of dog food in there."

"Well then, we have his dog. I say he, but maybe it's a she."

"We think it's a man, Megan." He paused. "If you have his dog, he may come there looking for it. I think you should ask Denver to take the dog."

Megan glanced at Bibi and Denver. Both were standing in the kitchen, watching her. "You have any reason to believe he's connected to what happened to Otto or Ted?"

"We just don't know." King said something to someone else. When he came back on the line, his voice became brusque. "We're going to need to talk with Emily."

"Now? She's asleep."

"The morning is okay. Can you have her meet us at her grandmother's property? Say nine o'clock?"

Megan's stomach tightened. "Is she in some kind of trouble, Bobby?"

"I told you I would share what we know—within reason. I can't tell you why we need to talk to her though. We should meet with her first."

"Okay, fine. I'll see to it that she's there at nine."

As she hung up, she saw Bibi filling a kettle with water. Her grandmother was feeling restless. Chamomile tea and a shot of brandy or whiskey or rum...Bibi's remedy for eyes wide open. Megan knew all this was weighing on Bibi: finding Otto, suspicions about Teddy, concerns that someone was watching the farm. She also knew Bibi was tough as old hide leather—and that no one should underestimate her. She decided to hit the issue head on, with Denver there.

"Whoever was at Emily's could be connected to what happened to Otto and Teddy," Megan said. "But the police can't be sure. They want to talk with Emily tomorrow."

Bibi didn't respond. She placed a chamomile bag in her cup and added a shot of whiskey, then another. She poured boiling water into the cup along with a heaping teaspoon of sugar. She carried the cup to the kitchen table and sat down.

"Are you going to say something?" Megan asked.

"You let me believe you were going to the Kuhl property with Denver." Bibi's voice was even and low—a sure sign of anger. "You went alone, knowing full well that her father may have just been murdered."

Megan didn't say anything. It was pointless to argue. She was right, and an apology would only sound hollow to both of them.

Bibi picked her mug up. "I'm going to bed. In the morning, I'll watch Lily so you can accompany Emily to meet with Bobby."

"Thank you."

"Don't thank me." She turned, her eyes piercing Megan's. "You promised. No walking around alone. Don't break your promises to me, Megan."

"I should have never made a promise I couldn't keep."

"What does that mean?"

"It means I run a farm. I have responsibilities. It's not practical for me to wait for someone to hold my hand."

"But you expect that of me?"

She had a point, of course. Being older didn't make her helpless—or any less resourceful. "I'm sorry, Bibi."

Bibi nodded. She waved to Denver. "Thanks for coming,

Denver." To Megan, she said, "Get some rest. Morning will come quickly."

Megan watched Bibi leave. Turning back to Denver, she said goodnight.

"I can take that dog back to the clinic, Megan," he said. "It would be safer for all of you. In case its owner comes looking."

Megan shook her head. Whoever had the dog had cared for it. From skin to nails to teeth, the pup had been loved. Her owner might come looking, but perhaps that would be a good thing—an end to all of this, a way of flushing him out. And if not, Megan would rather the dog stayed here rather than be shut up in a cage.

"The dog could stay at my house," Denver said. "If you're worried about her comfort."

Megan smiled. He was a generous man, and she needed to appreciate that. "And put your pups at risk? I don't think so. We have the barn here—she can safely stay separate."

Reluctantly, Denver agreed. He promised to check on Sammy the next day. Megan locked the door after him. Sadie followed Megan out of the kitchen, up to bed. A glance back told Megan that Gunther had stayed behind, his body against the door, always the guard.

Megan's last thoughts before sleep descended were of the Sauers' farm. She reached for Sadie, who was curled at the end of the bed, her mind grasping for a pattern in the chaos. As her eyes closed, she pictured that empty barn. No chickens. What if Sauer was closing shop? But what did that mean? And how did it fit with Otto Vance and Ted Kuhl?

Or did it fit in at all?

Twenty-Nine

Megan returned to where it all started: with the Breakfast Club. She arrived before eight and found Albert Nunez and Lou Brazzi at the large copper-topped table at the back of the store. Alvaro had made them omelets. Brazzi was still picking at his food and reading a *Wall Street Journal*. Nunez, half-finished plate shoved to the side, was paging through *Field and Stream*. Megan sat down with them in the empty seat next to Nunez.

"What can we do for you, Counselor?" Brazzi asked. He smiled. A steel-haired man in his late fifties, Brazzi had the only real estate law business in town. He made his own hours and was picky about the engagements he accepted. Megan had always liked him. Perhaps it was the kinship of lawyers—or the easy way he had around people.

"I want to talk about what happened with Otto and Ted."

Both faces shut down. Brazzi pursed his lips. Nunez snorted.

"What about it?" Brazzi asked.

Megan thought about how to ask her questions. She knew these guys would be offended by a frontal attack, but she had neither the energy nor the time to beat around the bush.

"In the days leading up to Otto's death, it seemed like Teddy and Otto weren't seeing eye to eye. I sensed a lot of tension in the group."

Nunez gave Megan a wary glance. "What does that have to do with anything?"

"I wonder if whatever was between them could have been more serious than any of us thought."

"Ted died of an allergic reaction," Nunez said. "Peanuts."

Brazzi shook his head. "I heard his death is suspicious. Bobby and his people are doing more tests."

Nunez frowned. "What kind of tests?"

"Not sure," Brazzi said. "But they're not certain the peanuts are really what killed him."

Nunez sat back in his chair looking agitated. He turned to Megan. "Are you saying Ted and Otto were murdered? And it was because of Oktoberfest? Because that's what all the bickering was about—who got to be the beer sponsor." He slammed a hand down on the table. "Utter nonsense."

Brazzi shot Nunez a withering look. "Ted had *everything* tied up in that brewery. Everything. It wasn't utter nonsense to him."

Megan glanced up in time to see Alvaro staring at her. He lifted his chin toward the door, where Glen Sauer was standing alongside his wife, Irene. Sauer, a beefy giant of a man with porcine features and a putty-like nose, was gripping Irene's shoulder and whispering in her ear.

Megan lowered her voice.

"I'm not saying Ted did anything to Otto, nor am I denying or confirming that what happened to Ted was due to foul play. I'm just worried—and I think there was more to the tension between the two men than anyone is letting on."

"Spoken like a lawyer," Nunez growled. "Ted felt like he got the short end of the stick and he was sore about it. That's it."

Brazzi stared pensively toward the Sauers. Megan stood. Clearly she wasn't getting anything new out of this crew. She left them and joined Clover at the checkout counter.

"What do you think?" Clover asked staring at the Sauers. "Why are they here?"

"Looks like they want Lou."

Indeed, Glen was making his way to Brazzi, Irene's shoulder still in his grasp. Neither looked happy. Megan and Clover stocked lip balms on the counter, all the while watching the Sauers with quick furtive glances.

"Is it just me, or does Lou Brazzi look carsick?" Clover whispered.

"As long as it wasn't Alvaro's omelet."

Clover laughed. "Lou's a good egg, but he doesn't look thrilled to be talking with Glen."

"I wonder what that's all about."

Megan saw Alvaro watching the conversation too. At one point, the cook leaned over the counter and asked Irene if she wanted some coffee. She shook her head, features pinched in distaste.

"Oh, no, she didn't," Clover whispered. "She just dissed Alvaro." Alvaro was the closest thing Clover had to a father figure, and she was fiercely protective. "I don't like the Sauers. Never have."

Megan felt the urge to escort them out of her café. She didn't have to make a choice. After a few minutes, Glen gave Brazzi a curt nod and he and Irene left.

The Kuhl property looked much less threatening in the daylight. It was a cool, sunny October morning, the kind of morning that made you want to sit outside on your porch watching the town awaken with a hot coffee in your hand and a warm blanket around your shoulders. Instead, Megan and Emily traipsed across town in Megan's truck, leaving little Lily with Bibi and Clay at the farm. When they pulled into the Cape Cod's driveway, they saw two police cars and King's unmarked.

Emily climbed out of the truck with trepidation, her slim face a mask of dread. Megan put a hand on her arm.

"It's going to be okay."

"I wish I knew what they wanted." She glanced around. "Why are there so many cops here?"

"I'm sure they just want to give you an update."

But that wasn't it. King walked over and handed Emily a warrant to search the property, the brewery, and the apartment on the other side of town.

"I need your father's laptop too. I believe you have it."

Emily nodded. "What are you looking for?"

King didn't answer. He glanced at Emily and said, "Come with me." Apologetically, he added, "Megan, you'll have to stay here."

Emily stopped walking. "I want her to come."

"She's not your attorney, Emily."

"But she could be." Emily looked at Megan. "You are an attorney, right?"

Megan said, "I'm not a criminal lawyer, Emily. And I'm not licensed in Pennsylvania." To King, she said, "Does she even need a lawyer, Bobby?"

Bobby sighed. "No, she doesn't. Fine, you can come too." He walked off, inside the house, and Megan and Emily followed him. When they got to the kitchen, King pulled some photos from a manila envelope and placed them on the stained Formica countertop. He stepped back.

"Do you have something you want to tell us, Emily?"

Emily studied the photos. Her face went from pink to fire engine red. She started to cry. "I'm sorry. It was my fault." She gulped. "I should have told you."

"Yes, you should have."

Megan looked at the photos over Emily's shoulder. They were murky black and whites. "Security footage?"

King nodded. "From the industrial park where the brewery is. Seems Emily was not completely truthful with us."

The pictures were damning. They showed Emily and a man who looked like Ted Kuhl sitting in Emily's old Pontiac. Ted's profile was clearly visible in the third photo. Each photo was time stamped—a match for the day before Ted's body was found in Mrs. Kennedy's tool shed.

"I was honest about everything else. *Everything*. But when I realized where he'd been hiding, I had to talk to him. There's an abandoned business near the brewery. He was there. The prior owner had given him a key. I found a copy in the safe deposit box." Emily's voice was shrill. She looked at Megan, eyes searching desperately for understanding. "Other than Lily, he's all I had."

Emily sobbed uncontrollably. Megan left in search of tissues while King stayed with his charge. When Megan returned, the police chief had an arm around Emily and was holding her close. His eyes met Megan's over the tall woman's head. They said "help me."

"Emily," Megan said sternly. "You saw your father before he died. You need to help us understand what happened after that."

Emily swallowed. Nodded. "Okay."

"What did he say to you?" King asked.

"Nothing. He wouldn't tell me anything."

King frowned. "You said you'd be honest."

"He just kept saying 'they'll be after you too,' and telling me to leave and not come back."

"Who is 'they'?"

"I have no idea. He wouldn't say."

"That was all?" King repeated. "That was the extent of your interaction?"

Emily was quiet for a moment. "I was happy to see him. I hugged him, just so relieved he was still alive. He scolded me for finding him, said it would have been better had I left him alone." More tears. Emily brushed them away with the back of her hand. When she could continue, she said, "I asked him what had happened, to help me understand why he left. He said he would tell me eventually, but for now, the less I knew, the better."

"He didn't give you any indication of who was after him?" King bent over so his face was level with Emily's. "Think. Picture the entire conversation."

Emily nodded.

"Okay, okay." She took a step back, widening the space between her and King, and then looked at Megan. "He touched the baby, and said Otto lost everything because of him." Her eyes widened. "That was it. 'Otto lost everything because of me. I won't put you in danger.'"

Megan and King exchanged a glance. "Whatever he told Otto, he felt that was the reason Otto died," Megan said.

"But Ted wasn't the one who killed him," King replied. "At least not based on this."

"My father wouldn't have hurt anyone," Emily said. "I told you that before." The tears started again, flowing down her face, creating a river of mascara and foundation. "But don't you see? I'm the reason my father died."

King and Megan looked at her. Around them, uniformed officers searched and sorted and fingerprinted, but Emily seemed oblivious to their presence. She stared at the white kitchen ceiling, tears still coming down.

King bent down slightly so they were eye to eye. "Why do you believe that? What else happened?"

Emily turned toward Megan. "That day at the farm, when you and Chief King were talking in the living room? I heard what was said. I didn't mean to listen...well, maybe I did. I heard about the Honda that had been following me."

Megan remembered. And she recalled how odd Emily had acted afterwards. "You think you led whoever that was to your father."

"Clearly I did. They must have found him and...well, you know the rest."

"It's not your fault." King called over a uniformed police officer. "Can you stay with Emily for a few minutes? Show her some of the photos you pulled. I need to talk with Megan."

Megan followed King outside into the unkempt backyard between the Cape and the broken-down trailer. King stopped in front of a rusty lawnmower so overgrown with weeds that it seemed part of the natural landscape.

"She's right. She probably led the killer right to Ted." King kept his voice low—barely audible. "Whoever was driving that Honda is our man."

"Nothing from the car?"

"Not a hair. But we did get some preliminary results from Forensics. Ted's last meal was likely some saltines and a bag of pretzels."

"No peanuts?"

King shook his head.

"Then what caused the anaphylactic shock?"

"Peanut oil. Injected directly into his bloodstream. We're still waiting on the toxicology reports to see if there was anything else in his system."

Megan let that sink in. So cruel. So premeditated. "Again, someone who knew him."

"Or who was able to find that out about him. He did occasionally wear a bracelet."

Megan thought about the Breakfast Club. Brazzi and Nunez. Was it possible they knew more than they'd let on?

As though reading her thoughts, King said, "We'll be interviewing King's buddies from the café, anyone with a nexus between Otto and Ted."

"Did whoever did this need medical training?"

"No. The coroner said anyone with access to needles and who's seen *M*A*S*H* or *CSI* or *ER*—and that's pretty much everyone—could have done it."

"Oktoberfest."

King cocked his head to the side. "What about it?"

"I've been thinking all along that the key is the Oktoberfest celebration. It seems really petty that two men could die over the beer sponsorship, but what if it's something different? Something unrelated to beer?"

"Like what?"

"I have no idea." Megan repeated what she'd learned about Ophelia's connection with Jenner. She thought about Denver's offhand suggestion—that Ophelia was a spy. "Ophelia may deserve some attention, Bobby. Things have been pretty weird since she came along."

"I can't see Ophelia killing two men."

"Perhaps not directly. Lana Vance told us both that she suspected Ophelia and Otto of having an affair. Maybe the deaths were personal. Ted found out what happened, and the killer took him out to keep him quiet too."

"We'd thought of that, of course." He paused. "Are you suggesting Lana?"

She had acted oddly when Megan went to see her. "Maybe. But not necessarily. Think about who has something to lose, Bobby. Right now we know of Lana—assuming the affair was more than a figment of her imagination. But even if it was, if she thought it was real, she could have acted."

"True."

"But besides Lana, who else could have benefitted or been harmed by Otto's and/or Ted's deaths?"

King sighed. "I guess that's exactly what we need to figure out."

The farm was quiet upon their return. Baby Lily was asleep in her playpen and Bibi was dozing on the armchair beside her, Sadie at her feet. Gunther, too, was resting—out by the barn where Megan found Clay and Porter.

Upon seeing her, Porter stepped back, wiped his hands on his jeans, and smiled. "We have something for you."

Clay, who was on a ladder in the main portion of the barn, stepped down. Sammy the dog was in her pen area, tail wagging. She jumped up on the gate and gave two quick barks at Megan. Mutton Chops, the barn cat, had curled into a ball beside Sammy's pen—clearly Sammy was used to cats.

"What's all this?" Megan asked. She scratched Sammy behind the ears, her eyes drawn to the rafters above her where Clay apparently had been working.

"I rigged a camera. This way, if whoever owns Sammy comes here looking for her, we'll get a photo."

"What a smart idea."

Clay climbed back on the ladder. He pointed to a tiny little device tucked above him. Megan never would have noticed it, even in daylight. "It's small and motion sensing," Clay said. "If someone comes in at night and startles the dog it will start recording. It's attached to an alarm, which we'll give you. You can put it beside your bed while you're sleeping."

"I love it." Porter handed her the small alarm. It looked like an egg timer, but heavier. "That's it?"

"That's it." Clay swung down off the ladder. "It was Porter's idea."

Megan turned to the younger man. He was chewing on a thumbnail, looking at her, his expression tight. His first defense was always to lash out, and even now he seemed to be waiting for Megan to say something before letting his guard down. She smiled and thanked him. His frame and features relaxed.

"I can sleep here," he said. "I'll bed down at the back of the barn in that small room." He gestured toward the oldest part of the barn, where just months ago men had trespassed, rooting for their own riches. "If someone comes—"

"Won't be necessary, Brian. But I really appreciate your concern. Both of you." She was touched by Porter's protectiveness and Clay's creativity, but she didn't want anyone staying there. She had to feel safe in her own home—and she and Bibi needed to do this on their own. "We have Gunther and Sadie, and with this camera and alarm, I think we'll be all set."

They both stood there, hands on hips, exchanging a look.

"Clover told me about Ted. That his death was no accident. Or suicide." Clay rubbed long-fingered strong hands against his pants. "And whoever owns that dog could be part of what's going on."

So much for secrets. At least Megan hadn't been the one to spill the coffee beans.

Megan gave Clay a hard look. "Gentlemen, we have a lot to do. The back bed needs to be mulched, the greens watered, and if we don't finish planting garlic bulbs soon we'll have no garlic for next year. Clay, please see to the garlic. Porter, you can help me mulch."

Neither said a word, but each heeded her requests, going off on their own in different directions.

Thirty

By mid-afternoon, clouds had settled in, blanketing Winsome once again in a shroud of muted gray. This time, the clouds didn't dissipate. Weather forecasters predicted a quick rain, but the storm stalled, pouring buckets of cold, stinging precipitation on the area, filling up creek beds and causing local flooding. At four o'clock, Ophelia and the Oktoberfest committee made the call to move the beer tasting inside Vance Brewery.

Megan wasn't going to go. While the tasting sounded fun, she was in no mood for a party, and she had too much to do at the farm. Alvaro was trying to finish the chili for the cook-off on Friday, so help was needed at the café. But the weather had dampened the desire to go out, and the café and store remained empty most of the day. Clover called at five to say she didn't need any backup. So when Denver offered to buy her a drink at Vance's brew pub, Megan agreed. Maybe she would have the opportunity to dig up more dirt on what was going on.

Despite the weather, the brewery was packed. The tasting was against the far wall, and a crowd was milling about between tables laid out with appetizers and beer samples. Over the speakers, the Rolling Stones crooned about getting satisfaction. A young businessman in a light wool gray suit nodded at Megan from two stools down. She smiled back noncommittally and took a seat at the bar, avoiding his probing gaze.

Pulling her wallet out of her purse, she said, "Hedy, a lager please. Whatever is on tap."

The youngest Vance nodded. She tipped a glass under a spigot and poured a straw-colored brew into a frosted mug. She placed it in front of Megan, reached beneath the counter, and grabbed a bowl of mixed nuts. This too she put in front of Megan.

"Decent crowd?"

"Pretty good, all things considered." Hedy wiped the bar down, her eyes on the crowd by the tasting. "I have to hand it to Ophelia, as much as I loathe her, she knows how to plan an event."

"That she does." Megan smiled. "Your mom around?"

"Nah. She's done here. It'll be me from now on." Hedy's smile seemed sad. "I'm taking over the management of the brewery."

"You'll be great. Is your mom okay?"

"Okay as she can be."

Hedy wandered down the bar, stopping to refill the beer for the young businessman. Megan drank her beer slowly while she waited for Denver to arrive. He texted her at five forty-five to say that he was running late. He was back at Mark's with their injured horse, but would be there soon.

"Another beer?" Hedy asked. She seemed more pleasant tonight, sparing a smile now and again and keeping the mixed nuts refilled. Maybe it was the prospect of running the restaurant.

"She'll have one," said a voice from over Megan's shoulder. "And I'll have whatever she's having."

Megan looked up to see Lou Brazzi behind her. The attorney had changed into dress pants and a tie since she'd seen him that morning, and his salt-and-pepper hair was slicked back from his face. He straddled the bar seat next to Megan and said, "Clover told me I could find you here."

Megan watched Brazzi from over the rim of her glass. She hadn't eaten dinner and lunch had been a baguette and cheese on the road, so she didn't want to imbibe too quickly. She needed her wits about her.

"What's up, Lou?" Megan asked.

"I wanted to revisit the conversation we had this morning. About Ted and Otto."

Megan's pulse picked up. She waited for him to say more.

Hedy came by with two beers and Brazzi handed her a twenty. "Keep the change." When the bartender left, Brazzi said, "I have no idea—beyond Oktoberfest—what was going on between those two. But I did have an odd conversation with Ted I thought I would tell you about. Just in case."

Megan nodded. "I'm all ears." The Stones had been replaced by Springsteen, and "Born in the USA" blared from loudspeakers. One high-pitched "yes!" rose above the rest of the hubbub back by where the tasting was taking place.

"This was a few weeks ago, mind you. Ted and I had arrived at your café early, before anyone else. I ordered oatmeal and fruit, like I normally do, and Ted ordered toast and coffee. He looked paler than usual. I was concerned he was ill or something. After a few minutes of chitchat, Ted said he had a legal question to ask me. He wanted to know how liens on real property were handled."

"Okay?" Megan said, looking for the connection.

"I asked him what he meant. What property had a lien on it, and under what circumstances would the lien be 'handled.'"

"And he said?"

"He got real quiet. Told me he'd run into some financial problems, couldn't pay some debts, and now there were liens on his mother's property, which he owned." Brazzi flattened his hands on the bar top. "He wanted to know if he came into some cash would he have to pay off the liens."

Megan considered this. The situation wasn't that unusual. If someone couldn't pay a large debt unsecured by real property, like credit debt or a secondary mortgage on real property, or if there were unpaid back taxes, the creditor could ask a court to place a lien on the property. It was like an IOU. The creditor would have to get paid when the property was sold.

"What kind of debts?" Megan asked.

Brazzi looked away. "Didn't say and I didn't ask."

"What'd you tell him?"

"That paying off the debts would be the right thing to do. He could try negotiating with them, but his creditors had a right to his property. Then he said, 'What if I sold the property?' I told him he wouldn't be able to sell it without satisfying the liens. He seemed agitated with my answer. Almost angry."

Megan thought about this in the context of what she knew. "Did Ted say how he was going to come into this money?"

"No. And when I asked him, he waved me away. Like he was embarrassed. Or it was beside the point."

"Which was it?"

"I guess the latter. He was dogged about his legal question, didn't hear much of anything else."

Hedy came back and asked whether they'd like another beer. Megan checked her phone—Denver was on his way—and then declined. Brazzi ordered a gin and tonic.

"So does that help?"

"I don't know. It could mean anything." Megan drained her beer, thinking. Maybe this *was* something. Like a motive for blackmail. If Kuhl had found out about Ophelia and Otto, he might have tried to blackmail Otto to raise capital for Road Master Brewery and pay off his debts. He could have rationalized that he was just getting what he deserved after losing the sponsorship.

She thanked Brazzi. "By the way, Lou—what did Glen Sauer want with you this morning?"

"You know I can't share that."

"Client privilege?"

Brazzi pursed his lips and nodded, ever so slightly.

Also interesting, Megan thought. What did Glen Sauer need with a real estate attorney?

Brazzi was staring into his beer when Megan's phone beeped. Another text. Denver got called away again and would likely not make it to the brew pub. Megan thanked Brazzi and excused herself from the bar. The joviality around her only made her feel more alone.

*   *   *

Later that evening, Megan relocated her laptop to the kitchen and booted it up. Bibi and Emily were watching reruns of *Pretty Little Liars* in the parlor, and Lily was awake but quiet in her swing. No one seemed inclined to go to bed.

Megan thought about her conversation with Brazzi. Clearly Ted had contemplated an influx of money, but he had liens on the Kuhl acreage he'd inherited from his mother—liens that had to be paid off if he was going to use the cash for his businesses. At least based on what Brazzi said. What person was willing to commit blackmail, but was worried about repaying debts?

That just didn't seem logical.

Megan considered what she knew, from the beginning. Otto Vance had suggested Oktoberfest. A committee was formed, and they selected Ophelia, the sister-in-law of Marty Jenner, to run the show. Ophelia had carte blanche to make decisions, and she handed out sponsorship in contravention of the committee's rules. One such controversy was the beer sponsor. Otto had tenure and a restaurant, but Ted's beer was award-winning. Upset, Ted challenged the appointment.

At the same time, Ophelia was accused of having an affair with Otto. An accusation she vehemently denied.

And at some later point, someone online was trolling Road Master, leaving mean-spirited reviews.

And then there was the mountain stalker and the lost dog. Related? Or related to the treasure buried on the farm's property? Or merely a coincidence?

Finally, Emily was followed by someone in a stolen Honda, which later turned up decimated by fire. And Emily's father was killed in such a way as to suggest an accidental allergic reaction.

What a crazy set of facts.

Megan started by looking up the Kuhl property. She had access to an online database that listed county properties—mortgage liens, sale prices, and other liens. It took about twenty minutes, but she finally found what she was looking for. Ted Kuhl did have liens on the property—to the tune of over $168,000. A good percentage of what that property was worth.

Megan kept coming back to Ophelia and Oktoberfest. Ophelia seemed to be the connection between all of these disparate facts. Megan again searched Ophelia's background. When that didn't turn up anything new, she looked up Janice Jenner, Marty's stolen-from-the-cradle bride. The search engine led her back to the wedding announcement. It seemed the most prominent thing Janice ever did was get married.

Frustrated, Megan again read the Jenners' announcement. She skimmed the description of the venue, the food, the bridal party, the prominent guests in attendance...and then she stopped. A picture on the bottom of the page caught her attention. She looked at it again, her breath catching in her chest. There, next to Janice and her father, stood a short man. Bald head, sinewy runner's body. A brunette clung to his arm, a glass of champagne in her hand. He wore a three-piece Italian black suit. She wore an ankle-length ruby-colored gown. The caption said, "The bride, Janice Dilworth Jenner, and father-of-the-bride Kevin Jenner, with New York developer Scott Hanson and his wife, Leigh."

She'd met these people before. Her mind flashed back to the open house at Washington Acres. The couple from New Jersey with the cute little girl. The woman's interest in Winsome, the man's quiet confidence. Scott and Leigh Hanson.

A developer and his wife. Land.

Megan's head spun with the possibilities. She searched Scott Hanson and found a dozen hits immediately. Known for large developments in New Jersey and New York, he was a proponent of planned communities. His latest, Peaceful Valley Acres, sat atop a hundred and forty acres of former New Jersey dairy farm. Two hundred "carriage house" townhomes, fifty condominiums, one hundred single family mega-homes, stores, restaurants, playgrounds. All with a nice iron gate keeping the riffraff out and the wealthy in.

He hoped to develop an even larger community. One for "sophisticated" professionals.

Megan could barely breathe. Synapses were firing, puzzle pieces were falling into place.

She dialed Denver's number, anxious to test her theory out on someone. He answered immediately. "Can't talk now, Megs. I'm with Ophelia. She wanted to review a few things for the article."

Megan said fine and hung up, disappointed. She couldn't very well tell him about Ophelia with Ophelia in his living room.

Ophelia in his living room.

Megan forced air into her lungs, again and again. A planned community. A spy in the house. A spy in Denver's house.

Megan had no idea how all this fit together, but she had a feeling that Scott and Leigh Hanson had not shown up at Washington Acres by accident.

Megan was the only one awake at midnight when she saw lights coming up her driveway. She stared out the kitchen window, surprised to see Denver's Toyota pulling to a stop beside the porch. Her mind flip-flopped with emotions—unsure where to land. Anger? Jealousy? Happiness? Terror? The truth was, she'd been fighting her internal demons ever since that first kiss in his bungalow more than six months earlier. The fight was still raging. Her heart and head slugged it out while she opened the door.

"What brings you here?" Megan asked.

Denver was wearing faded Levi's and a hungry look in his eyes. He didn't reply. He didn't need to.

He stripped off his coat and laid his hat on the table.

Megan took his hand, led him toward her. Her fears fell away as the distance between them closed.

Thirty-One

The alarm went off at 3:18 in the morning, waking Megan from a fitful sleep. She opened her eyes in a panic, then felt her dresser until her hand hit the tiny egg-shaped device connected to the camera. She hit the off button and leapt out of bed, grabbing her phone. She sprinted to the window, looking for light in the barn, and dialed 911. She got through immediately and reported an intruder at the farm. It could have gone off accidentally—Clay said that could happen—but Megan wasn't taking any chances.

She was alone, but the warmth of Denver's body stayed with her, calming her nerves. She pulled on jeans and a sweatshirt and waited. The police arrived by 3:29. They found the barn empty, except for Sammy, who was awake and whining in her pen.

"Doesn't look like anyone was here," the first officer said. "But we'll look around."

The two cops made a round of the property, sweeping their floodlights in the shadowed corners. Nothing. Chagrined, Megan thanked them for coming. She'd look at the camera footage in the morning to be safe, but it seemed like a false alarm.

Sleep was hard to come by. At 5:50, Megan crawled out of bed and into the shower. She stared at her reflection in the mirror, tracing the curves of her body with one hand, just as Denver had hours before. She saw her mother's clear Irish complexion and broad high-cheekboned face and her father's eyes. The face staring back at her looked tired though—tired and pale.

She toweled off quickly in the cool air and dressed in canvas cargo pants, a black turtleneck sweater, and boots. She dried her hair and pulled it back into a loose ponytail. She took her time brushing her teeth and putting on moisturizer.

She was stalling. She couldn't help it.

At 6:22, she made coffee and wolfed down a blueberry muffin and a large mug of java. Bibi was still asleep—unusual for her—and the quiet in the kitchen was deafening. Megan talked to Sadie and Gunther, hungry for company. At 6:46, she headed back to the barn, a pit forming in her stomach. She climbed a ladder, carefully detached the lens and memory stick, and walked the camera back to the house.

At 7:12, she hit play.

At 7:14, she saw him. Thick head of gray hair. Beefy shoulders. When he knelt down to pet Sammy, his face remained in the shadows.

Megan watched the murky footage again and again. Nothing more was visible. She had hair and shoulders and an excited dog. Could have been anyone.

Anyone.

He looked, however, like Marty Jenner. Same full head of gray hair, same bulky shoulders. Megan picked up the phone. This time she called King directly.

Megan waited until ten to dial her old firm in Chicago. She knew the person she wanted to speak with would be in by seven Central time, but she gave her another hour to get settled. Tina Yang picked up immediately.

"I thought it might be you. Recognized the area code."

Megan was happy to hear Tina's voice. They'd been summer associates together at the firm, and while Megan quit to become a farmer a year before she was up for partnership, Tina, a real estate attorney—a damn good one—had remained. She was a partner now.

"What can I do for you?" Tina asked. "Buying another farm?"

Megan laughed. "Not just yet. I actually have a whole different kind of question for you. About developers."

After a few moments of small talk, Megan gave Tina a quick summary of her concerns. "So if someone was trying to buy up land in Winsome, wouldn't they have to go to the zoning board first? And under Sunshine laws, we would know about it. They would have to notify the public about the meeting."

"Not necessarily. Think about it; why go to the trouble of getting approvals if you may not have the land locked up?"

"So you buy the land first?"

"You can, certainly. But a lot of developers go through a promoter. Think of a promoter like a matchmaker. They'll find the property, determine suitability, and eventually work with the township to procure approvals."

Megan frowned. "Sounds like a great deal of risk."

"There can be, but there can also be a huge upside. When the developer gets the land, the hard part has been taken care of. The promoter, whose interests are usually aligned with the landowners, can get a big cut of the profits."

Megan closed her bedroom door and sat down hard on her bed. "So no one in the town would have to know until everything had been lined up."

"Usually people talk. Once the developer—or promoter—comes knocking, word gets around fast."

"And then someone could act to get a better price or to stop the deal."

"Theoretically. Depending, of course, on the local zoning rules and what the property will be used for." Tina paused. "Is there development happening in Winsome? Cause it would be a shame to erode that small-town charm."

"I don't know. No one has said a word, which I found odd." Megan left out the fact that two people were dead—and definitely *not* speaking.

Tina said, "NDAs."

"Non-disclosure agreements?"

"Why not? I said promoter or developer, but the truth is that the deal can be a hybrid, and much more complicated. Your promoter or developer could be buying options to purchase land. To get paid for the option—which could be a handsome sum—the landowner must agree not to tell anyone about the deal." Tina paused. "Imagine you're a promoter. You see potential in an area, but you don't want to go to a developer until you're sure landowners will sell. You start approaching landowners. You offer them a sum of money—say $20,000—for the option to buy their land if certain conditions are met. To get that money, they have to agree not to mention the deal."

"The NDA."

"Exactly."

Megan thought about what Tina was suggesting. "Then once all of the properties are lined up, the promoter can sell the options to the developer for more than they paid."

"That's right. Or they can develop the land themselves."

Bingo. Megan considered Sauer and his mysterious conversation with Brazzi, a real estate attorney. Suddenly the lack of chickens in his chicken barn made sense. If you were planning to sell, why replace the animals? You'd be downsizing, purging the farm of assets before the sale. And if there was an NDA in place, you wouldn't be able to mention a word. Nor would your attorney.

She thought about Hedy's comments the night before, Lana's sudden reticence to talk. Perhaps someone had gotten to the Vance family. They owned a good chunk of handsome land in Winsome. An option to buy their land could come with an NDA—and enough money to shut up a grieving anger-fueled widow. And if that widow suspected her late husband of infidelity, she might be willing to take the money and run far from the business that introduced him to his lover.

While all of this made sense, it didn't explain either Otto's or Ted's death.

Megan asked Tina, "What might keep a developer from biting even after the promoter has done his or her work?"

"Hmm. Good question. Again, it depends on the project. If it's big enough, the developer will want everything to be perfect. He or she will be taking on a lot of risk."

Megan thought about the articles she'd found the night before about Scott Hanson's current projects. "How about for a large planned community?"

"How large?"

"Couple hundred acres. Stores, restaurants. A gated one-stop shop for the discerning resident."

"Oh, man, pulling something like that off would require location, location, location."

"Commuting distance to Philly, Allentown, New York City, and parts of New Jersey?"

"Are you talking Winsome? Add in a lovely historical town setting, pastoral views, and a decent school district and you just may have a winner." Another pause, then Tina said, "But the stars would have to align, because opposition could be steep. Zoning, taxes. Again, risk-reward analysis for the buyer. Everything would have to line up."

Darn right, Megan mused, thinking of Jenner. So why not limit those risks any way you can?

Thirty-Two

"Megan, why in the world would Jenner be here just to see his dog? And if that were his dog, why wouldn't anyone else know it? I've heard of hiding a mistress, but a dog?" King shook his head. "I don't think so."

Megan had to admit, now that she'd had some caffeine and time to think, this felt like a long shot. But Jenner was the only person who made sense as a promoter. And as a promoter, he'd have the most to lose.

They were at the farm's kitchen table. King played the footage again and again, just as she had. "Well, it's something, I guess. Although not much." King closed the laptop. He sat back in his chair and stretched. "Just doesn't carry himself like Jenner. Not that I can tell from this grainy footage."

The last few weeks had taken their toll on him, and King rubbed at the bruised-looking skin under his blue eyes. "I'll need to take the camera recordings. Maybe our team can do something with them." He tapped a finger on the table top next to the untouched plate of banana bread Bibi had given him. "I just can't figure out why a murderer would take the risk to sneak in here to visit a dog."

"It seems out of character, I agree," Megan said.

"Maybe he's not the murderer." Bibi placed a mug of hot coffee in front of King. "Drink, Bobby. You look like you need it."

"Thanks, Bonnie." King took the mug. He swallowed the hot liquid and placed the mug down on the table with a bang. Coffee sloshed out. "Maybe your grandmother's right, Megan. Maybe the dog is unrelated."

"Then why not just ask for your dog back if you know who has it? This footage proves that someone was watching me. Someone who followed me here and knows I have his dog." She frowned. "Someone who doesn't want to risk coming forward. And who looks an awful lot like Jenner."

"That he does."

Megan stood to refill her own coffee. When she sat back down, she said to Bibi, "When you came across Otto, did you call Jenner?"

"No. Just the police. Once I could get my darn phone to work right." Bibi finally sat down at the table. "Why?"

Megan didn't answer right away. Rather, she said to King, "Did you call Jenner?"

"We did. Once we confirmed Otto's death. It seemed only right, it being his solar farm and all."

"How long did it take Jenner to arrive?"

King's eyes narrowed. "Not sure—we were kind of busy with Otto. Anyway, I'm the one who called him, and I remember he said it would take a while. He was down near Philly."

"Driving around?"

"In his car. Alone. Why are you asking?"

"I think you should check the cell tower pings, Bobby. See if you can triangulate his whereabouts when he was called. And maybe the EZ-Pass records. If he came from Philly, he may have taken the Turnpike."

"No EZ Pass. We checked. Someone's already working on the cell tower—as a precaution because it was his property. Why?"

"I think he was in Winsome." Megan shared a high-level synopsis of her discussion with Tina and what she'd learned about Scott Hanson, the man who'd attended her open house.

King's skin paled, but not as much as Bibi's.

King said, "A planned development? Here? That would ruin this town." He shook his head. "I haven't heard a peep about development. You'd think I would have."

"Not with NDAs in place and lots of money to lose. Look, I don't have hard proof, but think about it. Sauer's acting odd—no chickens, no events on his property, yet he gets the sponsorship for Oktoberfest. Why? Someone wants to increase his farm's profile and value."

"Like the sister-in-law of the man who serves to profit," Bibi said.

"Right."

King took a deep breath, let it out slowly.

"You think Jenner recommended Ophelia so that he could help put this deal through?"

"Why not? If you knew you had a lot to lose—likely millions in promotional money just for matchmaking this deal—what better way to highlight the perfection of Winsome than have someone talented do it for you? Oktoberfest wasn't Jenner's idea, but it did present a fantastic opportunity to both smooth the way for a developer *and* build some good will with the town."

"It was Otto's idea."

King and Megan turned to look at Bonnie. Her hand was shaking, and her mouth was set in a firm narrow line. Bibi repeated, "Oktoberfest was Otto's idea."

It took Megan a moment to understand what she was suggesting. "You think Otto learned about the plan and confronted Jenner?"

Bibi nodded.

King said, "Makes sense."

Megan considered the facts. Otto's anger the morning of his death, his race to the solar field, uncharacteristically bypassing a stranded Brian Porter. Was he heading to meet Jenner? Or Ted? She said, "It does make sense. Otto would have been steamed."

King frowned. "You've both presented an interesting possibility, but I can't get any kind of warrant on an intriguing supposition."

"You can dig without a warrant, Bobby, and you know it. The cell towers, for one. Once you have your records you can see if

Jenner was lying about being near Philly. If he wasn't, then he couldn't have killed Otto."

King nodded reluctantly. "I'll see what I can do."

"You can talk with Sauer too."

"If there's an NDA, he won't talk," Bibi said.

"He will if compelled by law," King said. "Let me start with Jenner."

"Even if Jenner hurt Otto, why Teddy?" Bibi asked.

"Maybe Ted knew about the deal. Was threatening to go public." King rubbed his temples. "Otto could have told Ted in the course of their arguments about Oktoberfest."

Clarity came on like a floodlight. Megan sat up straighter. "There's another possibility."

They both looked at her, waiting. She shared her conversation with Brazzi. "I confirmed last night that there are liens against the Kuhl acreage, which is located *by the Sauers' farm*." Megan emphasized the last words.

"So?" Bibi said.

"I'm afraid I'm not following you," King said.

"The Kuhl property is an eyesore. The broken-down trailers, the overgrown fields. What if Jenner approached Ted first, hoping to secure an option for that property—to get it out of the way? But Ted said no. He knew to sell the land he would likely have to satisfy the liens—leaving him no better off than he was before."

"And when he figured out what Jenner was up to, and why Otto got the sponsorship over him, he told Otto," King finished.

Megan nodded. "All those emails between them, all those conversations."

"And Otto got mad," Bibi said. "He and Ophelia weren't having an affair. They were having an argument." She shook her head. "Poor Lana, thinking Otto was cheating on her all that time."

"Right. Only Ted never signed an NDA. In fact, maybe it was Ted's reaction that made Jenner start getting NDAs." Megan was getting excited. This all made sense. "Jenner wouldn't have expected him to refuse."

"Or Ted had an NDA and didn't care. He had nothing to lose." King glanced out the window, toward the barn. "None of this explains who was watching you that night at the Kuhl house. Nor does it explain your dog-petting visitor. Or, for that matter, who was driving the burned-out Honda."

Megan sat back, deflated. He was right. There were still holes. "I don't know," she said.

"Maybe we'd better tell Emily what's going on."

Megan glanced at her grandmother. "Why do you say that, Bibi?"

"Whoever killed her father may believe she knows more than she does. She could be viewed as a threat."

King's eyes widened. "You're right, Bonnie."

"Where is she?" Megan asked.

"She left earlier to run some errands," Bibi said. "But she should have been back by now. She's probably up at the barn with Clay."

Megan jumped up and looked outside. "Her car's not here."

A quick call to Clay told them that neither Emily nor Lily were up there with him. "Haven't seen her all morning," Clay said. "Is everything okay?"

"We hope so." Megan dialed Emily's cell phone. It went right to voicemail.

Megan looked at King, then Bibi. The look on both of their faces reflected her own anxiety. Megan felt the knot in her stomach tighten. "Bobby," she said, "I think your people should be looking for Emily."

"I'm already on it," King said. He stood. "Business as usual, please. It will be the best way to flush out whoever is behind this. In the meantime, I'll give you a call when we find her." He nodded at Bibi, whose skin was arctic white. "And you do the same. If you hear from Emily, let me know. As soon as you can."

Thirty-Three

It was hard to focus on work with everything going on. Megan arrived at the café at two, after King had left and after she helped Clay and Porter with some chores at the farm. Sammy the lost dog was settling in well, and Denver had given Clay the okay for Sammy to meet Sadie and Gunther. The three quickly became fast friends—and fellow canine conspirators. Their antics, at least, kept the goats in line and Megan's mind off of other things.

But at the café, it all came back. They'd had a good-sized lunch crowd, and customers still lingered. The chili cook-off was that evening, and the store smelled of cumin and chili and Alvaro's sweet homemade cornbread. Megan's mouth started to water the second she walked in, despite a stomach too twisted for food.

"Your Aunt Sarah was here looking for you," Clover said. She was helping Alvaro in the kitchen, and she placed a heaping handful of homemade potato chips on a plate alongside a Cuban sandwich and a small scoop of broccoli slaw. "She said it's important."

"Yeah, she's been wanting to talk for a while."

Clover looked at Megan, questions in her eyes. "You should call her."

"I will. Right now we have bigger issues to deal with." She asked Clover if Emily had come by the café.

Clover's unlined brow creased. "No, but Bobby called me. Asked that I call him immediately if I see her. What's going on?"

Megan debated how much to tell Clover. She opted for enough to keep her safe. When she was finished sharing, Clover was silent. She took a moment to pull off her gloves and wash her hands. Then she turned to Megan and said, "So...Jenner? I never would have thought him capable of something like that." Her voice was calm, but her shaking hands gave her away.

"Nothing's definite. The police are checking into it. For now, watch your back and keep an eye out for Emily."

Clover nodded. She pulled another order from a pile on the counter. After looking around to make sure no one was in earshot, she said, "Is the chili cook-off still on?"

"Bobby wants to maintain as much normalcy as possible. He's afraid canceling it now will tip off the perpetrators."

Clover smiled. "Perpetrators. You sound like him."

Megan left Clover in the kitchen and went in the back to check on Bibi. Her grandmother had seemed listless after King left. Megan knew she felt disheartened that such awful things could happen in her community, but Megan suspected the idea of a planned community had gotten to her as much as anything. There was nothing necessarily wrong with such things, but Winsome was still a small town. People knew each other, they cooperated. Doors were unlocked, kids played in neighbors' yards. There were no gates. A large development meant strangers—lots of them—and the demands that came with wealthy city people. It would be a change, maybe more change than an old-time resident could bear.

But Bibi seemed fine. She was gathering spices from the pantry and had an odd assortment of ingredients in a wicker basket. Oranges and cinnamon and walnuts and carrots. When she saw Megan looking, she said, "Orange-spiced carrot bread. For tonight."

That sounded delicious. "Will you be okay here at the café?"

"Where are you going?"

"I'm going to stop by Denver's clinic, and then take a ride to look for Emily."

Bibi's face tightened. "Take Denver with you. Please."

"I'll wait until he's through with his appointments, and then we'll go. Promise."

The clinic was nearly empty when Megan arrived. She sat in the waiting room, her foot hitting the floor with nervous little taps, until the receptionist told her Denver was free. What if things felt different in the light of the morning? What if she'd made a mistake? She found him in the surgery, washing up. He smiled when he saw her. And his smile melted away her apprehension.

"Everything okay, Megan? It's unlike you to come by this time of day."

"I was hoping you could do some veterinary hocus pocus and look to see whether anyone has reported Sammy missing." She smiled. "But mostly I wanted to see you."

"Now that I'm a famous country vet."

"Ah, Ophelia's article must have come out."

"I'll be signing autographs this evening, in fact."

Megan walked closer. "I was hoping I wouldn't have to wait until then."

He kissed her. She felt the now-familiar pull and kissed him back, her hands trailing the length of his back. "For you, maybe an exception."

Megan pulled away. "I never asked you about your evening with Ophelia." The words were out before she could help herself.

"Indeed. We didn't talk much, did we? Well, Ophelia and I left my house—turns out she's not terribly fond of dogs, and the feeling is rather mutual—and went to her office." He dried his hands on a clean towel and then walked out of the surgery, leaving Megan to follow. In his cramped office, he pulled something out of a folder and handed it to Megan. "I may have had an ulterior motive, I'm afraid."

"Oh?"

"I did some snooping of my own."

Megan glanced down. She was looking at a project plan.

Details of the Oktoberfest events were listed on the front two pages. Information about the Picnic on the Canal, Concert on the Green, the beer tasting, even tonight's chili cook-off. Megan had to hand it to her—Ophelia was very organized. The packet contained diagrams of the downtown area, contingency plans, and volunteers' phone numbers.

"Check out the last page," Denver said.

Megan flipped to the back, to a page listing Winsome businesses, with notes about each. Sauers' was first, followed by Vance Brewery and Merry Chance's nursery. A half dozen other businesses were listed as well. Each had a spot on the Oktoberfest lineup—including Denver's veterinary clinic, Mark Gregario's farm, and the Washington Acres café. "Priority List" was written at the top. Ideas for promoting Sauer Farm were written along the margins in neat slanted script.

"The main businesses are within a three-mile radius of Sauer Farm," Denver said. "The rest, like this clinic, are not. I thought that was interesting." He slipped on a pair of reading glasses and took the papers from Megan. "Seems to verify your thoughts about Ophelia. That she had a motive for choosing Sauer."

"It does more than that." Megan took the packet back. "You stole this?"

"I like to think of it as borrowing."

"How did you manage…never mind." As he told it, Denver had been a handful as a kid. An abusive father, trouble with the law. She imagined he knew all too well how to lift something unnoticed. She realized he didn't know the latest about what they'd found. She recounted as much as she could, as quickly as she could. She wanted to get out there to search for Emily.

"So the big businesses are land targets to be part of this planned community," Denver said, comprehending the scheme quickly. "And the others?"

"Made to showcase the charm of Winsome and its investment value, if I had to guess. For Scott Hanson's benefit. Or whatever developers Jenner invited."

"Sneaky swick. I can't believe he'd sell out this town that way."

"I can't either." Megan handed the documents back to Denver. "Won't she be missing this?"

"Maybe, but she had other copies. She's very organized. I understand why Jenner chose her."

Thinking of Jenner made Megan think about Emily. "Want to go for a ride with me?"

"Ye want to look for Emily?"

"How did you guess?"

"The only thing predictable about ye, Megs, is that you're unpredictable. I think about what a sensible woman might do, then I realize ye will surely do the opposite."

"That's not always true. I'm quite sensible."

Denver surprised Megan by pulling her forward suddenly. His breath was warm against her ear when he said, "No, you're not. Not always. But that's what I love about you."

Thirty-Four

They drove around for an hour with no luck. Megan called Emily's cell five times, but no one answered—and the calls went right to voicemail. A phone call to Clay told her that Emily never returned to the farm, and Clover texted her to say there was no sign of Emily at the café or in town. Emily had the baby with her. Had she run, afraid she'd meet with the same fate as her father? Or had she met with foul play? The thought of the latter terrified Megan.

"What do you want to do, Megan? It's starting to get late. The chili cook-off will have started and Alvaro and Clover will be missing you."

"I know."

They were sitting in Denver's Toyota, parked along the Kuhl property, the windows down to bring in some fresh air. The sun had sunk below the horizon, and beyond the mountain and Potter Hill, the sky was aflame with pinks and purples and an array of blues. Megan took a deep breath. It was a beautiful area. Someone was determined to capitalize on that beauty.

Denver's phone rang. He pulled the phone from his pocket and said, "I need to get this, Megs. It's Mark. His horse is still having issues."

"No problem. I'm going to take another walk around."

Denver nodded, looking less than thrilled. He reached behind the seat and pulled out a long metal flashlight. "Be careful."

Megan slid out of the car and onto the rocky driveway. They'd already looked in the house—Megan still had the key—and back behind the trailers. Now that the day had dimmed, the property once again took on an ominous feel. Megan was carrying the knife she found on Potter Hill and she patted her pocket, taking some comfort in its presence.

She walked along the property line, remaining in sight of Denver. She could see him speaking animatedly on the phone, no doubt taking in the horse's symptoms and doling out advice and comfort. She walked on, past the tree line and into the slim band of woods that separated the Kuhl home from the park. The air was cool and moist, redolent with the smells of damp leaves and wood smoke. Now that Megan figured out the development angle, she saw her hometown through a new lens. Its simple beauty became fodder for marketers. Its simpler way of life, an asset to be sold to the highest bidder—undermining, in the end, the very thing that appealed in the first place.

A tree swayed and the noise caused Megan to jump. She couldn't shake the feeling that someone was watching her. She figured it was left over from her last experience here, and she kept going.

Something on the Sauer property across the street caught Megan's attention. She squinted, then realized it was only the glint of metal in the dying sunlight. The Sauer property *did* look neater. No more refuse. No more old cars. No more—

Cars.

Like an old Honda. The Sauers bought old vehicles at auction. Some they fixed up, others they sold. They had connections. Knew where to get the best deals.

Was it possible? All this time she'd been thinking of Jenner, but someone else had a lot to lose—Glen Sauer. If his farm was to constitute the majority of the land needed for the development, clearly he stood to make a lot of money. What might he do to protect that opportunity? He had time—a farmer's schedule was busy, but flexible. He had means. And he had motive.

If Ted Kuhl had learned of the proposal and had gone to Otto, he may have talked with others. Others who also knew that Ted wanted the deal to fall through. Glen may even have been one of those others.

Megan waved at Denver. When she failed to get his attention, she texted Clover. "Are the Sauers at the chili cook-off?"

"Dunno. Saw Glen earlier. May still be here. Why?" Clover responded. "It's a hit. Everyone <3s Alvaro's chili."

Megan responded: "Good. Heading to Sauers' farm. Text me if you see them." With that, Megan texted Denver to let him know she was going to take a walk around the Sauer farm. Then she turned off the phone's ringer.

The Sauers' farm was quiet. Night was pressing in, so Megan kept to the outskirts, looking around occasionally to see if Denver was still in the car. Satisfied that he was there, she pushed forward.

It wasn't unthinkable to envision Glen Sauer as a killer. He had a cruel streak; just ask Gunther. And as a farmer, he would be used to giving medication. A shot of peanut oil into Ted Kuhl's vein would be no problem. He could easily subdue Ted—he probably weighed twice as much as the smaller man.

But Emily? If he hurt her too, where would this end? Who else would he need to quiet? And what about Lily? She was missing too.

Megan's sense of urgency heightened. She pulled her phone out once more. Not wanting to make any more noise than she had to, she sent Bobby King a text just in case, letting him know her thoughts about Glen Sauer.

She'd reached the spot where she'd followed Sammy. A few feet ahead was the path to the old chicken barn, and beyond that, the turkey shed and the barns that housed the cows. From what she could see though, nothing was out of place. She turned, realizing she'd lost sight of Denver's car. She was about to head back when something new caught her eye: a piece of jewelry on the ground near the stone chicken barn. She shone her flashlight on it. A gold cross, the one Emily often wore.

Heart thumping, she bent to pick it up. It felt light and insubstantial in her grasp, and she placed it in her pocket. She stopped and listened, holding her breath so she could hear more clearly. Nothing—no voices, no baby crying. But Emily had been here. She lifted her hand to open the chicken barn door, then noticed it was locked. A rusty chain was wrapped around the door handles.

It hadn't been locked just days ago. This was new.

Megan rattled the chain. It stayed affixed to the door.

She took the flashlight and pulled it through the chain. She tugged down on it once, then twice. Nothing. Breathing hard, she pulled the flashlight through again. This time, she summoned all her strength and gave a sharp downward thrust. Nothing. She did it again and again, each sound a sharp stab to her nerves. On the fifth thrust, the rusty chain broke.

Megan opened the door and shined the light inside. Emily Kuhl lay huddled on a dirty comforter, unconscious.

Megan ran in and knelt beside her. That was when she heard another sound at the door. Terrified, she turned. Denver was standing there with a finger to his lips. He jogged the ten feet to Emily and turned her over, placing his ear near her mouth and his hand on her heart.

"She's alive," he whispered. "Drugged."

"Lily?" Megan mouthed. Where was the baby?

Thirty-Five

"We've got to get her out of here," Denver said. "Hurry. I don't know what those daft bastards gave her, but her pulse is weak. Very weak."

"Where's Lily?"

"Call King. Hurry. Get an ambulance."

Megan nodded. She pulled her phone from her pocket while Denver picked up Emily. Emily was a tall, broad woman despite her thin figure, and lifting dead weight was difficult. Denver slung her over his shoulder with impressive strength, pointing toward the door.

"You take her," Megan hissed. "I'll go to the house and look for the baby."

"Don't confuse bravery with recklessness, Megs. The police will be on their way. Call King."

Megan already had her finger on the number pad, trying to get through. "I can't just leave a child—"

Only she never got a chance to finish the thought. There in the doorway lurked the silhouette of a person. And that silhouette carried a shotgun.

Irene Sauer was unnervingly quiet. She swung the shotgun, pointing it at Megan while she motioned toward the back of the barn. "Move it," she said evenly. "And put the woman down."

"What are you doing?" Megan asked. "Irene, be reasonable."

"Now." Irene clicked off the safety. "Please."

Denver placed Emily back on the blanket. Megan backed up so that she was behind the first pillar, her back to the rear of the barn. She tried to catch Denver's eye, but his attention was focused on Emily. It was hard to tell if Emily was still breathing.

"Ye may have a dead woman here," Denver said to Irene. "Do you want that on your conscience?"

"Give me your phones," Irene said. Her voice was low but commanding.

Megan slid her phone across the concrete floor. Denver did the same. Still looking at them, gun cocked, Irene picked up the phones. She backed up slowly toward the door, the shotgun pointed first at Denver, then Megan.

She slammed the door shut without another word. Megan could hear a chain rattle, the clink as a new lock fell into place.

"She's not going to make it, Megan. Not if we don't do something." Denver had his finger on Emily's neck, feeling for a pulse. "Her breathing is shallow and labored. I think they gave her a horse tranquilizer, or something like it. Too much maybe." His voice was calm, but Megan could hear the underlying urgency.

Megan glanced around, searching for an escape. Beyond the pillar, on the other side of the building, stood a high shallow row of windows.

Megan said, "If you can help me get up there, I can get through. I'll run down the road to your car and get help."

Denver shook his head. "Not alone. I'll go."

"You need to stay with Emily. I'm useless in a medical situation. Plus, I don't think you'll fit through the windows."

After a moment, Denver nodded. She was right and he knew it. What choice did they have?

"Here." Denver pulled his sweater off and handed it to Megan, leaving him in a t-shirt in the frigid barn. "Use it to cover your fist."

Denver knelt down and Megan climbed on his shoulders. His height made her eye level to the windows.

"Close your eyes," she said. She did the same, and shot her

hand through the window, protected by the sweater. Glass shattered, and the sound echoed off the cavernous walls. Megan tensed, expecting Irene to come plowing back in any moment. She used the sweater to pull out the biggest shards, trying to smooth the bottom sill so she could get through, her heart careening beneath her ribcage.

Denver glanced at Emily, whose chest was still. "Hurry," he said, his accent thick.

He knelt down again. Megan slid back to the floor. This time she climbed up with her feet planted squarely on Denver's shoulders.

"Now," she whispered. He heaved up and she pulled herself through the window. "A little more."

Denver stood straighter, pushing Megan's legs up with his hands and arms. Bits of glass sliced into Megan's arms and abdomen. She felt something wet drip down her forehead.

"Are you okay?" Denver's voice was a strained whisper.

"I'm fine. One more push."

Denver shoved her gently through the window. She slid down the smooth wood barn exterior, landing on her hip and right shoulder on the other side. Her head slammed into the barn siding. Quickly she stood up, ascertaining the damage. No broken limbs—just cuts and scrapes. She gulped in the cold fresh air, grateful to be out and alive.

Megan glanced around, trying to get her bearings. She could see a form in the distance, moving stealthily through the darkened property. Irene. Megan weighed her options. Head to their house and look for Lily? But if Glen was there, she'd be in trouble—and then they'd lose Lily, Emily, and Denver. Or go after Irene? Irene was broad and stocky, strong from her work on the farm. But she was also twenty-five years older. And she had Megan's phone. Without it, Megan would lose valuable time driving into town. Megan took off after Irene, determined to get the key, the gun, and their phones. She needed to call for an ambulance or Emily was going to die.

Irene stopped at a shed outside the cow barn. Megan could hear the cows inside, mooing and moaning. The sour smell of manure permeated the air. A door slammed, and Irene disappeared inside the shed. Megan took advantage of the lull, running and tripping through the path. She had trouble seeing out of her left eye. She swiped it. Red liquid stained the sleeve of her sweater.

The shed door opened again. Irene came out, only this time she was carrying the gun and something else. A few more steps and Megan could make out what it was: a gas can.

She was going to light the barn on fire.

With Emily and Denver inside.

Megan's head was pounding, her throat felt raw. She forced herself to take a step forward, then another, quietly closing the gap between her and Irene Sauer. Not quietly enough.

Irene froze. She looked around, then lifted the gun, deciding where to point it. Megan tried to hide in the shadows of the cow barn. Too late. Irene's gaze latched onto Megan and she began to rush forward, gun aimed at Megan's head. There was no time to think. Megan ran toward Irene. With a loud grunt she threw all of her weight at the older woman. Irene went down hard. The shotgun flew from her hand. The gas can tumbled to the cement.

Megan felt anger rage through her. She pushed Irene's face into the ground, making no effort to be gentle. With her weight centered on Irene, she reached for the gun with her foot, nudging it closer until she could grab the weapon. She pointed the muzzle against Irene's skull. Irene moaned.

"Don't move," Megan hissed. "Where's Glen?"

"In town."

Unsure whether to believe her, Megan felt Irene's pockets for the phones. Her mind flashed to Emily—and Emily's missing daughter.

"Where's the baby, Irene?" When the woman didn't answer, she pushed her harder against the ground. "Where is Lily?"

"In the house."

Megan couldn't very well get up with Irene under her. Her

mind waded through encroaching haze, determining its next step. She needed to call the police, but the gun weighed so heavily in her hands. Something buzzed in the distance. It took Megan a moment to realize the sounds she heard were sirens. Not near enough, but quickly closing in.

The ambulance seemed to take forever to get to the hospital. They'd needed backups—three in all. One for Emily and Lily, one for Irene, and a third for Megan. Megan was released into Denver's care after ninety minutes. From there she headed to the police station, where she gave Bobby King her statement.

"How's Emily?" Megan asked. "Will she be all right?"

Bobby's face swam before her. "You have a concussion," the doctor had said. From the expression on King's face, she still looked a mess.

"Emily," Megan repeated, "and the baby. How are they?"

"Lily was in the house. She was fine. But Emily?" King shook his head. "Lucky Denver was there." King stopped talking. He was tight-lipped and solemn. Megan didn't think Emily Kuhl was all right at all.

Thirty-Six

The apple-picking finale was moved to the next week out of respect for the victims. It was less a celebration than a day of fellowship and atonement. The crowds of tourists had dissipated, scared off, perhaps, by Winsome's fifteen minutes of fame on the evening news. Whatever the reason, Diamond Farm hosted a more temperate affair, with clusters of Winsome residents talking, drinking apple cider, and inevitably discussing what had happened.

Megan, Bibi, and Lily were there with Denver. Emily had made it through the night thanks to Denver's quick actions, although she would need a week to recuperate. She was staying at the farm, where Clay and Porter were available if she needed help. For her part, Megan was recovering nicely. She had stitches on her stomach, arm, and forehead, but the fogginess in her head had cleared. She stood by Denver with a glass of spiced cider in one hand and the handle of Lily's stroller in the other.

"Good to see you," King said to Megan. He was there with Clover, as much to let the townsfolk know things were okay as to enjoy the gathering. "You look much better than you did when I last saw you."

Megan smiled. "I bet."

"Thank you," King said. "For quick thinking. Things could have turned out much worse."

"I'm afraid we ruined the chili cook-off."

"Ophelia will never forgive you." King smiled. "Although she's dealing with her own legal issues, so I wouldn't expect many complaints from her right now."

"Jenner?" Bibi asked.

"Finally came clean—after we confirmed that he'd been in Winsome when I spoke to him after Otto's death. Not near Philadelphia as he claimed."

"The sweater vest?" Megan asked. "That always bothered me."

"Otto was carrying a recording device in the pocket. Jenner ripped the sweater and the device off Otto, they tussled, and Otto fell. It really was an accident—Otto's death, at least."

"Jenner was trying to keep Otto quiet?"

King nodded.

"Otto was angry when Ted finally convinced him of what Jenner was doing, how Jenner used Oktoberfest to up the price of the development. Jenner was the promoter, as you thought, and he figured he could get top dollar for matchmaking the deal if Winsome looked like the quintessential small, safe American town, and the Sauer farm was a sought-after provider."

"Ironic," Bibi said. "And Otto threatened to go public."

King nodded.

Megan said, "So he wasn't having an affair with Ophelia? All those emails and meetings were about this."

"Yes. Ophelia shared her role. The committee had no idea she was Jenner's sister-in-law. The threat of jail time is a great truth serum. At first Otto was trying to find out if Ted was telling the truth about the development plan. Then he confronted Ophelia— and Jenner got involved. They offered to buy him out. He refused. The meeting at the solar farm was a last-ditch effort to convince Otto, only Otto had other ideas."

"And his loyalty to Winsome killed him," Bibi said.

Denver, whose gaze had fallen on a group of Winsome residents pulling a wagon loaded with Granny Smith apples, turned his attention to King. Denver had fared better than Emily or Megan—but his haunted expression said he hadn't gone unscathed.

Denver said, "Irene Sauer. I never would have guessed—until I realized the horse tranquilizer she used on Emily was probably what was used to overpower Ted."

King nodded.

"You're right. We finally got the toxicology reports. They showed that Ted *had* been drugged, then the fatal peanut oil injected. It was meant to look like an accident. Irene is denying it, but even her husband seems to believe she did it."

"Glen wasn't involved?" Bibi asked.

"We think Irene acted alone. She wanted this for Glen. For their retirement. It was too much money to let slip away. When Glen told her that Ted was making noise, she acted."

"She's a big woman. Built the way she is, used to hauling feed and tending livestock, she could have dragged Teddy." Bibi frowned. "Farming can be a thankless profession, especially in today's world. I never much liked the woman, but I never saw her capable of this."

Denver said, "Irene should have known that the toxicology tests would turn up the drugs."

King crossed his arms across his chest. "She gave him just enough tranquilizer to subdue him—helped along by the alcohol. She took him to the shed—and that's where she injected the oil. She wanted it to look like he accidentally consumed peanuts. Drunk, running from his problems. She figured we'd look no further."

Megan thought of something. "The bad reviews. It was Irene, wasn't it, who smeared his name online. She wanted Ted to leave town."

King agreed. "We think so. But that will have to play out in court. Unless the woman decides to confess."

Megan was relieved to know that both Ted's and Otto's deaths were finally explainable. Horrid—but with answers. "Still...the way Irene burned the car, her willingness to burn down the chicken barn with people inside." Megan squeezed Denver's hand. He squeezed back. "Pretty cold-blooded acts."

"Irene did what she felt she needed to do under the circumstances," King said. "She'd followed a slippery slope and there was no climbing back up. Right or wrong, she thought she was making the right choices."

Where had Megan heard those words before? She glanced up at the trees, thinking about family and choices and treasures that would stay buried—for now. Birds called overhead. It was a perfect fall day, the cool air laced with the sweet smell of fermenting apples. Lily cooed in her stroller, and Megan knelt down to adjust her blankets. When she looked up again, she saw her Aunt Sarah across the orchard, talking to the older man Megan had seen eons ago sitting alone in the café. Megan watched the two of them—her tall, long-legged body and his broad shoulders and thick gray hair.

"The only thing I wish we could have solved was your mountain stalker," King was saying. "Never did figure that out."

"Speaking of stalkers, when Megan and Denver were at the Sauer farm, who called the police and for an ambulance?" Bibi asked. "Megan said it wasn't her or Denver."

A shadow passed over King's features. "That's a mystery too."

"Well, the only good news is that the development won't go through," Bibi said. "With Jenner in trouble and the Sauer farm sullied by Irene's actions, the buyers walked away."

"Could happen again," Denver said. "Just a matter of time."

But by now, Megan wasn't listening. Gaze on Aunt Sarah, she dialed Clay's cell. She had a favor to ask of him. And he agreed immediately.

Thirty-Seven

The man was standing by the farthest field, near the horse pasture. Mark's newest horse, the rescue with the lame leg, was outside, nibbling at grass by the fence. The horse looked well now, a white bandage on his left front leg the only indication of prior trouble. Megan watched the man watch the horse. She saw the tilt of the man's head, the breadth of his shoulders. She recognized others in the set of his jaw.

She approached quietly. "I have something of yours."

The man spun around. He seemed neither surprised nor happy to see her. Megan held out the knife. "I think this belongs to you."

"How did you know?"

Megan pointed to his hands, which held a universe of tiny burn scars. "Tell-tale sign of a knife maker."

He nodded. He had a broad face, clear skin, and deep-set green eyes. His nose was a little too big, and his tufty hair created a salty halo around his head. He was fit, if a little thick around the middle. Tall, broad, with the shoulders of a lumberjack.

"I guess I should thank you. For calling the police and summoning that ambulance Friday night."

A slight nod was his only reaction.

Megan stood there, wanting to say more. She knew he'd been the one in the woods. That he'd been squatting in the trailer on the Kuhls' property. That he may have saved Emily's life with a call to the authorities. She said none of these things, however. But she didn't leave. She let the silence press against them, trapping them in an awkward bubble.

Until a dog barked, then whined. Clay came running through the field, startling the horse. He held Sammy's leash, and the dog pulled him toward the man, tail swinging back and forth in mad little circles.

"Nora," the man said. A smile crept over his face. Megan recognized the smile as her own.

Clay questioned Megan with his eyes. She simply nodded. When Clay handed the man the leash, Megan turned to leave.

The man made no attempt to stop her.

Nearly two weeks had passed since the incident at Sauer farm, and Megan finally had the courage to stop by Sarah's cottage. The autumn leaves had mostly fallen, and brilliant hues had given way to mud browns. Her aunt was outside, raking the remaining leaves with an oversized rake. She stopped when she saw Megan and put down the tool.

"Come in for tea," Aunt Sarah said. "And a story."

Megan followed her aunt inside. Once settled in a chair in Sarah's kitchen, she had misgivings—she shouldn't have come. But it was too late for that.

"He was a hard-edged man," Sarah said. She was standing by the stove, waiting patiently for the water to boil, her back blessedly to Megan. "Poor, earning only what he could by doing odd jobs. His daughter was his pride and joy. His wife, an obedient little thing, didn't understand her demanding husband or her wild-eyed child. She just attended church and thought things would turn out fine if she followed the rules."

"Aunt Sarah—"

"One day he found out his daughter was pregnant. He couldn't imagine a bigger disgrace. Even more, he couldn't imagine a more bitter disappointment. He'd done what he could to make sure she had a better life than he'd had. He'd had her schooled, had her attend church, made all of the little sacrifices a parent makes for a child. And here she was, throwing it all away on a farmer's son from Winsome."

The whistle blew on the tea kettle and Sarah paused while she poured. When she turned to give Megan her cup, her eyes were misty. "He threatened to beat her within an inch of her life. Told her there'd be worse things coming if she didn't get married." Sarah put up a hand. "Before you say anything, know that your mother loved Eddie. Your mother loved him—and you—as well as a confused teenager could. But she had four adults telling her what to do, and she did it."

"Marrying my father."

Sarah nodded.

"Did Bibi know?"

Sarah sat across from Megan. Her face, so full and rich with character, contorted into a mask of pain. "Yes."

"She knew my mother was forced to marry my dad and she went along with it?"

Sarah sat there, mute.

"Well?"

"Don't ask questions if you're not ready for the answers."

"I'm here, aren't I?"

"True. You are." Sarah sighed. "Bonnie had your grandfather to deal with. He also thought they should marry. Bonnie figured that if your mother was living with them, she'd be away from John—that's your maternal grandfather's name, Megan—and safe. Duty was paramount. Childish whims went out the door in Bibi's eyes when Eddie and your mother decided to sleep together. Bibi had one real concern."

"The baby." She was thinking about me, Megan thought.

"Yes."

Megan looked out the window, at the last of the Macintosh apples, now rotten and prune-like, hanging from Sarah's two fruit trees. This kitchen smelled of cinnamon and ginger, but the tea was bitter on Megan's tongue.

"You knew he was here, in Winsome." Megan couldn't bring herself to say his name.

"Yes—eventually. We've kept in touch here and there throughout the years."

"You tried to tell me."

"Yes. He wanted to meet you, but was afraid you'd turn him away."

As he'd once turned away my mother, Megan thought.

"He asked me not to say anything or he'd leave. Promised he'd come clean in his own time. He's sorry, Megan. He never meant to scare you. He wants a relationship with you." Sarah's voice pleaded, cajoled, begged Megan to understand. "But he's a broken man, and a proud man, and I don't think he knows how to tell you any of this."

"Why are you helping him?"

Sarah took her time responding. "Because I feel sorry for him. Because I want to help you heal."

Megan wanted to say: And because you feel guilty—an emotion you can't seem to admit.

Megan pictured the Adirondack chair on Potter Hill. Once a symbol of fear and angst, she now saw it for what it really represented. Loneliness. Sadness. Regret. She took another sip of tea and turned her face to the window, letting the sun warm her skin until she felt human again.

Alvaro's Rustic Potatoes au Gratin

This simple dish is delicious on its own, but at the café Alvaro pairs it with grilled free-range chicken breast, a salad of fresh greens, and a slice of hearty French bread. Gruyere works well with this recipe too.

Serves 6-8.

Ingredients:
3 russet potatoes, peeled and thinly sliced
2 tbsp. + 1 tbsp. extra virgin olive oil
2 red bell peppers, seeds removed, cut into 1-inch pieces
8 oz Raclette cheese, grated (more or less to taste)
Salt and pepper

Preparation:

Preheat oven to 375 degrees.

Mix potato slices with 2 tbsp. olive oil. Spread the potatoes on the bottom of a large baking dish and cook them for about 30 minutes, uncovered, until the potatoes are mostly tender. Turn the potatoes over and add the diced peppers and remainder of the olive oil. Return the potato mixture to the oven, increase the temperature to 400 degrees, and cook the mixture for an additional 45 minutes (time will vary based on oven and size of pan), until the potatoes and peppers are tender and browned on the edges. Remove the pan from the oven, turn over the vegetables, and sprinkle the Raclette over the potato mixture. Return the pan to the oven and cook for an additional 5-10 minutes, until the cheese has melted. Sprinkle pepper and salt to taste.

Gardening Tips

Pests affecting your organic tomato plants? Try growing your tomatoes with a companion plant, such as basil, nasturtiums, or marigolds. Basil repels pests, and the peppery flavor of basil leaves pairs well with tomatoes in sauces and salads. Nasturtiums are said to deter insects such as aphids and certain beetles—plus the leaves and flowers of nasturtiums are edible and make a wonderful addition to salads. And not only are marigolds attractive visually, but they repel nematodes and other insects that harm tomatoes. Companion plantings work well in container gardens too.

WENDY TYSON

Wendy Tyson's background in law and psychology has provided inspiration for her mysteries and thrillers. Originally from the Philadelphia area, Wendy has returned to her roots and lives there again on a micro-farm with her husband, three sons and three dogs. Wendy's short fiction has appeared in literary journals, and she's a contributing editor and columnist for *The Big Thrill* and *The Thrill Begins*, International Thriller Writers' online magazines. Wendy is the author of the Allison Campbell Mystery Series and the Greenhouse Mystery Series.

The Greenhouse Mystery Series
by Wendy Tyson

A MUDDIED MURDER (#1)
BITTER HARVEST (#2)
SEEDS OF REVENGE (#3)
(Fall 2017)

Available at booksellers nationwide and online

Visit www.henerypress.com for details

Henery Press Mystery Books

And finally, before you go...
Here are a few other mysteries
you might enjoy:

KILLER IMAGE

Wendy Tyson

An Allison Campbell Mystery (#1)

As Philadelphia's premier image consultant, Allison Campbell helps others reinvent themselves, but her most successful transformation was her own after a scandal nearly ruined her. Now she moves in a world of powerful executives, wealthy, eccentric ex-wives and twisted ethics.

When Allison's latest Main Line client, the fifteen-year-old Goth daughter of a White House hopeful, is accused of the ritualistic murder of a local divorce attorney, Allison fights to prove her client's innocence when no one else will. But unraveling the truth brings specters from her own past. And in a place where image is everything, the ability to distinguish what's real from the facade may be the only thing that keeps Allison alive.

Available at booksellers nationwide and online

Visit www.henerypress.com for details

MURDER ON A SILVER PLATTER

Shawn Reilly Simmons

A Red Carpet Catering Mystery (#1)

Penelope Sutherland and her Red Carpet Catering company just got their big break as the on-set caterer for an upcoming blockbuster. But when she discovers a dead body outside her house, Penelope finds herself in hot water. Things start to boil over when serious accidents threaten the lives of the cast and crew. And when the film's star, who happens to be Penelope's best friend, is poisoned, the entire production is nearly shut down.

Threats and accusations send Penelope out of the frying pan and into the fire as she struggles to keep her company afloat. Before Penelope can dish up dessert, she must find the killer or she'll be the one served up on a silver platter.

Available at booksellers nationwide and online

Visit www.henerypress.com for details

FATAL BRUSHSTROKE

Sybil Johnson

An Aurora Anderson Mystery (#1)

A dead body in her garden and a homicide detective on her doorstep...

Computer programmer and tole-painting enthusiast Aurora (Rory) Anderson doesn't envision finding either when she steps outside to investigate the frenzied yipping coming from her own back yard. After all, she lives in Vista Beach, a quiet California beach community where violent crime is rare and murder even rarer.

Suspicion falls on Rory when the body buried in her flowerbed turns out to be someone she knows—her tole-painting teacher, Hester Bouquet. Just two weeks before, Rory attended one of Hester's weekend seminars, an unpleasant experience she vowed never to repeat. As evidence piles up against Rory, she embarks on a quest to identify the killer and clear her name. Can Rory unearth the truth before she encounters her own brush with death?

Available at booksellers nationwide and online

Visit www.henerypress.com for details